I0417869

Desperate Season

BOOK THREE OF THE SEASONS MYSTERY SERIES

MARYANN MILLER

Copyright © 2020 Maryann Miller

All rights reserved. No part of this book may be reproduced,
stored, or transmitted by any means—whether auditory, graphic,
mechanical, or electronic—without written permission of both
publisher and author, except in the case of brief excerpts used
in critical articles and reviews. Unauthorized reproduction of
any part of this work is illegal and is punishable by law.

Dedication

∙∙

This book is lovingly dedicated to all the folks who've read the first two books in the series and clamored for a new story with Dallas Homicide Detectives Sarah Kingsly and Angel Johnson.

** Here it is. **

Dedication

Acknowledgements

Many thanks to members of the Dallas Police Department who were so helpful in the initial research I did in creating the series.

Thanks also to Audrey Lintner of ALTO Editing for catching my mistakes and to Lauria for creating a great cover. And I'd be remiss if I didn't thank Five Star Cengage, who gave the series a chance by publishing the first two books in the series. It's a shame you stopped publishing mysteries. *Desperate Season* would have liked to live there first.

Author Note

· ·

While doing more recent research about the Dallas PD, I discovered that some things have changed since my initial research in the late 80s, including the location of the downtown headquarters. They have a brand-new building on Lamar St—The Jack Evans Headquarters. Departments and departmental offices have also changed, and there is no longer a CAPERS (Crimes Against Persons) division. Homicide now has a home of its own.

After some deliberation, I decided to keep the details as set out the previous two books for continuity for the readers. My apologies to the DPD for taking such liberties, but those liberties don't affect the heart of what the officers do. The real ones and my pretend ones.

If you enjoy reading this story, please do me a huge favor and write a quick review on Amazon when you finish. Those reviews mean more than you might know, and I thank you in advance for your kindness.

Chapter One

••

Sunday, March 4

Felicity wiped the sweat from her forehead with the back of her hand, then picked up her soccer ball. It wasn't so hot this early on a Sunday morning in March, but the workout brought out the heat in her body. She'd run laps, then practiced dribbling with her friend Maria for almost an hour. Now Maria was dashing off the field and called out, "See you tomorrow?"

"After school. I'll be here. I want more practice before the tournament."

"Me, too." Maria waved and hopped on her bike to ride home.

The two girls were the stars of their club soccer team, and they were proud of it. But not too proud. Felicity's mother told her what The Church had to say about pride, so she tried to contain her thrill over what she could do with her powerful legs on the soccer field. Today she'd managed to get past Maria eight times out of ten, and Maria played the best defense on the team.

Felicity checked her watch. Almost eight. She'd better hurry if she was going to make it home in time to clean up for ten o'clock Mass. She trotted over to the picnic bench where she'd left her backpack. At home earlier, she'd dumped her school books so there would be room for her soccer ball and a bottle of water. As far as she was concerned, those were more important than math or social studies. She had dreams. Big dreams of being a soccer star. She'd watched the Olympics when the American team had won gold, and that is what she wanted to do. Play for the United States and win. After that, maybe she'd become a coach. Help some other young girl find a dream that was worth hours of sweat and a multitude of sore muscles.

Hoisting her backpack, she hurried to where she'd locked her bike. A cool breeze blew across her face; it dried the beads of sweat and actually made her shiver. She didn't like being in the little park alone. She wished Maria had stayed so they could have shoved off together. Sometimes an older boy would hassle them, wanting them to buy some dope. "It's cheap," he'd say. "Just two bucks. And you can share."

She often saw him giving stuff to other kids who were there practicing soccer or playing on the swings and slides. They were little kids, even younger than she was, and some of them would take the little plastic bags of white powder. Felicity couldn't deny that sometimes she was tempted to join in whatever fun they were having after sniffing the drug. She could go along to get along. But then she thought of her Olympic dream. No way would she achieve that if she did drugs. The park was starting to fill up with other kids, and she knew she'd better hurry if she wanted to get out of there before the boy showed up.

After putting on her helmet, Felicity quickly unlocked her bike, pocketed the lock, and swung her leg across the seat. She hoped her parents wouldn't be angry if she was late. Especially her father. He got angry so quickly of late. She did not know what worried him, but something had changed him from the teddy-bear of a father he used to be to a mean old black bear that growled a lot.

Just as she brought the pedals around to shove off, Felicity heard a whisper of a sound behind her. Before she could turn to check it out, she heard a loud click.

Then, nothing.

Chapter Two

∙∙

Sunday, March 4

Sarah Kingsly eased back to a comfortable lope a quarter of a mile from home, then slowed to a walk for the final block to cool down. When she'd headed out for her run at seven that morning, it had been cool. Now it was already hot. When was she ever going to learn? It wasn't as if she was new to Texas and didn't know how hot it could get in early spring. The big joke around the department was that there were only two seasons in Texas, hot and cold, but most of the time it wasn't that much of a joke. There was none of that slow slide into spring that she remembered from her childhood in Tennessee. In Texas, you could be freezing your ass off one day and boiling the next.

Of course, if she'd come straight home instead of stopping for coffee at the convenience store, she would have missed the worst of the mid-morning heat. But then she would have missed the neighborhood gossip from Hussein, who owned the gas station. He spoke excellent English for an Iranian immigrant, and he liked it when Sarah hung around, even when she wasn't on duty. He'd once told her she just looked like a bad-ass cop even in her jogging clothes, and that was enough to keep the bad guys away. Of course, he politely called her Miss bad-ass cop, the mix of formality and slang always making her smile.

Pulling the neck of her t-shirt up, Sarah wiped sweat from her face, then dug the key to her apartment out of the pocket in her shorts. She reached out to insert the key in the lock and the door moved slowly away from her. She immediately went on high alert, easing through the opening and glancing in. It took a moment for her eyes to adjust from the bright sunlight to the dim interior of the entryway, and in that moment, she mentally scrambled for a reason the door would be open that didn't involve some maniac waiting for her. Since she had nothing for protection except her bare hands and a few keys on a key ring, she tried to convince herself that nothing was wrong. Perhaps she had inadvertently left the door open.

As soon as that thought formed, Sarah dismissed it. There was no way she'd left the door unlocked. Inadvertently or otherwise. She had never in her whole life forgotten to lock a door. Her mother had instilled the importance of security in Sarah the child by pointing out the crazy man on the next street who liked to go into people's houses and take things. It was rumored that he took more than things, but her mother had never elaborated on that.

Then there was the number one safety thing they were taught in the police academy—locked doors do deter most thieves. Although in practice, Sarah had found that thieves who were determined did not let something as minor as a lock stand in their way.

Thankful that her apartment was small, Sarah did a quick visual sweep of the living room and kitchen. It was hard to tell if anything had been disturbed. She wasn't the neatest of housekeepers, so the living room always had a "tossed" look to it. A second look around and she noted that her TV was missing, and something else registered. She didn't hear Cat. He usually came running out of the bedroom when she returned from her morning run. He knew it was time to eat, and not much stood between the cat and his food.

The silence grated on her nerves. She couldn't decide if it was good that she couldn't hear anything. That meant that whoever had been in her apartment was gone. But it also meant that Cat was gone ...or ... She didn't want to think about "or." She didn't care about the TV, but if someone hurt her cat, they'd pay for it.

Sarah slipped quietly into the kitchen and grabbed the big butcher knife from the wooden block on the counter. She'd rather have her gun, but that was in the drawer in her nightstand in the bedroom. No way was she going in there armed with just her keys. When the ring tone sounded on her cell phone, Sarah almost dropped the knife. *Damn*. She scrounged the phone out of the pocket in her shorts and answered in a whisper.

"Kingsly?" the voice of her boss responded. "What the hell are you doing?"

She resisted the impulse to ask him what the hell he was doing calling her on the first Sunday she'd had off in weeks. "I'm checking out my apartment."

"For what?"

"Someone took my television."

"Did you call 911?"

"Why? I'm already here."

She heard Lieutenant McGregor release a long breath. She worried that she might be the death of him yet. "Have you cleared the premises?"

"One room to go. On my way." She disconnected, then dropped the phone back into her pocket before pushing through the bedroom door, making it slam into the wall and anyone who might be lurking behind it. A quick scan of the room showed her nothing had been disturbed. Odd that someone would break in and just steal a television. Wasn't even a high-end set. She quickly retrieved her gun and cautiously opened the closet door. Nobody hiding there, and nobody in the bathroom.

But still no sign of Cat.

She'd never considered having a cat, or any other living thing depending on her for that matter. No pets. No houseplants. Nothing. But she had become quite attached to the little orange tabby who had arrived cold and starving on her doorstep right after John's death. Had it really been already over a year? Yeah. Closer to two years.

Now she imagined the cat outside somewhere, frightened. Or had the someone who'd broken in taken Cat? What on earth for? Heaviness settled in her stomach, and she sat down on the bed, trying to hold back tears that warmed her eyes. She swiped at the wetness. Get a grip, woman. It's just a cat for heaven's sake. But crying had come all too easy since John. He'd been her first and only partner after she'd gotten her shield fifteen years ago. Losing him and then having to kill the kid who'd shot him had been the lowest point of her life. Sometimes she felt like she was still down there in that deep black pit.

Shrugging off those dark thoughts, she reached out to put her gun back in the drawer and something nudged her foot. "Holy crap!" She jumped up, heart racing, and lifted the edge of the sheet that had slid partway off the bed. There was Cat, huddled in a shadowed orange ball. Sarah got down on her knees and held out her hand. "Hey there. You want to come out?"

His eyes were huge, the orange of his iris almost obscured by the black pupil. A sure sign he was terrified. Sarah waited, not wanting to reach in to pull him out and risk getting scratched in the process. Then her phone rang again, and the noise startled the cat. He let out a yowl and scurried deeper under the bed. Sarah leaned back on her heels and answered the phone.

"Is everything okay, Kingsly?" McGregor asked after she said hello. "I've got units on their way to—"

"Not necessary. Nobody's here. And nothing is missing, except my television. I found my cat."

"What?"

"Never mind. Call off the cavalry." Even as she said that, she could hear sirens in the distance drawing near. *Damn.* "Could you at least tell them to kill the sirens?"

Again, she disconnected and went to meet the officers. First, she closed her bedroom door. She'd deal with Cat later.

Just as the first patrol car pulled up in front of the apartment, her phone rang again. She didn't even have to say a word. McGregor was hot. "Don't you hang up on me again or I'll fire your ass."

"I'm not hanging up." Sarah opened the door to admit the patrol officers. "Why'd you call in the first place?"

"You need to meet Angel at a crime scene."

"Why me? It's my day off. And cops are at my door."

"You'll see when you get there."

With that, McGregor hung up.

If she hadn't been standing there looking at two officers who needed to take a report, she would've burst out laughing. They might find that reaction to a break-in more than strange for a seasoned detective, but she couldn't help but see the humor in McGregor's behavior—hanging up first so she couldn't hang up on him again. And he hadn't even told her where she was supposed to meet Angel.

After talking to the patrol officers who filled out an official report of the burglary, Sarah changed into her work uniform, which consisted of jeans and a white t-shirt, topped by a dark blue blazer. Then she called McGregor to find out where she was supposed to go. Forcing her to call seemed to make his day. He actually chuckled for a moment before giving her the address of the crime scene.

Then he told her what she was going to see when she arrived.

Damn. A dead kid. Sarah swallowed hard then slipped out of her bedroom, closing the door firmly again.

The patrol officers working her burglary called CSU to dust for prints, but Sarah didn't hold out much hope that they'd get any. Still, it was procedure. After getting assurance that the officers would watch for Cat when they went into her bedroom, she left her apartment in the capable hands of the Dallas PD.

~*~

Dread following close on her tracks, Sarah pulled into the small parking area next to the soccer fields. The minute McGregor had told her about the kid who had been shot, she knew she was not going to like this. Not that she liked any murder victim, but kids were the worst. Accident, disease, or murder. Didn't make a difference. Kids just shouldn't die. Period. They should live the full extent of years that took them to gray hair and wrinkles and lots of grandkids.

A few hundred feet from the parking area, Angel stood next to Walt, the medical examiner, who was hunched over a bundle on the ground. Sarah didn't want to go look at what was in that bundle, so she glanced over to where two uniformed officers were talking to a small cluster of people. She moved toward them and noted that one of the officers was Doug Grantham. Good guy who could have made detective years ago, but he liked being a beat cop. And Sarah liked it any time their paths crossed. He was a more seasoned version of Rusty, the rookie she'd met two years ago when dealing with the murders at the shopping malls, and she always appreciated working with someone that good at the job.

"What do we have, Doug?"

"Girl was shot." He made a vague gesture in the direction of Angel and Walt. "This guy here," he nodded to a young Black man wearing shorts, a red t-shirt and running shoes, "found her while he was jogging this morning."

Sarah looked at the witness. "Your name, sir?"

"Jeremy. Jeremy Wilson."

"Did you see anybody? Hear any gunshots?"

"No, Ma'am. There was nobody else around when I found her. And I almost didn't. This isn't my usual route to run, but I decided to cut through the park this morning."

Sarah glanced at the small crowd of gawkers that had gathered, and Doug seemed to anticipate her question. He was good at that. "They came when we pulled up with sirens and lights."

Sarah nodded, then turned back to the young man. "Did you touch the body, Jeremy?"

He swallowed hard, then offered a slight grimace. "I didn't want to. And I knew I shouldn't. But, well, I'm pre-med. Thought maybe I should make sure she was ...you know...dead."

As much trouble as he was having, Sarah wondered if Jeremy might reconsider his college major after this morning. But then, finding a little girl dead in a park is much different from treating some old man's gastritis.

"Any ETA on the crime scene team?" Sarah asked Doug.

"Any minute."

"Okay." She turned to Jeremy. "You need to stay here until the techs can get your prints."

Suddenly there was an edge of hostility in his stance and his expression changed from friendly to wary. "What for?"

At first Sarah wondered why the abrupt change. What did he have to hide? Then she stilled the impulse to ask him, remembering what Angel had told her about how young black men are taught from the cradle on up to be wary of the police. She wished it didn't have to be that way, but there it was. It wasn't going away any time soon, as

Sarah could well attest to after her experiences with racism on both sides of the coin. She spoke in a well-modulated tone, "If we get any prints from the area, we need to eliminate yours."

Jeremy gave a slight nod, and Sarah watched his shoulders slowly relax. "This officer will get you squared away with one of our techs and get your contact information. Then you can go."

That was met with another nod, and Sarah started to move away. "Later, Doug."

He acknowledged with a wave just as the CSU van arrived.

Sarah walked over to Angel and Walt, who had moved a few feet away from the body. A girl's bicycle lay on its side where it must have fallen when the girl was shot. She still had a backpack strapped to her back and a helmet on her head. The helmet was a deep red, matching the blood that had seeped into the girl's white t-shirt. The ground where the girl's head rested was dark and damp.

More blood.

"What a day," Sarah said as she stepped up to Angel.

"McGregor told me about the break-in at your place. You okay?"

"Yeah. Shit happens. The only thing they took was my TV."

Sarah could joke about it, but part of her still seethed when she thought about some stranger in her apartment. Some stranger with felony on his mind.

"You need me to handle this so you can go back?"

The offer surprised Sarah, but then a lot of things about her partner were surprises. They'd worked together for over a year now, but there were times when they seemed no closer to establishing the kind of bond most partners shared than they were on day one. Granted, day one had been a doozey of a PR move, putting them together to appease the black community who were fired up after Sarah shot a black kid. It didn't matter to the screamers that the kid had just killed a cop. It was just another case of white-on-black injustice that fueled the dissention in the city that never seemed to stop.

And sometimes the dissention permeated the squad room.

"Thanks," Sarah said. "Maybe I'll leave in a few minutes. Need to get my locks changed." She glanced over at Walt. "Any idea on TOD?"

"Rigor's just started, so I'm guessing three hours or so."

Sarah glanced at her watch. Ten-thirty. "Wonder why she was here so early on a Sunday morning."

"That's easy," Angel said. "Between the cleats she's wearing and the soccer ball Doug found in her gym bag, she was probably here practicing soccer."

Sarah turned back to Walt. "Anything else you can tell us?"

"Can't do much until the techs photograph everything. But COD certainly looks like a gunshot to the back of her head. Pretty close range."

"She was executed?"

Walt shrugged. "Could be."

Sarah took a step closer to the body. Such a little thing. "Who would want to shoot a kid like that?"

"I do believe figuring that out is your job, Detective." Walt delivered that with his customary wry humor.

Sarah laughed; the little joke releasing the tension that had been building inside. She shook her head, then looked over at Angel. "If you're sure you can handle this, I'll head out. Get my stuff taken care of."

"Go on. I'll get the ID and meet you at the station later."

A van pulled up and Sarah saw the logo for the Channel 8 News. "Shit." The passenger door opened and Bianca Gomez stepped out as the driver ran around to open the van doors. Sarah ran over. "Stay back," she called out. "You know the drill. We'd like to notify next of kin before you start splashing this on everyone's television screen."

Bianca made no move to get back in the van. "The people have a right to know when there's been a murder."

"The *people* you refer to are nothing but a bunch of vultures and you're the lead one."

"Oh, please. Aren't you getting tired of using the same old cliché?"

"Actually, no. As clichés go, it's a good one. So perfectly apt."

Bianca spoke through clenched teeth. "Are you going to move so I can do my job?"

"No. I'm going to stand here until you're gone. You'll be notified when there's a press conference at the station."

In defiance, Bianca motioned to her cameraman to get some long shots of the area. There was nothing Sarah could do to stop that, but she waited until they finished and got in the van. She didn't move toward her car until the news van was well out of sight.

Chapter Three

• •

Sunday, March 4

A rumble in her stomach reminded Sarah that she had not had breakfast. Coffee and a scone earlier did not qualify. Her normal Sunday-off routine was to follow up with scrambled eggs at home for her and Cat, but all thoughts of cooking had been chased away by discovering that someone had been in her apartment. She did a quick drive-through at McDonald's, getting there just in time to get coffee and a breakfast burrito. Unwrapping the sandwich, she tried to push the image of the dead kid out of her mind before she lost her appetite again. While the breakfast burrito was only a marginally healthier choice than a hamburger, at least it was neater. No catsup to come oozing out and drip down the front of her white shirt.

Shit! That image connected too closely to the dead girl, and Sarah dumped the sandwich back into the bag. Maybe Cat would eat it.

The apartment was much as she had left it, minus the crime-scene techs. She could see faint traces of powder on the stand that had held her TV where they had dusted for prints. She'd bet they got nothing but hers. Or maybe some from the TV repair guy she'd called out last month. He'd tried to talk her into buying a new flat-screen television, joking that her old Zenith was practically an antique. Maybe it was, but it was all she needed for the little she watched TV. She'd gotten it when everyone had to upgrade to digital, but that was as far as she was going with technology.

She threw her now empty coffee cup in the trash and put the half-eaten sandwich on the counter in the kitchen, then headed to the bedroom. When she opened the door, she saw Cat curled into a huge orange ball in the middle of her bed. At least she thought it was him. It could be an orange t-shirt she'd tossed there, but then the ball moved. Cat stood and stretched before hopping down to saunter over and rub on her legs. Obviously, he'd recovered from the earlier trauma. "You hungry, Cat?"

His response was a hearty meow. Waving his fluffy tail like a flag, he trotted off toward the kitchen.

Sarah fixed a bowl of cat chow and put a few pieces of the burrito in for a treat. She got fresh water for the cat, then called McGregor.

"Where are you?" he asked, barely giving her time to say anything.

"At my place. I did have a break-in this morning. Remember?"

"Yeah, well. Sorry. You okay?"

"I'm dandy." From the tone of his question, Sarah knew that was the answer he wanted. He didn't want to hear about how violated she felt and how much she wanted to smash someone for it.

She heard a deep sigh from his end. "Do what you got to do, then get in here as soon as you can. We got an ID on the girl."

"Just need to arrange for changing locks. Then I'll be in."

"Sooner than later."

"I got it."

Both locksmiths Sarah called were going to charge extra to come on Sunday, a *lot* extra, and she debated about spending so much on top of what it would cost to install the biggest, strongest lock she could get. What she had still worked, and patrols were going to be stepped up for a few days, despite her appeal to McGregor not to make that happen, so she should be okay overnight. She scheduled one of the locksmiths to come as early as he could make it in the morning.

~*~

Angel consulted the address that McGregor had given them for the dead girl, Felicity Santos, and told Sarah to stop in front of a white clapboard house. The patrol officers had apparently already been there to break the news to the family, and it hadn't taken long for grieving relatives and friends to gather. There were several cars in the driveway and one on what pretended to be a lawn. People clustered in groups of two and three, leaning on older cars, holding each other, some crying in great heaving sobs. The first time Angel had seen the way Hispanic people react to death she had been surprised to see how closely it resembled her own cultural experience. They mourned with great drama and in great numbers. No family suffered loss in solitude or very quietly.

"Too many people. Maybe we should wait until the parents are alone," Sarah said as she eased the car to the curb.

"That won't happen for a long time." Angel opened the passenger door. "Let's just do it."

Angel nodded to the people on the grass and the couple on the porch as she led the way to the front door. None of them spoke. They all had red, swollen eyes, ravaged by weeping, and she sent them silent messages of understanding. She rang the doorbell and a few moments later, a young woman opened the door. She was slim with long ebony hair down to her waist and large brown eyes that were carrying their own load of sadness. "Yes?"

"Mrs. Santos?" Sarah asked.

The woman shook her head. "She is my sister. I am Juanita Rios."

"We need to talk to her," Angel said. "And Mr. Santos."

"He is not here. He went with the officers to ... you know ... say for sure it is Felicity."

"I see. We are so sorry for your loss." Angel showed the young woman her badge and introduced herself and Sarah. "May we come in?"

"Certainly." Juanita stepped aside so the detectives could enter.

There were more people inside, and despite the open windows that created a cross-current of the cool spring breeze, the front room was stuffy. Too many bodies in such a small space, adding heat and the sweet-sour smell of nervous perspiration. A woman that Angel took to be Mrs. Santos sat on a sagging orange sofa with a man on one side and a woman on the other. While the younger sister was all lines and angles and wore tailored black slacks and a pale blue silk blouse, the elder was as round and plump as a beach ball encased in a dress emblazoned with large bright flowers of red and orange and purple. Her dark hair was pulled back in a bun. Juanita hurried over and spoke to the trio, then the man and woman got up, motioning to the others in the room to follow them out.

Juanita beckoned the detectives to come closer, and introduced them to her sister, Camille. Then she, too, started to leave.

"No," Camille said. "Stay."

Juanita looked at Angel as if to ask permission, and Angel nodded. Then she turned to the distraught woman on the sofa. "We are so sorry for your loss, Mrs. Santos."

"When can I bury my baby?"

Angel faltered for a response, glancing at Sarah.

"It could be several days," Sarah said. "We need to make sure we get every scrap of evidence from the—"

"What evidence?" Juanita asked, as if sensing it was a question her sister wouldn't ask, but would want to know.

"Anything that will help us find whoever did this." Sarah said, using that no nonsense tone that Angel was quite familiar with. Juanita gave a slight head bob, as if bowing to authority, and Angel nodded to Sarah to continue.

Sarah took a step closer to the women, maintaining eye contact with Camille. "Do you know how your daughter died?"

"Yes. The other police. He tell me. But I no understand. *Quién mataría a mi bebé?*"

"My sister asked who would kill her baby. We're all having a hard time with that," Juanita said, her English much better than her sister's. "My niece was an honor student. Active in the church youth group. We are at a loss to know how this could happen."

"Did you know Felicity was going to the park?" Sarah asked.

"Si. She go practice soccer," Camille said. "She practice every day. With her friend, Maria."

"My niece is on a club soccer team," Juanita said. "She works ... worked ... hard. She wanted to make the Olympic Development team."

"Did you notice any changes in her behavior of late?" Angel asked. "Any signs that maybe she had gotten involved with drugs?"

"No!" Both women spoke at once, then Juanita patted her sister's hand. "Felicity was dedicated to sports," Juanita said. "She would not do drugs."

"Often the family doesn't know," Angel said. "Especially in the beginning. And that park is noted as a hangout for dealers."

Juanita acknowledged the veracity in that with a slight head bow but then straightened her spine. "Still, I wouldn't believe it of my niece. She went to play soccer. Nothing else."

"People are not killed for no reason," Sarah said. "There has to be something."

"Could it have been a drive-by?" Juanita asked.

"No."

"How do you know?"

Angel sucked in a breath. How could she tell a grieving mother that her child was basically executed? That was one of the reasons they were pursuing the drug angle. Despite the protests from family, it was possible that Felicity had gotten into some trouble with a dealer.

"There was nothing at the crime scene that indicated a drive-by," Sarah said.

Angel shot her partner a glance that said, "thank you," then turned to the mother. "Did Felicity have any new friends? Anyone who might have pressured her into trying drugs?"

"I not know of such *amigos*." Camille paused to dab at a tear that had escaped and crawled slowly down a smooth amber cheek. "My girl busy always. No time for bad things. Maria no do bad things."

"Mrs. Santos ... Camille." Angel reached out to touch the woman lightly on the knee. "We are doing everything we can to find out what happened, but we have very little to go on. So, we have to consider that maybe she was involved in something she shouldn't have been."

"I no understand." Mrs. Santos looked from the detectives to her sister, then back to Angel, her eyes wide with alarm.

"Very young teens are doing drugs now. That's a fact. There's a new drug that is inexpensive and easily available."

Juanita leaned forward. "Are you talking about Cheese?"

"You know about it?" Angel asked.

"I wish I didn't, but I teach at the local middle school. Kids there are taking it. We had two students OD on the drug in the past six months."

Camille looked at her sister, eyes wide in alarm. "Felicity no do that."

Juanita patted the plump hand that clutched at her. "Shhh. I know."

The front door burst open and a tall, thin man strode in. Camille half rose from the sofa. "Emilio. These *policía*. They say Felicity do drugs."

Angel saw the muscles in the man's jaws tense as he looked from the detectives, to his wife then back again. He walked over and put his arm around Camille, who was now standing, then pointed at Angel and Sarah. "You no say bad things about my girl. Get out."

"That is not possible," Sarah said. "We are so sorry for your loss, but we do need to—"

"No."

The word cut like a saber, and Angel noted the look that passed between the sisters. There was no doubt that they were more than a bit cowed by the husband. But she reminded herself not to read too much into that. Spanish men went to great lengths to protect their women. Another cultural thing; one she wished was more prevalent in her culture.

Mr. Santos held on to his wife, but the grim set of his jaw did not falter, nor did the fire in his ebony eyes. "You go. No bother my wife."

"Is *bueno* Emilio." Mrs. Santos said in a weak voice.

"Not right," he said. "Leave us."

Juanita stood and gestured toward the door. "Please. Can this wait?" she asked. "Can you come back tomorrow? When emotions are not so raw?"

"Mr. Santos." Sarah did not move. "Our best chance of finding out who did this to your daughter is in the first twenty-four hours. Are you sure you want us to delay?"

Angel recognized that low controlled tone in her partner's voice. She'd used it before when trying to keep an interview cordial, but Angel also knew that there was a sharp edge to it that a witness or a perp would be well-advised not to touch.

"Any information you could give us might help," Angel said stepping into the conversational opening. She gave him a moment to think about that, then continued. "Do you have any idea of who might have done this? Something not related to drugs or to the park?"

He shook his head and glanced away, but not before Angel saw a flicker of something in his eyes. Anxiety? Fear?

"What kind of work do you do, Mr. Santos?" Angel asked.

"Trucking."

"What company do you drive for?"

"My own truck."

"Could one of your customers—"

"No." Santos shouted the word. "It is nothing from me. Now, you go. Leave us."

"Just answer one more question." Sarah again used that controlled tone that Angel knew all too well. "Where were you early this morning?"

Santos made a move as though he wanted to backhand Sarah, but his wife clung to his arm. "No, Emilio," she said.

Santos shook free of his wife and directed a torrent of Spanish at her and her sister. When he turned back to the detectives, Angel saw the fire of anger in his dark eyes. He didn't say another word as he turned and stalked toward a doorway that led from the front room to a darkened hallway.

Angel watched Juanita, who never took her eyes off the man as he took long, angry strides away, then caught her eye when she turned. "We are not trying to pin anything on your brother-in-law," Angel said. "Often we just have to ask tough questions."

"I understand."

Angel took out a card and handed it over. "Please. Call if you think of anything that might help."

The woman took the card, then walked the detectives to the door.

Outside, they paused on the front porch. Some of the people were still in the same places as before, like some tableau frozen in time. Angel remembered it was like this when her grandmother died. And when her best friend died. In both instances, time seemed to stand still for painfully long periods. As if everyone was holding their collective breath, hoping that time could be reversed and the death turn back to life.

"I think we should look hard at the dad," Sarah said once they were in the car. She had not started the engine yet and was looking back toward the house.

"Just because he went off on us? People deal with death in all kinds of ways."

"It just feels wrong."

"Is there any right way to behave when you lose a child?"

"I don't know." Sarah fired up the engine and slowly pulled around a parked car and the people still leaning on it.

They drove in silence for a few minutes, then Angel shifted to face Sarah. "I know we do need to eliminate him," Angel said. "But remember what happened last time you suspected a father of killing his daughter. The brass was all over us like hot tar."

Sarah remembered. It was not one of her stellar moments as a detective, but the father in question, a Dallas high roller, was so damn arrogant and condescending. And there had been reason for suspicion. When the story broke about his daughter working at a gentleman's club, he'd been more worried about how that would affect his image and reputation than the death of his daughter. Had that story not come out just after the body had been found, Sarah might not have wondered about him at all. As it was, preserving his reputation was a damn good motive for eliminating the daughter.

Still, Angel did have a point. They should go easy at this guy or they could risk having the whole Hispanic community up in arms. Seems like they couldn't do their job any more without worrying about what group they might piss off. All this PC crap was a royal pain in the ass.

Chapter Four

• •

Monday, March 5

Monday morning, Sarah was glad to finish her morning run early and make it home in time to meet the locksmith. Less than an hour later, the front door lock was changed, Cat was happily munching on his breakfast, and she was showered, dressed, and on her way to work. She might even surprise McGregor and make it to the station on time.

Angel met her at the elevator when she got off at the entrance to the CAPERS department. Sarah liked the name—Crimes Against Persons. Made her feel like the guardian police officers were supposed to be. Too often, the job involved horrible crimes and innocent victims that they hadn't been able to save, but every now and then, they did get there in time to help a woman escape from an abusive husband, or a kid from abusive parents, and that felt good.

"McGregor wants to see us," Angel said by way of greeting.

Sarah followed her partner, wondering if the abrupt comment meant anything other than the fact that Angel was in a hurry. Sarah wondered a lot; afraid that she had inadvertently said or done something to put them back to square one in their partnership. "Something wrong?" she asked.

Angel slowed her steps and let Sarah come alongside. "Sorry. McGregor just sounded like he wanted us there pronto. I think this latest dead girl was one too many."

"Any dead girl is one too many."

"Amen to that," Angel said as she opened the door to McGregor's office.

Every time she came in, Sarah marveled at the total disarray of the room. Boxes of files concealed most of the carpeting on the floor, and the stacks of files on his desk looked like they could create a paper avalanche at any moment. How he kept track of cases was beyond her, but he obviously had a system that worked for him and satisfied Chief Dorsett.

"Did you talk to Walt?" McGregor said, giving Sarah a nod to indicate the question was for her.

"Good morning, Lieu." Sarah pulled one of the battered metal chairs from the wall and placed it in front of his desk and sat down. "Yes. I did."

McGregor didn't respond to the sarcasm in her voice. He just waited for Angel to empty another chair of its contents, then he waved a hand at Sarah to continue.

"Walt's doing the autopsy this afternoon. Said he'd send the full report over later, but he did confirm that the girl was shot at pretty close range in the back of the head."

That got his full attention. "She was targeted?"

"Possibly."

"Christ." Mc Gregor wiped a hand through his thinning hair. "Who would do that to a kid?"

"Well, as Walt reminded me yesterday, that's what we need to find out."

McGregor glared. He was doing a lot more of that now that he was no longer drinking. Still, Sarah was glad he'd stopped. Not only had the move saved his job, but now his office no longer smelled like the back-alley vent from a bar. Like smokers who were unaware of the lingering aroma of stale tobacco, people who drank too much never seemed to know how the sour odor of liquor would seep from their pores. A few months ago, when she found out that he was going to AA, she'd asked if there was a twelve-step program for cussing. Maybe she should clean up her mouth. He'd looked at her and deadpanned, "Maybe you should."

As silly as some kind of program for curbing the urge to cuss sounded, Sarah knew it wouldn't hurt to at least try to limit the colorful language. How many times could she say "fuck off" to the brass and get away with it?

"Sorry, Lieu," Sarah said. "Just trying to inject a little humor here."

"Well, *humor* me, and tell me what else you've got."

"Actually, we *got* nothing, Lieu. Nothing at the crime scene and nothing conclusive from the family." Sarah finished by quickly filling him in on their interviews with the family.

"We are going to take a look at the father," Angel said. "Sarah seems to think he might be somehow involved. I'm a skeptic, but at least eliminating him will give us something to do."

"Can't imagine a father killing their own kid that way." McGregor shook his head. "I know fathers kill their kids all the time. But it would take a cold-hearted bastard to do it up close and personal. Is the father a bastard?"

Sarah thought about the guy's behavior. If they asked the wife, she might say her husband wasn't the kindest man. But was he rotten? Not like some people she'd helped put behind bars. "I'd have to say no. But he was evasive and basically shut us down in the interview."

"Wasn't just grief reacting?"

"Could've been," Sarah acknowledged. "But we've got to cross him off the list one way or another."

"Okay. Try again. But go at him easy."

When McGregor turned back to the papers on his desk, Sarah knew they were dismissed. That was his way. No wasted words. She stood and headed out, with Angel trailing behind. "When do you want to interview Santos again?" Angel asked.

"Let's see if we have anything from forensics or Walt first."

"Walt won't be doing the post until later today. Remember?"

"Right. But we might have something from Roberts."

Back in the squad room, Angel went to her own desk and Sarah noticed a blue folder on top of hers. She slipped out of her blazer, hung it on the back of her chair and sat down, opening the folder to find a forensic report. Leafing through the pages, Sarah noted that yesterday's crime scene had yielded lots of items. It was a public park after all, and Sarah wondered if any of the scraps of paper, cigarette butts, or fragments of fibers were going to mean anything to their case.

No shell casing had been found at the scene, which possibly meant the shooter cleaned up his brass, but a small bag that had contained dope was found close to where the victim had fallen. Some of that Cheese that had been showing up for months all around the city and in the suburbs. It had become the drug of choice for young teens. "Hey, Angel." Sarah waited a moment for her partner to look up. "CSI tech found a baggie at the park. It had remnants of Cheese in the corners."

"For eating or sniffing?"

Sarah chuckled. "The dope. What if the girl *was* there to score and something went wrong?" After a beat, she added, "Or what if the dealer approached her, but she refused? Made him mad?"

"Possibly." Angel paused for a moment. "But the way she was shot? That's not a typical MO for dealers. They don't usually use such precision when taking someone out."

"True. But that scenario fits better than one that has some kind of hit man killing a girl that young."

"Hit man? Where did that come from?"

"I'm not saying it was a hit. I'm just thinking out loud. Because of the close range of the shot."

"I seem to recall some detective telling me how we work on facts, not scenarios." Angel smiled and Sarah couldn't help but smile back. These brief moments of camaraderie always felt so good. Too bad it just took one moment of friction to wipe the smiles away.

Sarah sighed and turned her attention back to the report. She was much better off trying to solve a murder than fix the problems between her and Angel. After another half hour, she stood and stretched, then walked around to Angel's desk. "You ready for lunch?"

Angel slapped a file closed. "Sure. You find anything else?"

Sarah walked back to her chair and grabbed her blazer. "Nothing that helped. Let's see if we can prod a lead out of Santos."

They made a quick stop at a SUBWAY shop where Sarah had them add extra spinach to her Sub Club as a nod to nutrition.

Sometimes she did try to take care of her body and give it good fuel. Angel got the veggie sub. "You going vegetarian?" Sarah asked.

"Nope. Just don't feel like having meat."

After they ate, they drove the last couple of miles to the Santos home. The scene was much the same as the day before, with people in the yard and on the porch. Sarah nodded to them. "They going to stay here forever?"

"How should I know?"

The edge in Angel's voice gave Sarah pause. It was always such a surprise when the woman went from joking around one minute and polishing the chip on her shoulder the next. Sarah sighed, then said, "It was just an idle question. No need to get all twisted about it."

"Sorry. Just didn't know why you asked me?" Angel slid out of the car and waited for Sarah to come around from the driver's side.

"I asked you because you were the only other person in the car."

Angel didn't respond, and Sarah gave her a hard look. "Tell me you didn't think it was some racial thing."

Angel shrugged.

"Oh, for Pete's sake." Sarah shook her head and strode briskly toward the door.

_*_

Watching her partner, Angel wanted to kick herself for being so sensitive. Too often she acted off an instinct that had been carefully nurtured by her racist father, and propagated by the activists he invited into their home. She had never questioned it until recently, and the longer she worked with Sarah, the more Angel was discovering that racism really did cross the street at will.

A different Hispanic woman opened the door to their knock. This one was short, but not as rotund as Mrs. Santos. She seemed to understand English when Angel told her who they were and asked to come in. The woman obliged, leading them into the living room. Mrs. Santos was sitting in the same spot on the couch as she had been the day before, and for a moment Angel wondered if she had even moved in the last twenty-four hours. Noting the different dress the woman was wearing, this one with large orange flowers on it, she'd obviously moved at least once.

The other woman hurried through a doorway that led to a kitchen, then came back with Mr. Santos. He wore blue jeans and a crisp turquoise cowboy shirt with silver snaps. The tightness in his face was a clear indication he was not happy to see the detectives. Angel took a small step toward him. "We apologize for the intrusion, but we do need your help in our investigation."

"We'll try to be brief," Sarah added. "If you wouldn't mind joining your wife."

Santos hesitated for a long moment, then walked over and settled on the sofa. Angel glanced at Sarah, who gave a brief nod, indicating she should take the lead, so Angel pulled a small wooden chair from the corner of the small room and positioned it close to the couple. Sarah leaned against the doorframe to the kitchen.

"Do you have *hombre* who killed my *bebe*?" Mrs. Santos asked. While she had indeed changed her dress since yesterday, she had not lost that dazed look of someone slammed with deep emotional shock.

"No, Ma'am." Angel touched the woman's hand briefly. "We're doing our best."

"Chase drug dealers out of that park," Mr. Santos said. "Then no more shootings."

Angel took a breath. Now was the time to tell them the truth. "This was no accidental shooting," she said. "Your daughter was shot in the back of the head. Close up."

The pronouncement hung there in the silence for a few seconds, and Angel noted the reaction from Santos. The lines in his face tightened as he drew in a sharp breath and glanced away.

"What she mean, Emilio?" Mrs. Santos plucked at the sleeve of her husband's shirt, then continued with a torrent of Spanish.

He stilled her hands and responded with more hurried Spanish until she seemed to settle down, then he glared at Angel. "From who?"

"We don't know," Angel said. "Who do you think might do that?"

Santos seemed stunned by that question, so Sarah threw another one out. "Do you have trouble with anyone? Trouble that might have gotten out of hand?"

He broke eye contact again, but not before Angel saw a glint of fear in his eyes. She looked over at Sarah, who nodded. She'd seen it, too.

"Who do you work for, Mr. Santos?" Angel asked.

"Me. My own truck."

"Yes. You told us. But what do you carry in your truck? Who owns that?"

"Equipment. For electricity. Like that."

"From where?"

"*Méjico.*"

Angel exchanged another glance with Sarah, then faced him again. "You bring goods from Mexico?"

"*Si.*"

"And take them where?"

"Here … Texas. Other places."

"What other places?"

"North. Oklahoma. Colorado. Sometimes California." Santos started to sweat, little beads of perspiration forming in the furrows on his forehead.

"Do you ever take anything from Mexico besides equipment?" Sarah asked.

He shook his head and dabbed at the moisture on his face with a wrinkled bandana he pulled out of the pocket of his jeans.

The sound of the door opening, drew their attention, and the detectives turned to see Juanita walk in. Angel guessed the woman had just come from the school. She was dressed in a tan skirt and cream-colored blouse, accented with a scarf in bold reds, golds, and purples. A simple professional look for a teacher. She put her large black bag on an occasional table and went over to her sister, giving the detectives a questioning glance.

The intrusion broke the rhythm of the questioning, and Angel wished the woman would have chosen a different time to drop in. Juanita and her sister exchanged a few words of Spanish, then Juanita

35

looked back at the detectives. Her expression was anything but friendly. "Camille says you think my brother-in-law is responsible for Felicity."

It was an accusation.

Angel took a breath before responding. "We haven't said that. We're just asking questions. Most killings like this are not stranger-on-stranger. We always have to ask the family tough questions."

"My *marido* good man," Camille said. "He no do nothing wrong."

Angel gave the woman a slight nod, then focused on Santos. "Did you ever carry drugs in your truck?"

The question seemed to stun everyone for a moment. Then there was a flurry of Spanish from the two women on the couch. Angel held up her hand to stem the tide. "Did you, Mr. Santos?"

"No."

"Could drugs have been put in your truck without you knowing?"

Mrs. Santos started to cry and rock back and forth. Juanita soothed her for a moment, then glared at the detectives. "This is not right."

"Nothing about any of this is right." Angel waited a few seconds for them to realize what she meant and settle their emotions a bit. "We're just trying to find out who killed Felicity and why."

"Then go. Investigate." Juanita waved toward the door. "The killer is not here."

"Before we go, we need contact information for Felicity's friend, Maria," Sarah said. "Do you have a number?"

"Yes. We keep track of all of my niece's friends." Juanita went over and pulled a cell phone out of her purse, hit a few buttons then called out a phone number.

Sarah wrote the number in her notebook, then closed it. "Thank you."

"Now go. You have upset our family without reason."

Outside, Sarah paused halfway down the front walk and looked back. "I sure wish we could get a look at his business records."

"Yeah. Would be good to see his routes and destinations. See if they correlate with the known drug routes."

"Do you think he's moving drugs?"

Angel shrugged. "Not sure. But he's nervous. Like there's something he's hiding."

"We can ask McGregor about a warrant to search the truck, but I don't think it would happen. Not right now, anyway." Sarah got into the car and slammed the door. She pulled out her phone and called the number Juanita had given her. Because of the name, Maria, Sarah was expecting another Hispanic family, and was surprised to connect with someone whose ancestors may have made the Mayflower trip. The woman said the detectives could come over. Maria was there. She had stayed home from school and soccer practice.

It wasn't far to the address the woman gave Sarah. Made sense since the girls went to the same school and all.

The woman who greeted them at the door was tall with red hair and freckles across her nose and cheeks. "You're the detectives?"

Sarah nodded and showed the woman her badge.

"Hello. I'm Linda Finney. Maria's mother." She opened the door so they could step in, and then led them into a spacious kitchen. "Have a seat. I'll go get Maria."

While the house was similar in layout to the Santos home, Sarah noted that the austere decorations were a sharp contrast to the bold colors and numerous pieces of art that covered almost every surface of the other house. "I like this. Easy to clean."

Angel gave her a questioning look.

"No clutter. Did you notice coming through the living area? Not much to move when you have to dust."

"Who dusts?"

"Don't you?"

Before Angel could answer, Linda came back with her daughter. Maria was a smaller version of the woman, with a few less freckles. There were six chairs around a large oak table in the eating area, and Linda again invited them to sit.

Maria kept her eyes downcast as she took a seat. Maybe she was naturally shy or maybe it was just her reaction to the death.

Sarah remembered the time one of her classmates died in a flash flood after a torrential rain. She was shocked when she heard the news at school the next day. She hadn't known the boy very well, but she'd had a hard time looking at her teacher or her classmates, as if looking might involve having to talk about what happened and how she felt about it. It must be very hard for someone like Maria to lose a best friend. Sarah reached out and touched her hand. "We're so sorry about Felicity."

The girl nodded, but didn't look up. Her mother pulled a chair close and put her arm around the girl. "These detectives are trying to find out who would want to hurt Felicity, and they need to ask you some questions. Can you talk to them?"

Maria nodded again.

"Okay," Sarah said. "Tell us about yesterday morning."

Now the girl looked up. "What about yesterday?"

"We know that you and Felicity were at the park to practice soccer. What time did you start?"

"I don't remember exactly. Maybe seven o'clock." She glanced at her mother for affirmation.

"The girls try to get in an hour of practice on most Sunday mornings," Linda offered.

Sarah acknowledged with a nod, then turned back to Maria. "While you were there, was anyone else in the park?"

"Some boys playing way on the other side. I saw them when I left."

"Playing what?"

"Throwing a baseball."

"Did you see any adults?"

"Not in the park."

"What about outside the park?"

"There was a man. Near a car on the street."

"What was he doing?"

"Standing there. Leaning on the car."

"Did you get a good look at him?"

"Kinda. But I hurried past. I didn't like his face."

Sarah worked to keep any excitement out of her voice. "Would you recognize this man if you saw him again?"

Linda gave her a searching look. "Detective do you think—"

Sarah cut her off with a wave of her hand. "Maria. Can you tell me what the man looked like?"

"He was old. Older than my daddy. But not as old as my grandpa. In between. He had on green clothes."

"Green?"

Maria looked at her mother. "You know. Like the clothes cousin Barry wears sometimes."

Linda nodded. "I think she might mean Army fatigues. Barry just came back from Afghanistan. He wears them a lot."

Angel got out her cell phone and connected to the Internet, finding a picture of Army fatigues. She held the phone out to Maria. "Like this?"

Maria nodded.

"What color was his hair?"

"I couldn't see. He was wearing a baseball cap."

"So, his hair was short. It didn't show?"

The girl nodded.

"What color was the car?" Angel asked.

"Gray."

"Do you know what kind of vehicle it was?"

"Not for sure. But it did look a little like ours. The SUV."

"We have a Tahoe that we use most of the time," Linda said. "My husband drives a Nissan."

"Did you happen to notice the plate number?" Sarah asked.

The girl shook her head, then a tear escaped and slid down her cheek. "I'm sorry I can't help more."

"You're doing fine," Sarah said, then glanced at the mother. "Would it be okay for Maria to come down to the station and describe the man to a sketch artist?"

Linda glanced at her daughter. "Do you think you could do that?"

Marie seemed to brighten at the prospect of being helpful, and she nodded. Angel patted her knee. "If we showed you pictures of gray SUVs, could you possibly recognize the one the man was close to?"

"Maybe. I could try."

After making arrangements for the girl to come to the station, Sarah and Angel left. Walking out the car Sarah tried not to get too excited about the possible lead they'd just uncovered. Sometimes when it looked this easy at the beginning of a case, it really was too easy.

Chapter Five

●●

Tuesday, March 6

"When you called, you said you had some news." McGregor held up the coffeepot in a gesture asking if Sarah or Angel wanted coffee. Angel shook her head, but Sarah grabbed a mug off the shelf in the break room.

"We didn't get anything from Santos," Sarah said, holding the mug to be filled. "And even though I don't like his responses, we can look in another direction for now."

"We interviewed the dead girl's friend," Angel said, pulling out a chair at one of the small tables and sitting down. "She saw a man hanging around the park in the same area where the girls were playing soccer."

McGregor sat down opposite Angel, "Could it have been the shooter?"

"Possibly," Angel said. "He was at the scene, and Felicity's friend saw him start walking into the park as she rode off on her bike."

Sarah joined them at the table. "She's coming in to look at pictures of SUVs and try to describe the guy to Stimpson for a sketch."

"Since neither of you ladies were interested in the autopsy, I went this afternoon."

Sarah waved the sarcasm off. "Anything different from what Walt already told me?"

"Just confirmed and on paper. COD was a single gunshot wound to the head. Do you want the details of what the bullet did to the brain?"

"No, Lieu. If we wanted that, we would have gone to the autopsy."

"Walt retrieved the bullet. Looks like a .22 caliber from a revolver. That and a bit of powder residue confirm that is was the fairly close-range shot Walt thought it was. Also explains why there was no shell casing found at the scene."

"So, it definitely wasn't random," Angel said.

"Doesn't look like it." McGregor took a swallow of his coffee and then said, "And it wasn't sexual. The girl wasn't assaulted."

"Wonder if that'll be of any consolation to the family," Angel said.

Sarah pegged that as a rhetorical comment, so she didn't respond. She sipped her coffee, then set the mug back on the table. "Lieu? Why couldn't it be random? Some shooters kill just for the fun of it. Or it could have been a gang initiation. Some kid blooding-in."

"According to Walt, the weapon was within three to five feet of the girl's neck. Maybe a little closer," McGregor said. "Never heard of a random killing or gang initiation being done at such close range."

Sarah shuddered and shook her head. "It just seems so strange that this could be a hit. Who would put out a contract on a kid like that? And why?"

"If we knew the answers to those questions, the case would be solved," Angel said before getting up to get a bottle of water out of the refrigerator.

Sarah chuckled, then finished her coffee.

McGregor pushed away from the table. "When is the girl coming in to meet with Stimpson?"

"In the morning," Angel said. "She was pretty upset by the time we finished, so the mother wanted us to wait."

"What else are you working?"

"Checking the father's story," Sarah said. "We got some information on what companies Santos drives for, so I want to talk to the owners. See what routes he drives and how often."

"Okay, get your reports in before you leave today."

Back in the squad room, Sarah went to her desk and started calling some of the companies for which Santos drove. She took the top half of the list and Angel took the bottom. The most frequent trips Santos took were in and out of Mexico, and Sarah was surprised to see what the U.S. imported from there: Machinery, electrical parts and equipment, and even oil. Who would have thought? Seems like Mexico would import oil from the U.S. When she called a company in Mexico, Falco Electronics, she found out that the biggest percentage of what Mexico imports from the U.S. was electrical machinery and equipment. Weird. It was like the two countries were trading the same products. She asked the man at the other end why that was so, and he laughed. "They no tell me."

He did verify that Santos was one of the regular truckers with whom they worked, and a quick Internet search showed that Falco was a highly-respected business in Mexico. Did that mean it was unlikely they could be involved in any kind of drug running? Sarah leaned back and sighed. It was Mexico. There were no guarantees when it came to that southern neighbor.

She glanced up and saw Chad Smith weaving his way through the room. The detective stopped between her desk and Angel's. He flashed a grin that broke the dark contours of his face with perfect white teeth, and Sarah noted how handsome he was. How come she'd not paid closer attention before? She gave herself a mental shake. She had to stop looking at black men the way she had been looking at them of late. First LaVon and now Chad? No matter how enlightened she might be, there were still plenty of people who hated to see a white woman with a black man.

There was no need for concern, however, since Chad seemed to only be interested in Angel. "Ladies," he said, perching on the corner of Sarah's desk, but looking over at Angel.

"Where have you been hiding yourself?" Sarah asked.

"Been with Ryan. He's forming a task force to try to get a handle on the Cheese problem." He glanced at Sarah. "The brass have their shorts in a wad over it. The mayor of Plano called our illustrious mayor to demand that we stop the flow of drugs into their school system. Like those kids out there can't get the drug from anywhere else."

"Yeah, but by making the call she gets political points for being pro-active about the drug problem."

Chad laughed, then glanced back at Angel. "Did you miss me, too?"

She gave him a non-responsive wave, and Sarah wondered about that. Chad had made his interest in Angel clear from the first time they'd worked together, and Sarah thought that they had actually dated a few times. Now Angel seemed a bit frosty.

"You got some time to bounce some ideas around?" Sarah asked.

"Sure. What's up?"

Sarah quickly reviewed the basics of their case.

"Are you liking the father for this?"

Sarah gave a slight shake of her head. "Not seriously. I just can't imagine a father shooting his own kid like that. Walking right up behind her and bam." Sarah mimed the action and noted the grimace that crossed Chad's face.

"My thought exactly," she said.

"Although we are wondering if he's somehow connected," Angel said. "As my partner is so fond of saying, Santos has been acting kind of hinky. So maybe somebody offed the kid because of something the father did or didn't do."

"We were thinking maybe drugs," Sarah said. "Maybe he's transporting for someone. And that someone had her killed to punish the father for some transgression."

Chad shook his head. "If the father double-crossed some drug kingpin, it's hard to imagine they would go after a kid. More likely they'd just take out the father."

"But then they'd lose their driver," Angel said.

"They can always find another driver."

"McGregor once told me that hired killers never took contracts to kill a kid," Sarah said. "Sort of an unwritten rule. Like 'honor among thieves.'"

Angel looked at Chad and asked, "What do you know about the guys who are pushing the drug around town? Are they capable of killing a kid?"

"You never know what the low-level guys are capable of. Especially if they are sampling the wares."

"So, it is possible?" Angel asked.

"Possible, but not probable," Chad said. "There's still the way she was shot. That is not a typical MO for a pissed off drug dealer."

"Pretty much what McGregor said, too." Sarah let a breath out in a deep sigh. "So, all we have is a lot of maybes."

Chad stood and rapped the top of her desk with his knuckles. "Glad I could help, ladies."

Sarah didn't miss the look he gave Angel before he walked out. She leaned back in her chair and watched her partner busy herself with papers on her desk. Odd. Should she ask what the deal is between the two of them? For once Sarah held her tongue. It was none of her business unless Angel made it her business. "What do you think?"

Angel looked up. "About what?"

"The guy in the park that Maria saw. You think he had something to do with it?"

"I don't know." She leaned back in her chair. "On one hand I know the people connected to those Mexican drug cartels are heartless. Maybe they would send a guy to kill a kid."

When Angel stopped, Sarah prompted. "And on the other hand?"

"What kind of cold-blooded bastard would actually do it?"

Sarah nodded. That was a damn good question.

~*~

After a workout at the dojo, Angel decided to swing by her parents' house. Sometimes she just had a hankering for her mother's greens and cornbread. Since that was pretty much a staple side dish with any kind of meat, she was sure there would be some, and even if they had already finished supper, her mother would always heat her a plate. Her daddy said she was spoiled, but Angel just felt well-loved.

When she walked into the brightly lit kitchen, she was surprised to see LaVon leaning against the counter, a plate in his hands. Her father, Gilbert, was seated at the small kitchen table with a cup of coffee. He was wearing his blue coveralls with his name stenciled on the pocket, so he had not been home from work very long. Even though he owned the plumbing business and had two younger men working for him, he still liked to crawl under sinks. "Well, Mama, looks like another one of your chicks has come home to get a free meal," he said.

"You just hush now," Frances said to him before motioning Angel to sit down. "Let me fix you a plate."

"I told you I would be happy to stock the pantry," LaVon said to his father, who just hrumphed.

Angel sat at the table across from Gilbert, then turned to LaVon. "What are you doing here, big brother? I thought you had a standing date with what's her name on Mondays."

"Lois. Her name is Lois. And that ended months ago."

"Oh. I didn't know."

LaVon laughed. "You should be happy. You never liked her."

"That's not true."

"Okay. Then how come you never could remember her name?"

"You two stop it," Frances said, bringing Angel a steaming plate of greens. "I swear. Sometimes you two are worse now than when you was kids."

Angel's father hrumped again. "They's still kids."

"Saw the news report about that girl being shot," LaVon said, putting his plate in the sink and running water on it. "Your case?"

Angel swallowed and licked the corner of her mouth. "Yeah."

"Getting anywhere with it?"

Angel shook her head.

"Front page news when a white kid or Mexican kid gets killed," Gilbert said. "Reporters don't care when it's a black kid."

"Gilbert. You know that is not true," Frances said. "News was all over that story about the security guard what killed that black boy in Florida."

"Only after the Brothers made enough noise to wake the media up," Gilbert said.

Angel took another bite of her dinner so she wouldn't enter into this debate with her father again. The subject of racism was always like a piece of music on an endless loop. Sometimes she agreed with her father just to stop the loop from rolling, but more often lately she just wanted to challenge him. She set her fork down and took a sip of the water her mother had placed next to the plate, hoping that would keep her mouth shut.

"How's the partnership going?"

Angel choked on the water, and glanced at her brother. "Why do you want to know?"

"Making sure my baby sister is happy."

"I'm happy. We get the job done. Okay?"

"No need to get all defensive," LaVon said. "I was just curious."

Something about his tone made the words ring false, and Angel gave her brother a long look. It had been many years since he'd inquired about her happiness. In many respects he took after their father, not big on emotions, caring about them or sharing about them. She noticed that her mother also seemed puzzled, looking at LaVon with a bit of a frown creasing her broad forehead.

"Too bad you never did get that transfer back a couple of years ago," Gilbert said. "Get partnered up with one of your own kind."

"I never put in for a transfer."

Gilbert looked like he'd been sucker punched. "But it was decided."

"No Daddy. You decided. Not me."

"You're still my daughter and you will do as—"

"Stop right there. And listen. Because this is the last time I want to have this talk with you, Daddy. If that means I've got to stay away, then so be it. But I will no longer accept your orders or your racist attitude."

Frances gasped. "Now, honey."

"No, Mama," Angel patted her mother's hand. "I hate to say it, but I mean it. Daddy just has this great big hate for white folks. And that hate … It's like a chain keeping him trapped. And he just keeps trying to make sure that chain stays around us."

"Are you aware of—"

"Yes, Daddy. I am aware of the history. I am aware of the injustice. I am aware of the white folks who rue the day the first slave was brought here and black skin was introduced to white. But we have got to stop looking at everything through glasses tinted with racism."

Gilbert stood and pushed his chair back with such force it banged against the wall. As he stormed out, Angel was reminded of how many times that had happened throughout the years. Another endless loop. When her father did not like what was being said, he walked away. But he never walked out of their lives, which was a point in his favor and one of the things that she loved most about him. He was narrow minded and a bigot. But he was loyal.

Most times after a fuss up like this, she would wait for his temper to cool, then go apologize. But she wasn't going to do that this time.

"Angel, honey, you got to stop talking to your daddy that way." Frances said.

"No, Mama. I won't let this blow over like I have all the other times. This has got to stop."

LaVon clapped. "Bravo, little sis."

She gave him a hard look. "Quit that. This is not worthy of an ovation. I feel like I just shoved a dagger in his heart."

Chapter Six

· ·

Sunday, March 11

M elinda followed Ashley to the back of the restaurant toward the restrooms. The old Chinese lady who let them in had bought Ashley's story that she had an urgent problem. "You know, with my period. It came early."

Sometimes Melinda couldn't believe what her friend could get away with. If she tried to lie like that, it would never work. She couldn't hold eye contact for one second when telling a lie, but Ashley was so good she could probably pass one of those tests for finding out lies.

What they were doing was so wrong, but Melinda couldn't turn her steps around. Not if she wanted to save face. When Ashley had first asked her if she wanted some Cheese, Melinda was foolish enough to ask, "What kind?" She really thought Ashley had been talking about Velveeta. That was two months ago, and Melinda had tried to pass it off as a joke. But Ashley knew. She knew that Melinda had been brought up sheltered and wasn't one of those kids who waited for parents to crash, then snuck out at night to hook up or do drugs.

That's why Melinda was compelled to prove something to her friend. That's why she followed her down the darkened hallway, even though she'd rather not.

Ashley led them to the women's restroom and went to the far end of the counter. She pulled a baggie of powder and a straw out of her purse.

Melinda glanced quickly at the door. "What if that woman comes in? Shouldn't we go in a stall?"

"Chill. We'll be quick." Ashley laid a mirror on the counter and smiled at Melinda. "Can't do this off a toilet seat."

In a practiced move, Ashley got two short rows of powder on the mirror, then she handed the straw to Melinda. "You go first."

This part always felt weird to Melinda, and a little silly. That was until the drug hit. Then she just felt good. Spinning a little. Like she might just float up and away off the earth, but the prospect didn't scare her. Maybe she should just float away and never come back. Nobody would miss her. Not really. Her parents would pretend to be devastated, but she knew better. They were so wrapped up in their jobs, it might be a relief not to have her making her little demands on their lives.

She reached out to hand the straw back to Ashley. At least that's what she thought she did, but she seemed to be having trouble getting her hand to go where she wanted it to. It seemed to be operating outside the control of her mind. Ashley giggled and grabbed the straw. "Hitting you hard, is it, girlfriend?" Then Ashley bent to take her hit.

As Melinda watched her friend sniff the dope, her eyes blurred and she fought back a wave of nausea that started in her toes and gained momentum as it swept toward her stomach. The light around her slowly dimmed until the room was shrouded in darkness. What was happening? This wasn't like all those other times. Where did the high go?

"Ashley, I don't feel so good." She could hardly get the words out. She imagined they were baby birds fighting to crack through a shell.

"What's wrong?" The response was muted, as if Ashley were speaking through a heavy cloth.

"I don't know. I just …"

Those were the last words Melinda ever said.

Chapter Seven

•••

Sunday, March 11

Afficiency talking to a few of Felicity's friends from the soccer team, Sarah stopped at a donut shop. Cop stereotype be damned, she liked the BBQ Chicken sandwich at Dunkin' Donuts, and the coffee wasn't bad either. She ate the sandwich and took a refill on the coffee to go. A whole week had passed since the young girl had been killed, and here was another Sunday and another day off that wasn't going to happen. The only consolation was that nobody was getting a day off for the foreseeable future. Not while the pressure was on everyone in the department from the top down. Of course, nobody at the peak of the pyramid would be giving up a Sunday at the golf course.

Sarah was just stepping out of the coffee shop when her cell rang. She dug it out of her jacket pocket and noted the number. McGregor. "I'm on my way in," she said. "Stop nagging."

McGregor ignored the pathetic joke and told her to meet Angel at a restaurant where two girls had been found dead. He gave her the address, then abruptly hung up. Probably because he was as tired as she was of hearing about dead girls.

Sarah sighed, unlocked her car, and got in.

It took thirty minutes to get to the little dive on the upper section of Greenville Avenue. Thirty minutes during which Sarah finished her coffee, listened to some tunes from Travis Tritt, and tried to keep images of dead kids out of her head. She also tried to forget how many days had passed since Felicity's body had been found. They weren't even close to nabbing a suspect. The friends Sarah had

51

talked to this morning had nothing to share that was of any help. Other than soccer, none of them knew what Felicity liked to do. None of them could be sure the girl didn't do drugs, but most of them thought not.

Maybe she should have another go at Maria. The young girl was the closest thing they had to a witness, and maybe Sarah could jog some detail loose. It was a plus that the girl was so eager to help. She'd been great with Stimson on the sketch, but so far that had gotten the detectives squat. No matches on any criminal data bases. The girl had not been able to positively identify the SUV by make or year, which probably didn't matter anyway. There was no way to know if the vehicle even belonged to the man who'd been leaning on it. And he might not even belong on a possible suspect list. Not that they had one, but it was nice to dream.

When Sarah pulled into the parking lot of the restaurant, she found a spot between a patrol car and a large van with lettering, *Tian An Men, a Chinese Buffet and Take-Out.* She eased her brand-new Taurus into the space, making sure there was plenty of room between her car and the others. Her trusty old Honda had given up the ghost several months ago, so she'd decided to go American, but she wasn't sure that trading gas mileage for patriotism was the best of moves. And she still wasn't sure that trading in a dented old car was the best of moves either. She never had to worry about where she parked before. Or about car payments.

The restaurant was just one of the many little Asian places that had cropped up in recent years, and Sarah stepped into the large entry to be immediately surrounded by a sharp aroma of sesame oil and the prattle of a foreign language. Some of the wait staff clustered in a tight group by the front of the serving area, chattering with great excitement. In a far corner, she saw her partner, along with Ryan O'Donnell, talking to an Asian woman who could have been thirty or sixty. It was hard to tell. The woman was petite and rail thin, with jet black hair and a flawless complexion.

Sarah made her way over. "What do we have?" she asked. "McGregor didn't say much."

"Two dead girls in the bathroom," Angel said.

"He told me that," Sarah said. "Murdered?"

"Not directly," Ryan said.

"Care to explain?"

"It appears the girls OD'd."

"Okay. I'm confused," Sarah said. "We're already working a case. Why would McGregor send us here?"

"When this report came in, I was in the office with the Lieu," Angel said. "The brass got wind of this right away and were all over Dorsett like sap on a pine tree. Somebody told the commissioner that there were seven deaths in the last six months from this Cheese. He didn't like that. Told Dorsett to get on top of this any way she had to."

"And that included pulling us off the Santos case?"

"No," Angel said. "We're just supposed to lend a hand for a day or two. That way the press can show the public what a fine job we're doing."

One thing, perhaps the only thing that Sarah and Angel had in common was their dislike of the press and the department's penchant for doing things just to appease the public. Appeasing loud, screaming voices seemed to be the thing to do in this modern day, and it sure hobbled a cop when it came to doing the job.

"After McGregor talked to Dorsett, he must have called my boss," Ryan said. "Walsh told me you'd be coming."

Sarah looked to Angel, who merely shrugged

"So? We're working this together?" Sarah asked Ryan.

"Looks like it."

"Okay, then."

"Come on," Ryan motioned Sarah to follow him. "I got a couple of guys processing the scene and Walt is about to finish up."

"I'll talk to the owner again," Angel gestured to the distraught Asian woman sitting at an empty table.

Sarah nodded and trailed after Ryan. When they got to the restroom, Ryan stepped aside. "Go ahead," he said. "It's crowded in there."

Inside, Sarah caught the distinctive odor of death that comes with a release of bodily fluids. No matter how many death scenes she witnessed, the smell never got any easier to take. The odor at the morgue was only marginally better. She pinched her nose and walked over to where Walt was hunkered over one of the bodies sprawled on the floor. "Twice in one week, Walt. People might talk."

He glanced up at her. "You should start carrying a clothespin in your pocket, Detective."

"Funny, funny." Sarah didn't want to look at another dead girl, but she forced herself to do her job. The girl might have once been pretty, but death had not been easy. The aftermath of the drug overdose left her features contorted and her skin mottled.

Another one that was too young to die.

"How old do you think she was?" Sarah asked Walt.

"Eleven? Maybe twelve?"

"My God." Sarah gave a little shake of her head, then asked, "TOD?"

Walt leaned back on his heels. "This one's easy. Narrow window between the time they came in here and when they were found."

Damn. Maybe if someone had come into the restroom earlier...

Sarah let that thought drift away. Didn't matter now. Wishing wouldn't bring the girls back to life.

She stepped out of the crowded room and found Ryan leaning against the wall. "What's the story? How'd they get here?"

"Owner says the girls were in the parking lot when she pulled in." Ryan gestured to the woman with Angel. "She let them in to use the bathroom. Was busy setting up for the lunch buffet, so she didn't notice whether they left or not. Later, one of her staff found them."

"Do we have a timeline?"

"The girls came in just before nine. The waitress found them a little after 10:30. Patrol got here at 10:45. I made it about forty minutes later."

"Any ID?"

"Nothing yet. There are two purses in there, but we don't know which one belongs to which girl. I didn't want to look through them until the techs finished documenting the scene."

"Right. We'll check the purses later."

_*_

.Angel closed her notebook and gave the restaurant owner a brief nod. She knew enough about Far East cultures to know not to offer a handshake. What a weird week this had been. Like visits to the United Nations. She made her way over to Sarah who looked up and asked, "Anything?"

"Not much. Owner didn't know the girls. I asked her why she let them in if she didn't know them. She said because they were desperate to use the 'facilities'. Her word, not mine."

"She have any idea where they came from?" Sarah asked. "They're not old enough to drive, so they must have walked from somewhere."

"She didn't know. But she did say there are some apartments not far from here. They could live there."

"Maybe we'll get lucky. Find ID and addresses in their purses," Ryan said.

Angel nodded just as Walt stepped out into the hallway. "Finished. My team's coming to get the bodies. Should be here any second."

"What about the rest of the tech crew?" Sarah asked.

"They're winding it down," he said, peeling off his latex gloves. "Room should be yours momentarily."

Ryan hesitated a beat, then turned to Sarah. "If you and Angel can take care of the rest of this, I'll go with Walt. He said he could start the autopsies this afternoon."

"Sure thing," Sarah said. Better Ryan handling that than her. The last thing she wanted was to watch Walt cut another small body open. She'd seen too many. He always did the autopsies showing as much respect as he could to the dead person, but there was not much dignity in lying naked on a steel table while someone dug through your insides.

Angel and Sarah walked into the main dining room where the owner was seated at one of the tables, head in her hands. The rest of the staff was gone. Angel touched the woman's shoulder. She was so thin, Angel could feel her bones. "You okay?"

The woman jerked upright. "Bad for business. Bad for business."

"We're almost finished," Angel said. "Maybe you can open for dinner."

"No. Girls die. No work. No business."

Angel didn't know what to say to that. The woman had seemed calmer before, and Angel could deal with calm. She didn't know what to do with hysterics, and the woman looked like she was on the brink now. But at least she had some concern for the dead girls. That was a point in her favor. Too many store owners were only worried about the inconvenience of something horrible happening in their establishments. Not good for the bottom line, you know.

When the first team from the coroner's office came in with a gurney, the woman opened her eyes wide and sucked in a quick breath. Angel patted her shoulder before moving to block her view as the second team entered. Angel motioned toward the drink station that was toward the back of the room. "Could I have some iced tea?"

"Yes. Yes." The woman rose quickly and almost ran to get the drink, looking like a little bird with arms fluttering and legs taking quick, short steps.

Angel followed. That way the woman would not have to come back and see the bodies being taken out. As she passed Sarah, her partner gave her a quick nod, as if she understood Angel's move.

A few minutes later, the detectives were able to go back into the restroom. One CSI tech remained, but the rest had gone with the bodies.

With the dead girls out of the bathroom, Angel didn't feel that clutch in her belly that she always got when she walked into a murder scene. The first time she'd seen a woman sprawled across the floor in death, she'd nearly lost her breakfast. Maybe one day she would get hardened to it all, but this wasn't the day.

There were two purses in the room; one on the counter in the sink area and the other in a far corner on the floor. The detectives took the latex gloves the CSI tech handed them, then Sarah walked over to the purse on the floor. Angel picked up the other bag. It was made out of heavy blue denim with lots of spangles. Seemed like everything young people wore today glittered. Bling, they called it. She opened the purse to discover it was crammed full, so she carefully pulled out the first item, surprised to see it was a small day planner. With so many electronic calendar options available, she didn't think a young teen would have something like this. She opened it and looked at the calendar on the left. Nothing noted on any of the dates and nothing on the notepad. After pulling out a leopard-print scarf, a small bag with makeup, a hairbrush, and a couple of pens, she checked in various other pockets in the purse and found forty-three cents in change, a receipt from The Gap, and a condom. A condom?

"I found a phone," Sarah said, drawing Angel's attention. "You?"

"Not yet. But I found a condom."

"Really? Those girls were having sex?"

"One of them was."

"At twelve? Really? When I was twelve, I didn't even know about sex."

"The times, they are a changing."

Sarah shook her head, then started scrolling through the display on the cell phone. Angel pulled a few more items out of the purse, finally locating a phone. It was a cheap, Trac flip phone, and as Angel pulled it out, it rang. She answered and heard Sarah say hello.

Ending the call, Angel turned and saw her partner with the phone to her ear. "I just called a number for a Melinda," Sarah said. "So, we know one name."

"Not much good if we can't find a last name. Or put the right name to the right girl." Angel checked the phone for recent calls and found one for an Ashley. She pressed "call" and the phone in Sarah's hand rang.

"Who am I?" Sarah asked.

"Ashley."

"Is she listed in contacts? With maybe a last name, too?"

"I'm checking."

Angel scrolled though a long list of friends before finally finding the name. "Ashley Munroe." She spelled it out. "Odd spelling. Isn't it usually M O N R O E?"

"Yeah. But the different spelling might make it easier to track down."

"We done here?" Angel asked.

Sarah nodded. "I'll meet you at the station. Let's see what we can find on a Munroe family."

"Okay." Angel gave the contents of the purse, and the purse, to the CSI tech, who started bagging everything.

Traffic was jammed on Central Expressway because of an accident, and Sarah slammed the brakes just in time to avoid the car ahead of her. Since there wasn't an ambulance at the scene, Sarah figured that nobody had been seriously injured, but the drivers who always had to slow down and gawk had traffic backed up for half a mile. Vehicles inched along at a slow crawl until passing the site where a small sedan had rear-ended an even smaller sedan.

By the time Sarah made it to the station, Angel had found a promising listing for a Munroe family. "The address is close enough to the restaurant that it could be our girl," Angel said.

Sarah looked at the paper Angel handed her. "Let's go see."

"Okay. I'll swing by to check if Roberts has some pictures ready," Angel said. "You want to let the boss know?"

Normally Sarah hated to pass up an opportunity to trade barbs with the head of the forensic team, but she nodded and then went down to McGregor's office.

"Hey, boss," Sarah said, when he looked up from the papers on his desk. "Angel and I found a possible residence for one of those girls. We're headed there now."

"Okay."

Sarah turned to go back out, but McGregor called out. "Wait. Forgot to tell you that Simms thinks he has a lead on your burglary. Might be able to get your television back."

"That's good. I hope he catches the bastard, but no big loss on the TV."

McGregor had already put his attention back on what he'd been working on, and he just gave a slight wave of acknowledgement.

From there, Sarah went to get a departmental car. She preferred not using her personal car as much as possible, especially after incidents like earlier on the expressway. If she was going to slam into another car, she'd rather not do it with her own. She called Angel's cell to let her know she was ready to go.

~*~

It didn't take long to drive to the address on Willow Grove Road. The homes in the area were a mix of restored historic buildings, with a few mini McMansions thrown in. The neighborhood didn't reek of as much money as the area where the real wealthy of Dallas lived, northwest of the downtown area, but it had enough of the odor to turn Sarah off. She was the first to admit that she didn't like rich people. Maybe because they didn't know how to act like ordinary people? Or maybe just because Sarah had grown up poor and had suffered more than a little discrimination from "others." She knew Angel was well aware of how she felt, so she turned to her partner after parking in the circular drive in front of a stately home. "Maybe you should take the lead on this. I might say something to upset the rich white folks."

Angel laughed. "Like I won't?"

"No. You're much more polite than I am."

"How about that. Something we agree on."

Sarah chuckled as she slid out of the car, grabbing the folder with the pictures of the dead girls from the dash. These moments of joking around were so infrequent with Angel, but they felt good. It was at times like this that it felt like they were close to being real partners.

Almost.

Sarah walked around the hood of the car and followed Angel to the front door. It was a work of art, heavy dark wood with an intricate flower pattern carved in it and a fair-sized stained glass window about chin high. The image in the glass was abstract, so Sarah was at a loss as to what it was supposed to depict. It was eye-catching, though, with bold reds, golds, greens, and blues on a white background.

Angel pushed the doorbell, and Sarah nodded at the window. "Know what that is?"

"Haven't a clue."

The door was opened by a petite woman wearing black yoga pants and a turquoise workout tank top. She was trim and fit and very tan. "If you're selling something, I'm not interested," the woman said, turning as if to close the door.

"We're detectives with the Dallas PD, Ma'am," Angel showed her badge. "I'm Angel Johnson and this is Sarah Kingsly."

The woman turned back.

"Are you Mrs. Munroe?" Angel asked.

"Yes. Celia Munroe."

"Do you have a daughter, Ashley?"

Celia nodded, alarm flashing in dark brown eyes.

"May we come in?" Sarah took a step forward.

"What is it?" The woman looked quickly from one detective to the other. "Has something happened?"

"It would be better to talk inside."

The woman who had stood so ramrod straight a few moments ago, seemed to shrink and fold into herself just a bit as she moved back. Her eyes were still riveted on the detectives, but her voice was a whisper. "Please tell me Ashley is okay."

Stepping in, Sarah saw that the foyer opened to a living room ahead and a bit to the right. A large Grandfather clock stood sentinel in the foyer. Sarah touched Celia's shoulder and guided her to a sofa across from a TV that was paused, the large screen showing women in some totally unnatural positions.

"Is anyone here with you?" Sarah asked.

"No. My husband is gone on a golfing outing. We have no other children." Celia looked from one detective to the other, eyes wide with apprehension. "Please just tell me about Ashley."

"I'm afraid we have some bad news," Angel said, sitting down beside the woman, while Sarah sat in an occasional chair across from them.

"This morning the bodies of two girls were found in the Chinese restaurant on Greenville. Victims of an apparent drug overdose."

Celia gasped, clutched at her throat, then gave a weak laugh. "And you think it was Ashley?" She paused just a beat. "It couldn't be Ashley. She doesn't do drugs."

"We found her purse. And her cell phone." Angel said. "Both at the scene."

"Maybe someone stole them and left them there. You said the dead girl was a druggie. Druggies steal all the time." Celia glanced at the TV screen. Perhaps thinking that if she could resume the workout, she could go back in time. There would be no police here telling her this awful news.

Sarah recognized the evasive tactic. She'd done this too many times herself when needing to avoid the painful stuff, and she struggled with finding the right words to bring the woman back. Angel rescued her.

"We're pretty sure that isn't the case."

Despite the softness of Angel's words, Sarah saw the pain they inflicted increase with every tick of that tall Grandfather clock. The woman paled and then choked. It took long minutes for Celia to pull her eyes away from the frozen image on the TV screen, then she wrapped her arms around her stomach and let out a low keening sound that threatened to go on forever.

Sarah gave her a few minutes, then said, "We need a positive ID on the girls. Can you look at some pictures?"

A sudden burst of emotion pushed Celia to her feet. "I don't want to look at pictures. Take me to Ashley."

Angel rose and put a hand on the woman's arm. "That isn't possible right now."

"When? When can I? Oh, my God. I can't believe this."

"Please, Mrs. Munroe. Please sit down." Angel tugged on her arm, and, after a moment, the woman sank to the sofa so quickly it was as if her legs had simply stopped working.

Angel waited a moment, then took the folder from Sarah and opened it. "These are the two girls," she said. "Is one of them Ashley?"

It seemed to take forever, but Celia finally glanced at the pictures, then choked on a sob and glanced away.

"Mrs. Munroe," Sarah said. "We need to know for sure if one of them was your daughter."

Without looking, Celia whispered. "Ashley ... she ... the one on the left."

Angel waited out more painful moments while Celia fought the battle between stoicism and total collapse. It looked like collapse was going to win, and Angel put a hand on the woman's shoulder. "We are so sorry for your loss."

Those words hung there for what seemed like forever, then Angel broke the silence again. "We need your help, Mrs. Munroe," Angel said, removing the picture of Ashley. "Can you tell us who this other girl is?"

After another long hesitation, Celia looked over and studied the face. "I'm not sure. It could be her friend, Melinda. But I only met her once. Ashley has ... had lots of friends. It's hard to keep up."

"Do you know Melinda's last name?" Sarah asked, pulling her notebook out of her jacket pocket.

Celia shook her head and glanced away. "I'm sorry. Ashley may have told me once. I don't know. I forgot."

"That's okay." Angel touched Celia's arm in a gesture of comfort. "Do you know where Melinda lived?"

"No."

"Did she go to school with Ashley?"

"Maybe. I'm not sure, but I believe so." Celia seemed to brighten just a bit at the prospect of being helpful. It always amazed Sarah how people in these first stages of shock and grief would clutch at anything to feel better, if even for a second or two.

"What school?" Sarah asked.

"Montblair. A private school. Ashley's in sixth grade."

"Thank you, Mrs. Munroe. This is all we need." Sarah closed her notebook.

"Is there someone we can call for you?" Angel asked. "Your husband?"

"I don't know." Celia wiped trembling hands across her face, then looked up as if suddenly remembering. "My sister lives in Plano. Maybe she can come over until Frederick gets home."

Celia gave the number to Angel, who then walked to the foyer to make the call. It was always better to do that away from the person who had just been body-slammed with bad news. Sarah stayed until Angel came back, hating every moment she had to watch this poor woman dissolve.

"She's coming," Angel said. "Do you want us to stay until she gets here?"

Celia took a deep breath, then raised her chin a notch. "No. I'll be okay. It won't take her long."

"We'll see ourselves out." Sarah stood as Celia nodded. "We'll lock the door."

Again, a nod. There was nothing else to say.

"You were good in there," Sarah said as she walked toward the car with Angel.

"Yeah, well, I've always had an affinity for someone's pain." Angel slid into the passenger seat. "And that woman was suffering the worst pain imaginable."

"None of it's easy."

"What now? Go back to the station and try to get someone at the school?"

"The only possible employee at the school on a Sunday would be the janitor." Sarah pulled out her cell phone. "And it's late enough that he's probably gone for the day. I'll check with McGregor. See what he wants us to do."

"But there's another mother out there who needs to know about her daughter."

"Is it going to matter if we bring her the bad news today or tomorrow?"

Angel hesitated for just a moment then shrugged. "Guess not."

Sarah connected with McGregor and told him what they'd gotten from the mother. "Want us to try the school tonight to see if we can get a lead on this Melinda?" She listened for a few moments, then disconnected. "He's going to send a Uniform over to see if anyone is as the school. He'll let us know. Otherwise we'll get on this first thing in the morning."

"That's a relief. I really didn't want to have to do this one more time today."

~*~

After Sarah had taken them back to the station to get their own cars, Angel went to her favorite place to get rid of frustration, the dojo. She needed the intense physical sparring to work off the anger over the senseless deaths of two young girls.

Normally on a Sunday evening she would be at her parent's house for dinner, but not this week. She had not gone back since the blowup with her father. She'd talked to her mother a couple of times this past week, but countered her mother's pleas for Angel to make up with her daddy. In time, she probably would. Home was a sanctuary and there were times she really needed that sanctuary. But she wanted to let him stew long enough to know she was serious about asserting her independence.

Angel went into the locker room and opened her workout bag, pulling out her dobok and black belt. She changed quickly, hung her street clothes in the locker, and padded barefoot out to the main workout area. There were only a few people out on the floor, one being Randy, the dojo owner, a small Asian man of indeterminable age. Angel found an open mat and performed the opening salutations, then started working patterns. The first few were simple, increasing in complexity as she worked. Sweat beaded on her face and trickles of moisture ran down her spine. She pushed herself hard for nearly thirty minutes, then stopped and stepped back.

Randy came over with a towel. At five seven he was barely taller than Angel, but there was a lot of power in that small frame. There was also a lot of wisdom under that thatch of black hair laced liberally with streaks of silver. "Bad day, today?"

Every time he spoke, Angel knew that if she closed her eyes, she could forget that he was Asian. He had the look all the way, but he spoke perfect English. Not even a hint of the pidgin English so often associated with Asians. Angel didn't even know what country he was from. He never said. He never said what his real name was, either. He was just Randy.

Angel took the towel and wiped her face. "It's never a good day when children die."

A wave of pain crossed his face, and Angel wondered for a moment if he had personal experience of that truth.

She knew better than to ask.

"You want to spar?"

Normally Angel welcomed a chance to go up against the Master, but today she was just too emotionally spent to focus. In martial arts, it was never a good idea to fight if you couldn't focus. She shook her head.

Chapter Eight

• •

Monday, March 12

Mid-morning on Monday, Sarah and Angel were in the Lieutenant's office, after being summoned there by a harried-looking boss. Sarah recognized the signs. The heat was really coming down the pike.

"What do you have on those OD victims?" McGregor asked. "Did you get an ID on the second girl?"

"We're working on that," Angel said. "Going to the school the first vic attended. There's a good chance both girls went to the same school. It's spring break, but we were lucky. The headmistress was in this morning. We're set to meet with her this afternoon."

"Anything to help us figure out where the girls got the drugs?"

McGregor posed that question to Sarah who shook her head. "Way too early for that, Lieu."

"I know." He wiped a hand through his already messy hair. "But if we don't get a handle on this Cheese problem, every suburb in a fifty-mile radius is going to be on the commissioner's ass. And the heat will eventually burn our asses."

"Looks like that's already happening, boss."

McGregor sighed, but didn't respond.

"Why is finding the dealers our problem?" Angel asked.

McGregor glared at her, but before he could start yelling, Sarah jumped in. "She's right. The drug side of this belongs to Webb and his guys in Vice. Not us."

"Yeah. But Dorsett got word to put every department on this until the drug is gone."

"And I just bet that word came from the commissioner who got it from Price. Looks good if he can tell the press that 'we are doing everything we can in finding the culprits who are bringing this dreaded drug into our fair cities.'"

Sarah did such a good imitation of the PR director that Angel laughed and even McGregor smiled.

"No matter where it originates," McGregor said. "The mandate is clear. So, you are to offer as much assistance as you can."

"Before or after we handle the victim notification?" Sarah said that with enough sarcasm that McGregor shot her a hard look. She softened her tone. "Okay. Sorry. We're out of here."

"Good," he said to their departing backs.

~*~

While Montblair was not quite as pretentious as the private schools in the wealthier parts of town, the stately Georgian building still had a certain air of money and class.

"Not as upscale as the last school we visited." Angel said, exiting the passenger side of the car.

"Nope. Think we'll luck out with the headmistress?"

"What? Helping us? She already said she would."

Sarah chuckled. "No. I meant if she would be pleasant."

"She already is. She was nice on the phone."

The parking lot was nearly empty, just three cars pulled close to the building, but that was not a huge surprise. Not many teachers would be on site during spring break. What was a bit of a surprise was the guard at the front door. He looked like a cross between an English Bobby and a Canadian Mountie—red jacket, blue trousers, and a small narrow-brimmed black hat, but his manner was anything but comical. He also had cop eyes, the kind that are not threatening but don't miss a thing. "May I help you?" he asked.

"We have an appointment with the headmistress," Sarah said, showing him her badge.

He took both badges and carefully inspected them before using his cell to call DPD to verify their identities. "No disrespect intended," he said. "But I'm sure you understand. We've had to tighten security since those latest school shootings."

"Of course." Sarah took her badge back and clipped it to the waistband of her jeans.

"I'll get one of our administrative assistants to take you to Ms. Hornbuckle." The officer made another call on his phone, and in a few moments the door opened to reveal a short, rotund woman who reminded Sarah of her third-grade teacher. The woman's wardrobe, which consisted of a tailored brown skirt, ruffled blouse, sensible shoes, and large wire-rimmed glasses, was even more dated. It looked like something out of the 60s or 70s.

"This is Ms. Wilson," the officer said. "She'll take care of you."

The detectives followed Wilson down a long corridor, the walls adorned with posters and some art work that almost looked professional. It was eerily quiet with no students around, and Sarah was aware of every footfall on the tile floor. The corridor ended in front of double doors that looked like they were carved out of golden pine. Wilson opened one door and led the detectives into an anteroom that had two desks. One was occupied by a young woman who could have been a student, the other was empty. Sarah presumed it was where Wilson worked.

The woman walked to another intricately carved door and knocked before opening it a crack. "The detectives are here to see you, Ms. Hornbuckle."

"Come in."

Wilson opened the door wider and stepped aside to usher in the detectives. Ms. Hornbuckle was a sharp contrast to her assistant. An attractive blonde with a bright, open smile, she wore a casual dark suit with a splash of color in the scarf that appeared tossed around her neck, but had probably been carefully arranged that morning. She rose from her chair and reached over to gesture to two chairs in front of the desk. "Please sit down, Detectives. I understand you want to talk to me about Ashley. We're just devastated."

"We appreciate you making time for us, Ms. Hornbuckle," Angel said.

"Not at all. And please call me Alicia." She offered them another big smile. "Would you like some coffee? Water? Anything?"

Sarah glanced at Angel, who shook her head.

"No, we're fine," Sarah said.

Alicia nodded to her assistant. "That will be all, Frances."

After the door clicked shut, Sarah asked. "What can you tell us about Ashley?"

"She wasn't the best student, but she tried. Came from a good family."

"Did you know she took drugs?"

The woman's smile faded. "Not at all. I was shocked when you told me about the circumstances of her death."

"What about other students? Do any use drugs?" Angel asked.

"No. Of course, we can't monitor them all the time, but we do try to watch for the signs. It used to be that teachers and administrators only had to worry about this in the upper grades." Alicia leaned back with a sigh. "It is really disheartening to see it creeping into the middle schools."

Unlike the last headmistress they'd dealt with, Sarah realized she could like this young woman. There was none of that haughtiness and pretension that had almost dripped off the other woman. Alicia really seemed to care about her students.

"We're hoping you can help us ID the girl who was with Ashley." Sarah slid a picture across the desk.

Alicia looked, then sucked in a breath. "That's Melinda. Melinda Nebors. She and Ashley are ... were ... inseparable. Besties, as the current jargon goes. Oh, my God." She pushed the picture back and glanced away, but not before Sarah caught the glint of tears brimming in the woman's eyes.

Sarah gave her a moment to compose herself, then asked. "Can you give us her contact information?"

"Of course." Alicia wiped her cheek. "Frances has it all on her computer. I'll have her take care of it."

"Are you going to be okay?" Sarah asked.

"Yeah," Alicia offered a weak smile. "I'm going to go home and hug my daughter. Then figure out how to handle this with the rest of my students."

Out in the parking lot, Sarah paused before getting into the car. "Now there's a teacher who deserves to be a teacher."

"And should get paid a lot more than I bet she gets paid," Angel said.

The women got into the car, but Sarah didn't start the engine.

"We just going to sit here?"

"No. I'm just not in a hurry to bring bad news to another person."

Angel fastened her seatbelt. "Me either."

~*~

Much later, after dropping Angel at the station and switching the department car for her own, Sarah went home. She stopped at the market on the way and picked up some roasted chicken and fried okra for supper. Okra was a vegetable. Right.

Cat greeted her with throaty meows that gained volume the minute he smelled the chicken. Sarah put the groceries on the counter, then went to change into shorts and an oversized tee. Properly dressed for dinner for one, Sarah served up the food, giving Cat an ample portion of the chicken, and started to eat, soon discovering she wasn't all that hungry. The images of the dead girls and the distraught parents kept taking control of her mind. Felicity's parents. Ashley's mother, Celia. And the Nebors. Mrs. Nebors had fainted upon hearing the news about Melinda, falling against her husband, who'd been beside her on the sofa. They had barely been able to answer any of the most rudimentary questions, so Angel and Sarah had left. A fuller interview could come later.

Chicken and okra now cold and congealing on her plate, Sarah pushed it aside. Sometimes she hated her job. Fucking hated it. Having to tell parents their child is dead was the worst thing possible. Especially these girls who were so young. They should have been living their time of childhood exuberance and innocence and parties with friends. Not involved with drugs and druggies and killers. *What the fuck is happening to our world?*

Standing abruptly, Sarah gave the rest of the chicken to a delighted Cat and tossed the okra. Then she poured herself a hefty glass of Blackberry Moonshine, a new liquor she'd recently been introduced to by LaVon. She carried the drink to the living room, flicked on the TV for company, and considered calling him. For all of about five seconds, before realizing she was in a really pissy mood. Not the best time to be talking to anyone.

~*~

Tyrone tucked a white handkerchief into the breast pocket of his slate gray blazer and walked into Ricky's Pool Hall. He saw Franklin seated in a far corner with a glass of iced tea on the table in front of him. Franklin, who had been known to shoot anybody who dared call him Frank or Frankie, was addicted to iced tea. Sweet. He did not share Tyrone's addiction to pot or tobacco. He was addicted to sweet tea. Had a glass in front of him at all times. He also did not share Tyrone's penchant for fine clothes and shoes buffed to a blinding sheen. Franklin looked like the hoodlum he was, complete with slouching jeans and a hoodie. Tyrone always wondered why his partner had to advertise.

"Did you see this?" Franklin asked without preamble. He slid a newspaper across the table while Tyrone lowered his bulk into a chair.

Tyrone didn't have to ask. He saw the headline right away.

"Cheese" takes another life

"See what the police said?" Franklin leaned across the table and poked a pudgy finger on a section of the story he'd already marked. Next to the penciled star was a statement by the police commissioner, "We will not rest until we get every person responsible for this plague on our city put behind bars."

"Strong words," Tyrone said, leaning back in his chair and crossing his feet at the ankles, careful not to scuff his Salvatore Ferragamo loafers. "Are we worried?"

Tyrone knew that Franklin hated to even think about being scared, let alone admit it, but they had not gotten where they were without knowing when to be aggressive and when to exercise caution. Tyrone had learned that principle of success in business school. Franklin had learned it by coming up hard on the streets, and Tyrone had always been a little surprised that such different paths had led to the same conclusion.

As expected, Franklin bristled. "Ain't afraid of no cops."

"I'm not afraid either. But I am going to advise our employees to be extra careful about cutting the heroin."

"Got to keep the supply going."

"True. But if we can avoid another death that could possibly be connected back to us, we minimize the risk."

The only response was a grunt, so Tyrone leaned closer to emphasize his words. "You know I'm right. I've always been right."

Because Franklin was so tough on the exterior, some people made the mistake of thinking that he was top dog and the strength that held the business together, but Tyrone was the pillar of this partnership. He could say that without having to sound boastful. It was simply true. Despite the fact that he sampled his product from time to time, he knew how to keep his head in any situation. He knew how to analyze changes in the marketplace or the neighborhood and act on those changes. And he was articulate enough to give their enterprise an air of legitimacy. Who expected a gang leader to talk like a Harvard grad?

Franklin had the muscle and intimidation. Tyrone had the brain.

"Okay." Franklin took a swallow of his tea. "We'll do it. But not 'cause I'm scared."

"Of course not."

Chapter Nine

....

Wednesday, March 14

C had bent his wrist, cradled the ball and pushed it as he jumped, sailing the basketball high over Ryan's head. When he heard the swish of the net, he smiled. He hadn't lost the touch.

"You used to play for the NBA or something?" Ryan asked, taking the ball on the bounce.

"B-ball paid my way through college. Didn't need it after that."

The detectives were at the park where the young girl had been shot, hoping to snag the "shitty little dealer," as Ryan liked to call the guy who worked this area. They were trying not to look like cops. Hence the one-on-one game they figured make them blend in with the few others who were there tossing footballs, or skating the winding concrete path through the park. This effort was part of the full-court press the department had launched in light of the screaming headlines and disgruntled politicians. Bianca Gomez, the media thorn in everyone's side, had started doing a special nightly report on the local news. It was called "Killer Cheese." When Chad saw that last night, he'd choked on his beer. Was she picking out a title for a book?

Ryan dribbled around him and charged the basket. "Hey. You gonna let this white boy win?"

Chad laughed and moved quickly into a defensive position. Considering that he had about four inches on Ryan, it wasn't hard to block the shot.

They played for about ten more minutes, then Ryan slowed a dribble and gave a head nod toward a skinny black kid who had just walked into the park. Chad moved and intercepted the ball, turning so he could get a better look at the kid. Why the hell did they all have to be so obvious? Dark hoodie, dark pants about to slide off the kid's skinny ass, shades, and that "drug dealer" shuffle.

"That's Damian," Ryan whispered as he snagged the ball back and dribbled slowly away.

Chad waited a moment, then moved slightly toward the kid. "Hey, brother. Wassup?"

Ryan had turned his back on the kid, and Chad waited to see what the kid was going to do. He'd stopped walking and was just staring at them. Then Chad saw the kid shift his weight to his toes. "He's gonna run."

Almost as if the words were a command, the kid took off, racing away from Chad to the left. As Chad sprinted after him, he saw Ryan drop the basketball and tear off on an angle that would put him ahead of the kid. That is if the kid continued to run blindly and not veer off to the right. That possibility was hampered a bit by the creek that meandered through the park and the steep banks on either side. But the kid could probably jump it if he wanted to.

Luckily, he chose not to, and the detectives were closing in when the kid suddenly tripped and went down. Ryan grabbed him by the back of the hoodie and pulled him upright. "Damian, my man. If you learned how to use a belt, you wouldn't be tripping over your clothes."

Chad just shook his head when he saw the kid standing there, jeans in a heap at his feet.

"If I turn loose of you, you gonna run again?" Ryan asked.

The kid shook his head.

"Then pull up your pants and sit down over here." Ryan pointed to a nearby picnic table.

"Homeboys can't see me talking to the cops."

"They won't know we're cops," Ryan said. "I'll have my partner here act like my body guard, and I could be some rich white dude buying some of your product."

Chad stepped off a few paces while the kid flopped on the wooden bench. Ryan sat next to him. "So, Damian. You work this park on Sundays?"

"Sometimes."

"You here that day the girl got shot?"

"What day?"

"Don't act stupid. I know you're not stupid, Damian." Ryan leaned in close. "Were you here and did you see anything?"

"The girl was dead when I got here." The kid looked from Ryan to Chad, then back again. "Honest."

"Honest was never in your vocabulary, kid." Ryan stood and grabbed Damian by the arm. "Let's finish this at the station."

"Wait! Wait! I didn't do nothing."

"You'll have plenty of time to convince us when we get there."

_*_

Ryan stashed Damian in an interrogation room and left him alone. "He can stew for a little while," Ryan said to Chad. "Meet me back here in fifteen."

Chad gave a mock salute. "I'll see if Sarah and Angel want to sit in."

"Okay."

Ryan went down the hall toward the break room, and Chad headed in the opposite direction, the basketball he'd retrieved from the court still under his arm. He was glad to see that Angel and Sarah were at their desks. He bounced the ball a couple of times as he walked toward them, drawing a comment from Burtweiler who was at his desk. "Go play outside, little boy."

Chad laughed. It was okay for Burt to call him "boy." Burt had kin who'd died at Auschwitz. He'd learned about bigotry and discrimination in ways Chad would never know, and that gave him a pass. Plus, Burt was a good guy.

Chad palmed the basketball, then leaned a hip on Angel's desk. She eyed the ball, then raised her eyes to his. "Thought we were all working."

"Ryan and I just nabbed a possible in the park killing."

Angel stood. "Really?"

"Yup. Got him sweating in interrogation." Chad turned to glance at Sarah. "Thought you two might want to come and see how the pros do an interview."

Angel just shook her head, but Sarah laughed as she stood, pushing her desk chair back. "I'll be happy to step in any time you men need help."

"He's in interrogation room two," Chad said. "I'll be back after I put my toy away."

A few minutes later, Chad joined the women outside the interrogation room where they could see Damian seated at the table. Sweat stained the neck of his black t-shirt and dotted his forehead. One leg was bouncing up and down in an erratic rhythm.

"Your boy looks nervous," Angel said.

Chad shrugged. "It could be nerves or hunger for a fix."

"You think this guy killed the girl?" Sarah asked.

"He was there. But he said the girl was already dead when he found her."

"Bet he said he didn't do nothing, too." Angel shook her head. "Nobody ever does anything."

Sarah nodded then turned to look through the one-way glass at the suspect. "I'm no expert on drug dealers," she said. "But this kid doesn't look tough enough to shoot anybody."

"Don't underestimate these little punks," Angel said. "They learn mean in the cradle."

"This from a nice middle-class girl like you?"

"You don't have to be on the streets to know what happens there."

Sarah glanced at Angel. Hmmm. That was a side of Angel that Sarah had never suspected. Before she could ask her partner more, Ryan came striding down the hall. He greeted the women then nodded to Chad. "You ready?"

Damian looked up with wide, frightened eyes as the door opened and Ryan and Chad stepped in. Ryan took the chair across from Damian, and Chad leaned against the wall near the door.

"You gotta let me go," Damian said. "I didn't do nothing."

"Yeah. You already told us that," Ryan said. "And if you can prove that, we will let you go. But first, I'm going to read you your rights."

Damian started to stand and Chad stepped over to push him down. Ryan went through the required warnings, then asked if Damian understood his rights. Damian nodded. "Okay," Ryan said. "Tell us about that Sunday morning. Seeing the girl. What did you do?"

"Nothing. I started through the park. Then saw her just lying there. So, I beat it out of there."

"You didn't touch her?"

"No, man. Ain't gonna be nowhere near a dead body."

"How'd you know she was dead?"

That question made Damian squirm and the answer tumbled out of him. "There was blood. An' I didn't see her moving. You know, breathing."

"See anybody around the area? Any of your rivals maybe?"

"Didn't see nobody else."

"Okay," Ryan leaned back in his chair. "Had you seen her at the park before?"

"Yeah."

"Ever tried to sell her anything?"

Damian shifted and glanced away.

Chad took a step closer. "Now is not a good time to start being evasive, Damian."

The silence stretched for another minute, then Ryan asked, "You still working for Tyrone?"

The briefest of nods was his answer.

"So. Maybe we take a little break here. I go talk to Tyrone. Tell him you're being all friendly with the cops."

Stark terror made the whites of the teen's eyes show. Chad put a hand on the table and leaned into Damian's face. "Now. Did you ever sell the girl drugs?"

"No. She wouldn't."

"Wouldn't what?"

"Take any. Not even free samples."

"Did that make you mad?"

Damian sucked in a breath. "What you saying, man? I tole you I didn't do that girl. Tyrone ...he ..."

"Tyrone what?" Ryan asked.

"He said never mind about the girl."

"Never mind what?"

"She got all in my face one time. Yelling and screaming that she was going to call the cops." Damian shifted again. "Tyrone said to leave her. Find other customers."

"He wasn't worried?"

Damian shrugged, and Chad exchanged a look with Ryan. In Chad's mind, it didn't sound plausible that Tyrone would ignore a threat like that.

"So, what did you do?" Chad asked.

"Nothing. Stayed away. Didn't go back to the park for two weeks after that. Give her time to chill out."

"What time did you go on Sunday?" Ryan asked.

"In the morning."

"What time?"

"I ain't got no watch. But it was early. I had to ... to take care of some business. Then go to my mama's for church. She likes me to go to church with her on Sundays."

"Oh, I bet you're a perfect little saint," Chad said.

"It's the truth, man. My cousin was getting baptized. Mama made me go."

On the other side of the one-way mirror, Sarah laughed. "Do you believe this kid?"

Angel shook her head. "But I bet that holds up. Nobody would make up something like that for an alibi."

They listened as Ryan got the timing of when Damien was at the park narrowed down a bit more. Church services started at 10:30, so he said he had to be at his mother's house a little after ten. The church was just a few blocks from her house, and she lived less than a mile from the park. Damian probably was at the park no earlier than nine or nine thirty.

"Well, crap," Sarah said. "If he wasn't at the park any longer than to have seen the body and skedaddled, then he must have been there just a few minutes before the body was discovered."

"But after she was killed."

It wasn't a question. More of an affirmation of what Sarah was thinking, so she didn't respond.

"That still doesn't rule out the possibility this could be related to him and his gang," Angel said. "A while back, didn't Chad say something about a turf war going on between a couple of gangs?"

"But it still comes down to the way she was shot. That would work for executing a rival gang member, but an innocent bystander?"

The door to the viewing area opened and ADA Jessica Franklin stepped in. "McGregor says you got a possible suspect in that park murder."

"We were hoping," Sarah said. "But hope is getting thin."

They watched as Chad and Ryan exited the interrogation room, leaving Damian to write out his statement on a legal pad Ryan had given him. A few moments later, the detectives stepped into the viewing room. "We're a long way from filing charges, counselor," Ryan said, nodding to Franklin.

"I was here for another case, and McGregor suggested I come by to see if you had anything for me." Jessica turned to the window. "What's his story?"

Ryan quickly outlined what had prompted them to bring Damian in. "I'll admit we may have acted on adrenaline. But we got so much pressure on us it's amazing we can walk upright."

"Some people would argue that men still drag their knuckles on the ground." Jessica said, a smile assuring the joke.

"Nice try, Counselor," Ryan said. "But I'm still stressed."

That comment elicited a laugh from everyone.

"Call me when. You notice I said 'when' and not 'if' you catch the killer. I'll make sure he doesn't see the light of day for a long, long time."

Chapter Ten

••

Thursday, March 15

A s Sarah walked into the squad room early Thursday morning, her cell rang and she answered to hear McGregor's clipped order, "Conference room A. Pronto."

She laughed. She was never sure if he was so curt because he didn't like phones, or this was just the way he liked to do business. Sometimes she thought curt was just fine. Cut through all the excess and get to the point. Other times, she thought a friendly "good morning" to accompany the message would be nice.

Sarah entered the room and saw why McGregor scheduled the meeting here; this many people would not fit in his office. In addition to McGregor and Angel, Ryan was there with his boss, Lieutenant George Walsh. They were polar opposites when it came to looks. Ryan could double for Mel Gibson any time, and Walsh was a heavier version of Laurence Fishburne. If one could imagine a heavier version of the actor. Sarah took a seat opposite Angel, noting that she sat close to Ryan. The electricity between the two was hard to miss, and Sarah remembered that the interest had started over a year ago. Had they carried that interest beyond the flirting stage? If so, Angel sure knew how to keep it secret. Not that they shared secrets like that.

Would they ever?

McGregor walked to the head of the table and stood. "Before we got pulled into these drug cases, O'Donnell and Walsh were already planning something that could make a dent in the problem. They can tell you about it."

McGregor nodded to Walsh, who pushed back his chair as if he was going to stand, then apparently changed his mind. It took a lot of effort to move his kind of bulk.

"We know who's in charge of the drug scene in most of Dallas," Walsh said. "We just haven't been able to get to them."

"Them?" Sarah asked.

"Yeah," Ryan said. "Two guys, Tyrone and Franklin." He pushed two mug shots across the table to her.

"Right. The names that scared the piss out of Damian."

Ryan nodded.

Sarah looked at the men in the photos, noting the cold, dead look in the one named Tyrone. She poked the face. "He's not one to mess with, I'm guessing."

"Nope." Ryan took the photos back.

"We've arrested some of the punks on the street," Walsh said. "But we can't get to those guys at the top."

Walsh paused, his silence inviting comments or questions.

"Nobody willing to deal?" Angel asked.

Walsh shook his head. "We've offered, but no takers. So, we have to get to the top guys another way."

"How? If everyone around them is scared shitless?" Sarah asked.

"Ryan here has a CI he thought we could use."

Sarah glanced at Ryan. "Damian?"

Ryan laughed. "No. He'd piss his pants and blow the whole deal. I've got this girl—"

"Girl?" For a moment Sarah flashed on the last drug case she'd been involved in. That one hadn't ended well. John had been killed, and he was a cop. How could they ask a civilian, a girl, to put her life at risk?

As if sensing the reason for her hesitation, McGregor cleared his throat and caught her eye. "Not all stings end badly," he said.

Still, Sarah had a hard time shaking the image of her former partner bleeding all over the alley floor, not far from the kid Sarah had to shoot to protect herself. Too many stings do end badly. And they still weren't sure of the motive for Felicity's murder. It could be connected to a drug deal gone all wrong.

Ryan, too, seemed to pick up on what Sarah was thinking. "This girl is smart," he said. "Street savvy. Nothing's going to happen to her."

"Once he gets her set up," Walsh said. "Ryan'll run her as usual."

"Is Chad in on this?" Angel asked Ryan.

Ryan shook his head.

"He's with Burtweiler and Simms on that real estate lady killing," McGregor said, leaning back in his chair. "That one's generating some heat, too. So now we've got two PR fires burning."

Sarah was aware of the attention the murder of the agent was getting in the press and elsewhere. Real estate agents were afraid to show houses because of the woman who was knifed to death in a vacant house. One leading Dallas agency had even called to request police protection for her people. As if that could even be possible.

"Okay, that's it for now." McGregor gave them all a nod and headed for the door. Sarah watched as Ryan turned and winked at Angel before following McGregor. Walsh was so intent on heaving his bulk out of the chair, he didn't appear to notice the exchange.

Sarah walked the long way around to her partner, giving Walsh time to get out the door. She tapped Angel on the shoulder. "What's with you and Ryan?"

"What do you mean? There isn't anything."

"Come on. I saw the little wink."

"Oh, that." Angel glanced away for a second to pick up her notepad from the table. "That's just his way."

"So, there's nothing …?" Sarah finished the question with a back and forth of her hand.

"Of course not. I don't date co-workers or …"

Angel didn't finish her sentence, but Sarah knew what was left out. She'd met Angel's father enough times to know he would not be happy if his daughter was with a white man. She was also sure that he would have some pretty strong reactions if he knew his son was getting involved with a white woman.

Especially this white woman.

That and her complicated relationship with Angel had kept Sarah from responding to LaVon's overtures at first, but the man was persistent. So far, they had only had dinner twice, and he'd taken her riding a few times, but each good-night kiss had grown with intensity. An intensity that was getting harder and harder to ignore.

"Sarah?"

"What?"

"Are you ready to go talk to the Nebors again?

"Uh, sure."

~*~

The interview with the distraught parents didn't provide any tangible information. Like the mother of the other girl, these parents had no idea their daughter was doing drugs. They had no idea where she got the drugs. "Cheese?" the mother had said. "It's really called Cheese?"

"Yes," Angel had told her. "Because it looks like Parmesan cheese."

"Oh my God."

"We read about this in the newspaper," Mr. Nebors said. "But didn't pay a lot of attention. Never thought it would—"

His statement ended in a cough that Sarah was sure covered the beginning of a sob. The man obviously didn't want to crumble in front of strangers. She wondered if he'd let go with his wife, or would he keep his grief separate, private? Private grief between spouses wasn't good. It could tear them apart.

Angel handed her card over to the man. "If you think of anything that might help, call."

"Um, yes. Yes, we will."

As the detectives were leaving, Sarah thought those people would probably never use Parmesan cheese again.

Back at the station, she'd barely settled at her desk after reporting to McGregor, when her cell rang. "Kingsly here."

"Detective Kingsly, you might want to come down here."

She recognized the voice of one of the patrol officers she'd worked with before, Rusty.

"Where are you?"

"At an apartment fire. South Oak Cliff."

"Why are you calling me? If something's not right, you should call the arson squad, not homicide."

"Because one of the burn vics asked for you."

"What's her name?"

"Amber. Amber Robinson."

Amber? Then Sarah remembered. It had been over a year since Sarah had heard from the girl. That was shortly after Amber had been attacked by the same person who had killed her friend. Sarah had thought the young woman was ready to make a change. Stop dancing at the gentleman's club where the horror had started and do something positive with her life. Sarah had even offered to take her in until she could get a job and a place of her own. But after a day in the hospital, Amber had announced she was not comfortable living with a cop. Especially not a cop who had more rules than her mother.

After that, Sarah had pretty much given up on the young woman, but she'd sometimes wondered if she could have tried harder to steer her down a different path. Sarah knew from her own reluctance to take advice, that sometimes people needed a bit more prodding. Or maybe a lot more prodding. A cattle prod came to mind and made her smile momentarily. Then she sighed and asked Rusty, "Why did she want you to call me?"

"According to her, there's nobody else to call," he said. "And her apartment's a goner. She said you offered to help her before."

"What about her parents?"

"Won't let me call them. Said they disowned her."

No big surprise there, Sarah thought. The girl kept making stupid decisions. *If I was her mother, I'd sure as hell disown her.*

"Is she hurt?"

"EMT's think she broke her arm, and she could have a concussion. But she's refusing transport until you come."

Great. Sarah drew in a breath, then let it out in a long sigh. "Give me an address. I'll be right there."

The acrid odor of burned wood was strong in the area as Sarah got out of her car and walked toward the fire scene. Firefighters were still working around the apartment building, long arcs of water cascading down on areas that had not been touched by the fire but could possibly erupt if embers were smoldering somewhere within the walls. She always marveled at how quickly and easily they moved, despite the heavy protective clothing and gear. She couldn't imagine working with more weight than her light jacket, weapon and holster, and handcuffs.

An ambulance was parked to one side, away from the main activity, and Sarah spotted Rusty standing at the rear of the vehicle. She walked over and saw Amber sitting just inside the open doors. An EMT was taping a bandage to a cut on her head and one arm was in a sling. "I fell running down the stairs," Amber said.

"Thanks for calling me," Sarah said to Rusty, who nodded and moved off. Then she turned to the young Hispanic EMT. "Is she going to be okay?"

"Should be, but she needs that arm in a cast. And she should have a CT scan to make sure there is no head bleed."

"I don't have insurance," Amber said, her voice drawing Sarah's attention.

"I told you to get a better job." When the girl flinched, Sarah almost regretted the smart remark, but she hadn't been able to hold the words back. And maybe that was okay. Maybe this was part of the extra prodding.

"If we take her to Parkland, they'll have to treat her. Insurance or not," the man said.

"Okay, do it," Sarah said.

"What about after?" Amber asked, a stricken look on her face.

"One step at a time. Go get yourself taken care of. We'll talk about after later."

Watching them settle Amber on the gurney, Sarah wondered what after would be. Should she arrange for a hotel room for the girl? That was an expense she couldn't afford, but what was an alternative? The first time Amber had been in trouble, she'd made it clear that she didn't want to crash with Sarah. Not that Sarah wanted her to, but ... Was there a way she could force the parents to take Amber back?

Sarah sighed as her cell phone rang. She held up a finger to Amber, then answered. She listened for a moment, then ended the call.

"I've got to go back to the station," Sarah said to the girl. "Let the medics take you to the hospital. Later we'll figure out something beyond the hospital."

"I can't pay for no hospital."

"Don't worry. I'll handle it." Sarah turned and walked briskly away. *I don't fucking need this.*

So much for her campaign to stop swearing.

Chapter Eleven

•••

Thursday, March 15

The scene in the large conference room could have been an instant replay of the morning briefing, except this time Helen Dorsett was present. That did not bode well. The Chief of D's didn't come to briefings unless she'd been getting pressure from above. That didn't mean God, although sometimes the commissioner thought he was God. When Brett Price, the prince of PR, walked in, looking resplendent in his three-piece pin-striped suit, Sarah knew her instincts were right. Someone had turned the heat way up on one of the cases.

Sarah set her coffee down on the polished surface of the table. Then she slipped her dark blue blazer off, hung it on the back of a chair, and sat down. Whatever was going to happen, it wasn't good.

Dorsett, looking a little shabby in her tan suit that was rumpled in the back from too many hours at her desk, walked to the head of the long table as Price settled into one of the side chairs and adjusted the creases in his pant legs. "A report just came in about another OD," Dorsett said, pushing at a wisp of gray hair that had escaped her signature bun. "Another young girl. This one only ten."

Silence followed, and Sarah tried to envision what the others here who had children or grandchildren might be thinking. It was hard enough for her to get her mind around the fact that kids that young were taking drugs. She couldn't imagine how she would feel if she had a relative who might be one of those young kids.

"When the commissioner heard about this one, he exploded all over me." Dorsett gave up on the attempts to control her hair, the wisp brushing her cheek as she moved.

"I've released a brief statement to the press." Price straightened in his chair in a familiar pose that was supposed to show how important he was. Sarah didn't give a rat's ass what Price thought of himself. To her, he was just a weasel. He'd throw anyone in the department under the bus just to protect his job and his image. "The commissioner will have a press conference later this afternoon. Nobody else will be authorized to talk to reporters."

As if I would, Sarah thought.

"In the meantime, we'll proceed as planned." McGregor glanced at each of the detectives before settling his gaze on Ryan. "Where are you with the CI?"

"Some Uniforms are picking her up. I'll stash her for a couple of days to get her ready."

"We'll put her through the system," Walsh said, shifting his bulk in the chair. "Let word get around that she was arrested. That'll strengthen her cover."

"Anything else?" McGregor looked at Ryan.

"This is what we've managed to put together on the cartel we think is responsible for the black-tar heroin." Ryan stood and slid folders across the smooth surface of the table to McGregor, Angel, and Sarah. He glanced at Dorsett and Price. "Sorry I didn't bring more copies. Thought I was just meeting with the—"

Helen cut him off with a wave of her hand. "Perfectly okay, Ryan. And there's no reason for us to stay. Y'all are on top of this." She motioned to Price, then turned back to McGregor. "I need something to feed to the commissioner for the press conference later."

"I'll give you what I can."

"Okay." Helen nodded and headed toward the door, leaving a faint odor of a sweet perfume in her wake.

McGregor motioned to Ryan to continue.

"What we know," Ryan said, sitting back down. "Is that for years the Sinanola Cartel handled all the drugs coming into Mexico from South America. They didn't move it themselves, though. A group known as the Herrera Organization transported tons of cocaine from South America to Guatemala, and then north to Mexico and the U.S. But more recently the Los Zetas have taken over Mexico drug trafficking. They bring in cocaine, marijuana, as well as the black tar heroin that's used with OTC drugs to make Cheese. A local gang cuts it and distributes the Cheese."

"Is it the Crips or the Bloods for the local gang?" Angel asked.

Ryan shook his head. "A merger of the two, which surprised the hell out of us, when it happened."

"When was that?" Angel asked.

"About a year ago. Seems they realized the benefits of joining forces and staying local."

"Is that the one Damian works for?" Sarah asked.

"Yeah."

"One of our problems," Walsh interjected. "We keep arresting the same kids over and over again. Kids like Damian."

"That's how we got our CI to cooperate," Ryan said. "We arrested her three times for misdemeanor drug possession. Once we got the feds involved, she knew things were getting much more serious. Made her willing to work a deal."

"The leaders are good at staying under the radar," Walsh said. "Send kids out to do the grunt work. So, if we can nail their asses, it'll stop the current river of Cheese in its tracks."

Sarah couldn't quite get an image of a river stopping in its tracks to stick in her mind, but she knew what Walsh meant. Cut off the head of any snake and the body dies.

"We get federal charges for the gang leaders," Walsh continued. "They won't ever see their grandchildren. If they live long enough to have grandchildren."

Angel motioned to get Ryan's attention. "Earlier you mentioned two guys. Tyrone and Franklin. They the leaders?"

Ryan pulled a couple of mug shots out of his folder and slid them across the table. "Tyrone Vane and Franklin Gibbs. Both from the same neighborhood. They've taken over the west side of the city. Call themselves The Westies, and they've terrorized the neighborhood.

Residents are scared of retaliation for reporting crimes, so they look the other way."

Angel took a long look at the two young men, then passed the pictures over to Sarah, who also studied them carefully. Then Angel turned to Walsh. "Are we just looking to bust this local group, or are you aiming higher?"

"The Feds are going after the big guys," Walsh said. "Strike a big blow in retaliation for the deaths of a couple of agents. A guy from ICE was killed last month, and a DEA agent bought it two weeks ago. The Feds'll put all their energy into finding those responsible."

McGregor's phone buzzed and everyone waited while he answered a call that lasted all of ten seconds and ended with him saying, "Okay." Then he stood and pushed his chair in to the table. "Let us know when you have that CI, Ryan. Kingsly, Johnson, you're with me."

"What's up Lieu?" Sarah stood and grabbed her folder.

"Tell you on the way." McGregor strode out of the room with the women trailing. "Burt brought in a suspect in that real estate killing. He thinks she might respond to a woman's touch in interrogation."

"Now? In the middle of this?"

He stopped so quickly, Sarah bumped into him. "Yeah. Now. You got a problem with that?"

"Uh. No." Sarah took a step back, recognizing that the pressure cooker was close to exploding.

McGregor strode ahead and Sarah glanced at Angel. "Flip you for it."

"No way. I think the Lieutenant meant that Burt was looking for a softer touch. You haven't been soft since I've known you."

There was a slight edge to Angel's tone, that slight edge that always snuck up behind Sarah and whapped her. Once they'd gotten past the roughest edges of their partnership early on, it seemed like most days they could sail along together just fine, then a high wind would blow in and the partnership would threaten to capsize. Trouble was, Sarah would get so relaxed she wouldn't see the wind coming.

McGregor called over his shoulder. "Tag team her. Do what you do best."

Sarah and Angel walked into the small room adjacent to the interrogation room where they could look through the glass and see the suspect. Simms was there, watching his partner who was in with the woman. Simms could not deny his Indian heritage. American, that is. Except for the fact that he was a bit smaller, he always reminded Sarah of an actor who played the role of an Indian in every old Western movie she'd seen. Jay something was his name. She should look it up on the Internet sometime. If she ever had time for research that did not involve a crime.

Sarah nodded to Simms. "Caught a break, did you?"

"Yup. She's looking good for this."

"McGregor said you wanted someone fresh in there?" Angel nodded toward the interrogation room, where Burt sat across from a woman about forty. A legal pad and pen lay on the table between them. Nothing was written on the paper.

"She's not responding to either of us."

"I can understand with Burt, but she resisted your charm?" Sarah asked.

"And I even took my war paint off."

Sarah chuckled then asked, "What's her name?"

"Belinda Samuels."

"What's her story?" Angel asked.

"Not much so far," Simms said. "She works with the vic, but hasn't said much beyond name, rank and serial number."

"Seriously?" Sarah asked. "She really do that?"

Simms turned to give her a look.

"Okay. Sorry. So, what do you have on her?"

"Got a break when the real estate office manager reported an apparent embezzlement. Turns out the lady's been stealing for a couple of years."

"How does that connect to the murder?" Angel asked.

"We suspect the vic found out before the manager did and was going to report it."

"Evidence?" Sarah asked the question while checking out the suspect. In her fashionable leggings, topped with what looked like a cashmere sweater and one of those hairdos that had that casually-thrown-together look but had probably cost a fortune, she didn't look like a killer. But few do until you look into their eyes where the evil couldn't hide. Sarah wondered what kind of evil she would see in this woman's eyes.

"Slim. Her prints were found at the scene, but she's shown that property to clients, so prints don't mean anything." Simms let out a deep sigh. "If we want to build a case, a confession would make a good foundation."

"Okay." Sarah turned to Angel, "Go try your charm. Maybe she'll break for you, and I won't have to do a thing but watch."

Angel traded places with Burt, and for the next fifteen minutes she prodded the woman from different angles, but Belinda didn't vary from, "I didn't kill Francine" or, "I don't know what you are talking about." But at least she didn't lawyer up.

In the viewing room, Burt and Simms set up a stereo of frustrated sighs and finally Sarah couldn't stand it anymore. "Maybe it's time for me to go in," she said.

"Want some war paint?" Simms asked.

She smiled. "No. I'm good."

Sarah walked into the interrogation room, strode over to the table and stuck her hand out to Belinda. "Ms. Samuels. I'm Sarah Kingsly. Nice to meet you."

The young woman took the offered hand in a limp handshake.

"Want me to leave so you can visit with your new friend?" Angel asked.

"No. Stay," Sarah tightened her grip on Belinda's hand. "We're just going to chat about the missing money and what that has to do with her killing Francine."

"I already said I didn't do it." Belinda tried to pull her hand away, but Sarah didn't release her grip. "Let go of me."

"Didn't do what? Steal the money or kill your co-worker?"

"Neither one."

"Sarah, you might want to let go," Angel said. "Her fingertips are turning blue. Wouldn't want her fingers to fall off."

Sarah released her grip and sat down in the other chair facing Belinda. "I'm so sorry."

The apology seemed to fluster the woman as much as the initial approach had. She rubbed her hand and glanced from one detective to the other. "What is this? Some kind of good cop/good cop routine?"

"Not a routine at all." Sarah leaned back in the chair. "We're just here to help you see the mistake you're making."

"What mistake?"

"Trying to convince us you're not guilty."

Uncertainty furrowed the woman's brow for a moment, but she remained quiet.

"We know you did it," Angel said. "And officers are gathering the evidence now. So, we could just sit here and wait."

"Good idea," Sarah said to Angel. "You want some coffee?"

"Sure."

Sarah turned to Belinda. "What about you?"

"What evidence?" Belinda asked.

"Oh, didn't my partner tell you?" Sarah asked. "We're tracing the knife back to you."

"But you can't. I—"

"You what?" All trace of friendliness was gone as Sarah stood and leaned into Belinda, faces only inches apart.

"Nothing. I—Nothing."

Sarah let go of the table and turned to Angel. "You might want to go now. I may have to get rough here. You wouldn't want to get blood on your new suit."

"You're right." Angel stood.

"Wait. Wait." Real fear was in Belinda's eyes now. "You can't do that. I'll ... I'll report you to the Dallas Review Board."

Sarah laughed, but the sound was not pleasant. "Been there. Done that."

"She's really not a nice person," Angel said with a nod to her partner. "And she never worries about breaking rules."

There was another long moment of silence while the woman glanced frantically between the two detectives. Then Angel moved toward the door.

"You're just going to leave me with her?" Belinda's voice was a high squeak.

"Well, yeah. Unless you want to save us all some trouble and tell us what happened."

Again, the frantic eye movement and a hard set to the woman's jaw. They waited so long; Sarah worried that the woman wasn't going budge. Angel reached for the doorknob, and then Belinda slumped in her chair like someone had pulled a plug and all the strength had drained from her body and spilled out of her toes.

Then the words tumbled out. "I didn't plan to kill her. I just wanted to frighten her so she wouldn't report me. I was going to pay the money back. Nobody had to know. But she had to get all high and mighty. 'It was a crime', she said. 'And a sin.'" Belinda raised her face and some of her spirit seemed to come back. "Who was she to talk about sins? She was bonking the manager."

Sarah wasn't even surprised at the absurdity of that statement. All kinds of people had all kinds of weird notions of right and wrong.

Angel stepped back to the table and slid the legal pad and pen across to Belinda. "Write it all down."

"You got this?" Sarah asked.

"Yeah." Angel sat down opposite Belinda.

Sarah walked out where Burt and Simms were smiling. "I love you ladies," Burt said kissing her cheek. "Come have a drink with us after we get our perp squared away."

Sarah briefly considered going to celebrate with the guys, but changed her mind, realizing she couldn't be cheerful. Her mood was anything but pleasant. Despite this win, there were still too many losses, and she was tired of all the harm that people inflicted on each other. She was tired of those who took the high road and tried to justify their crimes. And she was tired of people like Belinda who acted like it was their right to rid the world of people they did not like.

She would go home, hold her cat, and maybe get drunk in private.

Chapter Twelve

• •

Friday, March 16

A slight throbbing in her head was the rude awakening the next morning. Sarah knew she'd tipped the bottle one too many times last night. A shower and an Advil helped marginally, but she skipped her instant coffee at home, fed Cat, and stopped by the convenience store for a good cup of coffee.

When she walked in, she saw a couple of guys at the counter. One had the image of a swastika on the back of his leather jacket. Hussain was behind the counter, apprehension obvious in his expression. Sarah gave him a nod on the way to the coffee dispensers, then stopped when one of the guys called out, "Hey, raghead. Go back where you came from."

Sarah turned and walked back, getting closer to the men than was comfortable for them. "Maybe you should go back where you came from."

"Back off, lady."

"I'm no lady. I'm a cop."

The man took a half step back. "We ain't doing nothin'."

"That's right. And you take your *nothin'* and get out of here." Sarah waited until the men finally moved, mumbling their way out the door. She smiled at Hussain. "Assholes."

"Yes. But very scary assholes."

Sarah got her coffee and stayed at the shop for a while making sure the men didn't come back. Then she got a refill and headed out. She had to stop by the hospital before going to the station. Amber had called just as Sarah got out of the shower to say she was going to be released later that day. In addition to the broken arm, Amber had a concussion and some internal injuries from the fall, so she'd been kept for observation. Sarah hated to think of what the bill was going to be. Maybe she should just let Parkland absorb the cost like they did for others who didn't have insurance. Police detectives didn't have tons of money stashed in off-shore accounts.

Even with two days to think about it, she hadn't been able to come up with a place for Amber to stay. The girl was too old to go into the CPS system, and there were no relatives willing to lend a hand.

Sarah had been surprised to find that Amber had told the truth about not having any kin around. Sarah had thought that was just a convenient lie, but after searching online and through the databases available to law enforcement, she'd only found one distant cousin in Washington state. When Sarah called the man, he'd said he'd broken ties with the family and certainly did not want to invite some harlot into his home. Harlot? What the hell did he mean by that?

When pressed about that, his response had been there was no other reason for a cop to be calling about Amber unless she was in trouble. And that trouble was either drugs or prostitution.

Sarah had hung up on him.

So, the issue still wasn't resolved as she walked into the hospital room. Amber was up and dressed and obviously anxious to leave, packing some personal items into a plastic bag the hospital had given her.

"I thought you were getting released later," Sarah said.

"Talked the doc into letting me go now. Is that a problem?"

"Where do you plan to go?"

Amber shrugged.

"You can't just leave without a place to live."

Amber pulled the string that closed the bag and looked at Sarah. "Maybe I could stay at a shelter until I'm able to work again."

"Oh, for heaven's sake." Sarah ran her fingers through her hair, took two steps away, then turned back. "God help me, but I can't let you do that. Come on."

Amber hustled to catch up as Sarah strode out the door. "Where are we going? Can I hang with you at the station?"

"No. You cannot 'hang' with me at the station." Sarah paused for just a moment and gave Amber one of her sternest looks. "And don't you dare do one thing that will make me regret where I'm taking you."

The tone of Sarah's voice seemed to take some of the starch out of Amber, and she apparently could not voice the question that was in her eyes.

"I'm taking you to my apartment," Sarah said. "When I come home from work tonight, we'll come up with a long-range plan."

"I haven't changed my mind about not wanting to live with a cop."

"And I haven't changed my mind about not wanting to live with a girl who makes such stupid choices. So, there you are."

That seemed to stun Amber for just a beat, then she asked, "What will I do?"

"I don't know. But the same conditions apply as the last time I offered to help. No drinking. No doping. And no dancing."

"Not even a little two-step?"

It was the first glimpse of humor the girl had offered, and Sarah couldn't hold back a smile. The humor was one of the things she'd liked about Amber when she'd met her before. That and her grit. Angel had said that Sarah made the connection because Amber was probably a lot like Sarah had been as a teen; funny as hell sometimes, but a lot of times a real pain in the ass. Sarah had wondered how Angel could peg her so well. They'd never had one of those girlfriend chats sessions to get to know one another. Hell, sometimes they couldn't even talk about a case without getting all crossways.

Sarah sighed and motioned to Amber. "Come on."

~*~

Angel looked up from her desk as Sarah strode into the squad room, noticing that her partner's hair was more of a mess than usual, and a frown pinched her eyes. "Everything okay?"

"Just dandy." Sarah shrugged out of her jacket and slung it across the back of her desk chair, then sat down and swiveled to face Angel. "Guess who I just dropped off at my apartment?"

For just a moment, Angel was at a loss, then a realization dawned. "Not Amber?"

"Yup. She signed herself out of the hospital and had nowhere to go."

"So now I can't be telling folks how mean you are anymore?"

Sarah chuckled. "Maybe we should protect my reputation. It does come in handy sometimes."

The other day when Sarah had told her about the fire at the apartment complex and the connection to Amber, Angel had suspected that the girl was going to complicate her partner's life. Looks like she was right, but before she could comment, her cell phone vibrated on her desk. She picked it up, said her name, listened for a moment, then said, "Okay."

To Sarah's inquisitive glance, Angel said, "That was Ryan. He's got the CI in one of the interrogation rooms. Wants us to come and meet her."

Angel's first thought when they walked into the dingy gray room was, *My God, she can't be eighteen.* A thin, petite girl wearing jeans and a tank top, she looked all of twelve. Angel caught the girl's eye. "How old are you really?"

"Old enough."

"Marcella. Your smart mouth isn't needed here," Ryan said, leaning on the table to get in her face. "I told you we could help you out, but only if you help us out."

"Don't mean I have to kiss no ass." Marcella threw her long black hair back in a gesture Angel had seen many girls use when trying to show a bravado that didn't reach below the surface.

Sarah stepped forward. "You know what, Ryan? Let's just cut her loose. There are plenty of others out there who might like your deal. They might even talk nice. We can always use this one as a patsy. Put the word out that she's working for us and use that to cover the real CI."

Angel was pleased to see the girl cast a frightened glance at Ryan. People might object to Sarah's tactics, but she did have a way with making a threat stick.

"Is she for real?" Marcella nodded to Sarah.

"She is that," Angel said. "You do not want to get on her bad side. In fact, you might not want to get on any side if you are not ready to cooperate."

The girl took a moment, and Angel could tell she was considering all the options. "I do this? Work for you? Mean I have to quit using?"

"As law enforcement officials we'd have to say yes," Ryan said.

"And as someone who hates to see a girl throw away her life, I agree," Angel added.

"What do you care about my life?"

A little bit of the tough girl was back, but Angel decided not to rise to the bait. It seemed senseless to let this little slip of a thing make her angry. If the girl was over five feet tall, it was only by a couple of inches and she was thin to the point of emaciation. Probably due to spending more money on drugs than food.

It would be nice to save this one.

Ryan and Sarah seemed okay with letting a silence reign for a few minutes, so Angel did too. Finally, Marcella started to fidget in her chair. Silence always did work wonders.

"What do I got to do?" Marcella asked.

Ryan motioned for Angel and Sarah to take the two banged up metal chairs opposite Marcella, then pulled a matching chair for himself from the corner. "We want to get to whoever is bringing the black heroin into Dallas," Ryan said.

"I don't know who that is."

"We didn't think so," Angel said. "We just need you to find out."

"How?"

"Who're you getting your Cheese from?" Ryan asked.

"This boy at school. Ricardo."

"Then the first step is to find out where he's getting it," Ryan said. "Then we'll work from there."

"Everybody knows who owns the west side." Marcella gave a bit of a sneer. "You so stupid you don't know?"

The attitude pushed Angel's last button. She hated the smart-alecky street kids who tried to act all tough like that. She slowly stood and loomed over the table. "It's not polite to call people stupid. And it is really not smart to call a police officer who could lock you up stupid."

Angel paused to give the girl a moment to absorb that. "So, I would suggest you think back to what your mama told you about respecting authority. And in case she forgot, pretend I'm your mama. Got it?"

"My mama ain't no n—" The girl bit off the rest of the word when Angel leaned even closer and held her gaze without blinking. Tension crackled in the room, then finally Marcella nodded.

"Good." Angel sat back down and turned to Ryan. "Do you have any more questions for this young lady?"

"Just one," Ryan said. "Are you in or out?"

Marcella closed her eyes for a moment, then let out a long sigh and a single word, "In."

They spent the next few minutes outlining how Marcella would work with them, then Ryan had her taken back down to booking. "You were right about putting her through the system," he said to Angel. "She'll be safer without even a hint that she is working for us."

"I just hope that's good enough," Sarah said.

"It will be."

Even though he was answering Sarah, he never took his eyes from Angel. His look and his cocky grin was enough to undo her. She gave him the briefest of nods, before turning and walking away. As she passed Sarah, she caught a flicker of a smile on her partner's face.

Damn.

Sarah turned to Ryan. "You going to do anything about that?"

"What?"

Sarah nodded in the direction Angel had gone. "That."

"There's nothing to do," Ryan said. "She's made it clear she doesn't cross the racial line."

"Damn shame," Sarah said. "I think it might be good for her."

Ryan's response was a deep blush that surprised Sarah.

It was a day filled with surprises.

~*~

Sarah unlocked the door to her apartment and stepped in, balancing the pizza she'd picked up on the way home. Amber sat up from where she'd been dozing on the couch, Cat nestled against her stomach. "Need some help?"

"No. I've got it. Come on into the kitchen."

"You didn't tell me you had a cat."

"You allergic?"

"No."

"Then it's no problem. Right?"

Amber shook her head.

"Great." Sarah put the pizza box on the counter, slipped off her jacket and eased out of her shoulder holster. "Paper plates are in the cabinet." She nodded to the one she meant. "You can handle those one-handed. I'll be right back."

Sarah locked her gun in the drawer in the little antique dresser she used as a nightstand. She'd bought the piece after finding out the drawer had a lock and the antique store owner actually had the key. Then she hung up her holster and jacket, and went back out to the kitchen. Amber had managed the plates and had found the silverware. Sarah gave Cat his dinner, then opened the refrigerator and asked, "What do you want to drink? I have water and water."

"I'll have a beer."

"You'll have water."

"You've got beer. I saw it."

"No beer."

"I'm old enough to drink."

Sarah turned and glared at her.

"Okay. Almost old enough."

"And old enough to know you don't drink when taking pain meds."

When Sarah lifted the lid on the pizza box, the sweet aroma of basil rode the steam, and her mouth watered. She hadn't realized how hungry she was until that wonderful smell hit her. Cat was drawn to the tantalizing odor, and she gently pushed him back to his dish. "No pizza for you, buddy."

Amber chuckled and sat down at the table. Sarah served two slices of pizza for the girl and for herself.

"Did you think about what we talked about this morning?" Sarah asked after eating her first slice and picking up the other.

Amber nodded.

"And?"

"How can I find another job? I don't even know where to start."

"Try the want ads? Or better yet. Go back to college. Work toward a well-paying career."

Amber laughed. "Do you know how much money I make at The Club?"

"Do I care?"

Silence followed, and Sarah could feel the heat of Amber's anger permeate the room, but the girl had the good sense to keep her mouth shut. Sarah waited a few beats then sighed. "Obviously you can do whatever you want," she said. "I'd just like to see you in some profession that doesn't have so many inherent dangers."

Amber took a bite of pizza and chewed it carefully, then said, "I'll think about it."

"Okay. What did the doc say about when you would be out of the sling?"

"Four weeks. Maybe."

Sarah swallowed hard. She hadn't thought about how long it takes for a bone to heal. How long Amber might be depending on her. "Do you have any money?" Sarah asked. "Enough to live on until you're working again?"

"Not much. I lost most of my cash in the fire."

"You had money in your apartment?"

"Yeah."

"How much?"

"I don't know. A couple'a thousand."

Sarah choked on her water. "You kept that much in your apartment? You don't use a bank?"

"I like to have cash for shopping."

Sarah didn't know what to say. This girl was a paradox. Definitely not as stupid as some of her behaviors would indicate, yet prone to moments of sheer idiocy. This is why Sarah had given up on her last year, and she was damned close to giving up again. But just like she couldn't turn away that kitten a couple of years ago, she couldn't turn away a kid in need. And that's what Amber was. A kid, despite her chronological age.

"Okay," Sarah said. "You can stay until your arm is healed. But you can't be a freeloader. You'll have to pitch in around here."

"Can I help you with your case?"

Sarah was thankful she hadn't taken another sip of her water or a bite of pizza. "Are you serious?"

"I helped you catch Tracy's killer."

"Right, and you almost died in the process."

Amber shrugged and pulled another piece of pizza out of the box.

"You can help me out around here. Do some cleaning. Take care of Cat."

Amber pointed to her sling.

"I haven't forgotten," Sarah said. "But there are things you can do with one hand. Can you cook?"

"I make a mean Ramen noodle."

Sarah shook her head. "Okay. So, you won't make supper, either. You can at least pour cat chow into a bowl, can't you?"

"Sure."

"Good. That's your first assignment. I'll think of more later."

After cleaning up the kitchen, with Amber's limited help, Sarah got clean sheets from her tiny linen closet and took a pillow from her bed to the couch for Amber. No way was she going to give up her bed for the girl. Amber had a few toiletries she'd gotten from the hospital, but that was all. No clothes. No nothing. Amber was still wearing the scrubs one of the nurses had given her, so Sarah gave the girl one of her t-shirts and some shorts to sleep in. She did not look forward to taking the girl shopping. Not only would this be a big hit to Sarah's credit card, she dreaded the prospect of shopping. It was her least favorite thing to do. Well, one of her least favorite things. Which is why her wardrobe consisted primarily of jeans, t-shirts in assorted colors, and blazers, also in assorted colors, to cover her holster. She did own two dresses. One for when she had to be in court and one for weddings and funerals. That was enough in her book.

Chapter Thirteen

••

Friday, March 15

Angel walked into the tavern and glanced around. Four cops in uniform sat at the long, wooden bar. She didn't often come to the station hangout, preferring to go to Pete's Bar and Grill in her old neighborhood. Some of the people there didn't even know she was on the job, and that was fine with her. Sometimes anonymity could be a girl's best friend. She was here this evening because the frustration of the current case made her want to be with her blue friends instead of her black friends. She walked to the end of the bar, nodding to a couple of patrol officers who turned to check her out, and sat on a barstool.

The bartender, a tall, lanky man of middle age, walked over. "What'll it be?"

"Scotch. Neat."

That raised one eyebrow and the bartender asked, "Any particular brand?"

"Do you have Macallan's?"

That raised the other eyebrow and Angel suppressed a smile. She often got that reaction. Not that she went to bars to drink on a regular basis, but the times she did, her choice of drink seemed to take the bartenders a little off guard. LaVon had introduced her to fine scotch some years ago. It was when he passed the Texas bar and they were celebrating. After that, Angel had a hard time drinking anything else, although she would humor her father and have some of his Jack when he offered.

The bartender set the drink on a paper napkin, and Angel picked up the glass to take a sip. In addition to introducing her to fine scotch, LaVon had also instructed her on the proper way to drink it. One does not throw it back like a shot of whiskey. The scotch had a woody aroma and the first small swallow went down smooth, warming her insides along the way.

She set the glass back down and looked around the room. She'd thought Sarah might be here, but maybe her partner had gotten hung up at home with that girl. Why she'd taken her in, Angel had no clue. But then, she often had no clue about what her partner might do. Things were a bit better on the partnership level. They seemed to work with less friction than they had in the beginning, but there were still moments when Sarah would get all crazy and unpredictable.

"Hey, turn that up, will you?"

Angel looked toward the uniformed cop who was pointing at the television. She glanced at the screen to see the face of Bianca Gomaz, the evening news anchor at Channel Eight. Angel moved closer to the patrol officer who had called out to the bartender. "What's up?"

"She just said they arrested Chapo Guzman in Mexico."

Angel frowned.

"The drug lord. You never heard of him?"

"Oh. Right. The name eluded me for a moment." They waited for the bartender to turn the volume up and then a hush fell on the whole place as everyone listened to Bianca give the rest of her report. "Guzman was head of Sinaloa drug cartel, which controls trafficking routes along the U.S.-Mexico border, and his arrest was the result of a joint effort with the Mexican police, the DEA, and Homeland Security.

"In a pre-dawn operation, Mexican soldiers captured Guzman in the Mexican Pacific resort town of Mazatlan, but according to Mexican Attorney General Jesus Murillo Karam, authorities had been closing in on Guzman for months.

"Ongoing efforts by the police in Mexico, as well as U.S. agencies, yielded an abundance of intelligence that helped them track a pattern of behavior that eventually led to the arrest.

"Joaquin "El Chapo" Guzman had been the subject of a massive manhunt ever since his escape in a laundry cart from Mexico's Puente Grande prison in 2001. In 1993, he'd been sentenced to twenty years in prison for murder and drug charges.

"Currently, Guzman is being held in a jail in Mexico City, but officials say he will be sent to Altiplano No. 1 Prison in the Santa Juana neighborhood of Almoloya de Juárez, where he will join another notorious drug leader, Miguel Treviño Morales. After facing a long list of charges in Mexico, he could be extradited to the United States to stand trial for crimes committed on American soil."

"Holy shit," Angel said.

There was a flurry of other responses, but Angel only focused on the young cop next to her, shocked when he said, "They should shoot the bastard."

"Can't do that if he is already in custody."

"Maybe he could try to escape when they transfer him." The cop smiled when he said it, but Angel sensed he really meant it. And on some level, she wanted to second that motion. She was surprised when that thought flashed through her mind. Even a year ago, she would never consider shooting an unarmed prisoner. She held herself above the actions of too many white cops who were shooting unarmed Black men all the time. What was happening to her? Was she morphing into some kind of hard-ass cop who operated outside of the rules like her partner?

That was an interesting question.

But a more interesting question was what this arrest was going to do to the drug trafficking business here in her little corner of the world. Would the good guys benefit, or only the bad guys?

~*~

In another part of town, Tyrone and Franklin were huddled at a table in a corner of their favorite pool hall. They'd just seen the same news report. "Oh, man, we're totally fucked," Franklin said.

Tyrone waved a dismissive hand. He was mellowed out after sampling some of their product before meeting Franklin.

"Don't be flapping yo hand in my face. Serious bidness here."

"Chill, man. It doesn't mean anything." Tyrone motioned to the TV as if Franklin might have forgotten what had started their conversation. The TV was now muted, but the face of Bianca Gomaz still filled the screen. "I would sure like to sample some of that Spanish pussy."

Franklin slammed his palm on the table. "Forget about yo dick for one minute, nigger. Our whole setup could come crashing down. This was no fuckin' street runner arrested."

Tyrone slowly turned to face his partner. "There really is no need to shout."

Franklin started to protest, but Tyrone leaned closer, stopping the other man with a glare. "I mean it. Not only are you spoiling my incredible mood, you are drawing attention."

Franklin cast a glance around the room and noted that people had stopped playing pool. Tyrone made a "play on" motion to the couple at the nearest pool table, and they did. Everybody who frequented Ricky's Pool Hall knew what kind of power Tyrone and Franklin had in the neighborhood, and pretty soon the clacking of balls being sent to table pockets could be heard again.

"Nothing is going to fall apart." Tyrone kept his voice soft and level. "The way things happen south of the border; there will be a new guy in charge before we need another shipment."

"What if that don't happen?"

"It'll happen. Trust me."

Tyrone watched as Franklin took a sip of his tea, then carefully put the glass down. "You better be right."

Tyrone just smiled.

~*~

Saturday morning Angel walked into what could have been a cop flash mob at the station. Officers from every department were crowded into the CAPERS area and the buzz of voices was loud and annoying. She saw Sarah at her desk and made her way over. "What's going on?"

"Did you hear about the arrest in Mexico? The drug trafficker?"

"Saw it on the news."

A hush fell on the room when Helen Dorsett walked in. "Must be big news here, too," Sarah said. "That's twice this week she's paid us a visit. I don't remember last time that happened."

Dorsett was wearing a big smile, along with her blue suit and white blouse. Her trademark bun had an early-morning neatness to it. Angel could remember seeing the chief late in the day when it would be hard to tell if she'd ever pinned her hair back.

"I'm sure you all have heard the news by now," Dorsett said, leaning against the wall so she could face the officers. "But in case you missed it, yesterday we struck a big blow on the drug business in Mexico with the arrest of Joaquin "El Chapo" Guzman."

She paused as cheers and applause filled the room, then waved for quiet. "We don't know what the repercussions are going to be, but the DEA, Border Patrol, and Homeland Security are beefing up border security."

"What about the gangs here?" Burt asked. "Will we be seeing turf wars?"

"That's certainly possible," Dorsett said. "So, everyone needs to look sharp out there."

Walsh stood. "If I may, Chief?"

"Certainly."

"There's no doubt we'll see a domino effect. New configurations among the cartels." He eased his bulk onto the edge of a nearby desk. "The Gulf cartel and the Zetas have become weaker in recent months. So, they'll probably try for more power Leadership will probably shift to Zambada, another top Sinaloa leader. He's known as 'Mayo'."

"'Cause he likes mayonnaise?" Burt asked.

"Funny. I'm laughing my ass off," Simms said.

A few snickers swept through the room, but subsided quickly. Angel figured that was in deference to Chief Dorsett. Angel waved to get Walsh's attention and asked, "What does this mean for us?"

"Not much. Unless the supply of drugs gets cut off."

"That wouldn't be so bad, would it?" Sarah said. "We could go a few weeks without any drug deals in Dallas."

"Short term that would be fine," Walsh said. "But drugs are going to get here one way or another. If the locals who control the Dallas market need to find a new supplier, that could lead to some violence."

"We moving ahead with the plan from the other day?" Angel asked.

Walsh looked to Dorsett for a nod before responding. "Nothing's changed," he said. "Ryan got the CI moved through the system, so she's good to go. One of our undercovers picked up chatter about her being arrested, so her cred has been established."

Ryan pulled away from the wall he'd been leaning against. "It could take a while for her to move up the ranks, though. So, it's not like we can nail the top guys right away."

"What do we do in the meantime?" Sarah asked.

"Tie them to the dead girl in the park," McGregor said.

"Even if they're not?"

The moment of silence that followed cut like a knife, and Angel was glad she was not on the receiving end of McGregor's glare. At times like this, she almost wished he was still drinking. He had been a lot more mellow then. Not this guy who was as potentially as explosive as a vial of nitro.

Ever the peacemaker, Angel sighed, then said, "Chances are they're connected, but they probably didn't do it themselves."

Ryan nodded. "They would have some kid do it. Maybe a new recruit who had to blood-in."

The term slipped easily off his tongue, but Angel had a hard time imagining a kid of nine or ten assaulting or killing someone as part of the initiation to be accepted into a gang. It made her gut ache to picture Nick, one of the young boys she knew in her neighborhood ever doing something like that. Yet some kid from some neighborhood did it every day.

"Fine," McGregor said. "Adult, or kid, or goddam donkey. I don't care. Just find out who did it."

"Simms and I can lean on a couple of our CIs," Burt said. "See if they heard anything."

"What about your guy, Damian?" Sarah asked Ryan. "Worth another go?"

"Yeah. It's been a few days. Time enough for him to have picked up something. The streets are like one big rumor mill."

That drew a chuckle from the officers, which McGregor quelled with a wave of his hand. "Okay, people. Back to work. See Murphy for the new assignments."

As the officers dispersed, Angel watched McGregor in conversation with Dorsett. McGregor didn't look happy. Angel nudged her partner and pointed to the duo on the other side of the room. "You think McGregor's catching hell over there?"

"No. Dorsett's smiling. She wouldn't smile if she was reaming him a new one." Sarah shrugged. "She's probably just passing on the heat from above. If you can get rid of it, you don't feel the burn."

Chapter Fourteen

••

Sunday, March 17

S arah relaxed into the rhythm of the horse the way LaVon had told her to in the few brief riding lessons he'd given her. They hadn't been formal lessons. Just him working to get her over her skittishness around horses, and in a way, it was helping her get over her skittishness about their growing attraction. That was scarier than any four-legged creature.

Even though she'd grown up in rural Tennessee, Sarah had never taken to horses. Not the way some young girls do. She'd developed a fear of the beasts when a bee stung one of her Uncle Zeke's big draft horses, and it went tearing across the field like a locomotive. That locomotive was heading straight for the fence where Sarah was standing on the rail, and terror froze her to the spot. Just when she thought the horse was going to crush her, it had skidded to a stop in a swirl of dust that choked her.

She'd vowed then she would never get that close to a horse again.

So much for vows. And so much for never dreaming she would consider dating a black man. Prejudice ran deep in the hills of Tennessee, and Sarah doubted that any of her remaining relatives would look favorably on this. She wasn't even sure how she felt about this, whatever *this* was. She'd worked hard to throw off the shackles of bigotry her family had tried to wrap around her, but, as Angel was always so fond of pointing out, there were traces of generational prejudice that still clung to Sarah like some unpleasant perfume.

Yet, she couldn't deny the attraction to this long, tall man. She glanced over at LaVon and felt that little tingle that she kept hoping would go away. Outfitted in jeans and boots and a white hat, he could have substituted for The Marlboro Man, and who could resist a cowboy?

Today they were riding along the Trinity River bottom, signs of spring ready to emerge in the buds on the trees and the hints of green on the vegetation lining the river. They maintained a slow walk and the side-to-side rocking motion of the big bay mare she was riding was comfortable and soothing. Sarah settled into the ride, realizing that she was much more relaxed than the first time they'd gone riding. LaVon was astride his stallion, a big black beast that obviously took a lot of strength to control. She could see the muscles in LaVon's arms tensing as he held the reins while the stallion danced and pranced and tossed his head, white flecks of foam forming on his neck.

"Why's he so nervous?" Sarah asked

"He's not nervous. He's just showing off for the pretty lady. Trying to get her interested." LaVon nodded at the mare that was ignoring the other horse. Then LaVon looked at Sarah in a way that made her blush.

"At least someone has some good sense."

LaVon laughed. "She don't know what she be missing."

He kicked the stallion into a fast trot and surged ahead. Sarah couldn't help but smile. She'd noticed that when LaVon was feeling particularly playful, he'd turn on the jive talk. That reminded her of how Chad would kid around with Angel. Obviously, that kind of self-deprecating playfulness was part of the black culture that Sarah had not really thought about much until partnering with Angel. And now …? What could she call what she was doing with LaVon?

Oh, hell. Don't call it anything. She urged her horse forward and the mare took off after the stallion. She had just about closed the gap, when LaVon pulled up. Stopping next to him, Sarah saw a man and two young boys on horseback heading their way. All three were black.

"Friends of yours?" Sarah asked.

"Because they're black?"

The edge in his voice was so much like his sister's, it cut at Sarah, and she didn't know what to say. Should she explain that she'd only asked because she thought he might know them from the stable? Would he see that as a cover for something else? It was so damn hard to keep filtering everything she said for fear of offending.

There was a strained silence for a few moments, then LaVon reached across and lightly touched her hand. "Sorry. That was unfair."

Sarah nodded, but was still unsure of what to say. She glanced at the other riders coming up the narrow trail. They all wore cowboy hats, and the man had his pulled low over his face. They were riding two abreast, with one behind, but there was no room to pass that way. There was some jostling and head tossing by the horses as the riders pulled up to pass in a slow single-file walk. The man raised his hat a fraction and exchanged a look with LaVon that Sarah did not want to even try to interpret. The other two riders just nodded briefly as they urged their horses on.

"I've seen them here before," LaVon said after the riders had passed. "The man, anyway. Often he's riding with different boys."

"You think there's something hinky going on?"

"Hinky?" LaVon asked, then seemed to get her meaning. "I don't know. Not in the sexual predator kind of way. But I'm pretty sure the man is part of a gang that controls West Dallas."

Sarah took a hard look at the man's retreating back, trying to bring back the image of his face. Was it one of the men from the pictures Ryan had showed them at the briefing? It was hard to tell. She hadn't gotten a good look at his face today because of the canted angle of the hat as he passed her. She gave in to an impulse, turned her horse and called out, "Tyrone."

The man reined in his horse and glanced over his shoulder just as LaVon came up beside her. "What the hell are you doing?" he asked in a low whisper.

"Just confirming your suspicion." Sarah urged the mare closer to the other riders who had all pulled up their horses. She stopped about ten feet away from the man who had motioned the boys to stay behind him and asked, "These boys your family? Or are you training some new mules?"

"Don't know what you talking about, bitch."

The boys looked confused, but Sarah didn't doubt the man knew exactly what she was talking about.

"It's Ms. Kingsly bitch to you," Sarah said. "But no harm. Enjoy your ride."

Sarah could feel the heat of the man's gaze as she turned and walked the mare back to join up with LaVon. "You mind explaining that little act?" he asked.

"Wanted to get a closer look at his face. Angel and I are working with Vice in a big crackdown on drugs. We're focused on that Dallas gang, and I'd bet my badge this guy is one of the leaders. Sure looks like him."

"You couldn't be mistaken?"

Sarah shook her head. "It's his eyes. I've seen those eyes. They look empty. Like there's nothing behind them, but your gut tells you you're wrong about that."

"I see him here frequently." LaVon shortened the reins to keep his horse at a walk. "He has four horses and comes out with one or two boys at a time. I've seen him with girls, too."

"Have you ever talked to him?"

"He's never been friendly. So, I keep my distance."

They were quiet for a while as they followed the trail that wound through the wooded area and led back to where they'd started. Sarah enjoyed the stillness where the only sound was the clump of hooves on the dirt and an occasional call from a Mockingbird. It was cool in the trees, and when they broke into a clearing, the abrupt change in temperature made sweat trickle down the middle of her back. Moving into the glare of the sun, she was glad she'd taken LaVon's advice and bought a cowboy hat. Or should she say cowgirl hat? The first time she'd worn the hat she'd felt a little silly. She'd wondered if she should also get a sheriff's badge and a holster with one of those old Colt revolvers so common in Western movies. Remembering that, brought a chuckle.

"What?" LaVon asked.

She shook her head. "Just playing a fantasy in my head."

"Does that fantasy involve me?"

The directness of his question brought the heat of a blush to her face. She wasn't quite sure how to answer, so she just smiled and urged her mare forward. She could hear the soft sound of his laughter behind her.

Back at the stable, LaVon unsaddled the horses and carried the heavy saddles to the racks. Sarah grabbed a brush out of the bucket near where her horse was tied and brushed the moist tangle of hair where the saddle and cinch left their mark. The mare seemed to like the attention, leaning into the brush strokes the way Cat would sometimes do. Except Cat didn't threaten to push her off balance.

Sarah pushed back, but the mare just leaned harder, almost knocking her off her feet. LaVon stepped up and stuck his fingers in the hollow where the mare's belly met her haunch. She immediately stepped away. "That's a trigger point for a horse," LaVon said. "Poking there will always make them move. Especially if you do it hard enough. It does take a lot to make a thousand pounds of horse move when it doesn't want to."

LaVon grabbed another brush and worked on his horse, smoothing out the ruffled hair from the saddle. "I talked to the boy who cleans the stalls. He confirmed that the man we saw is named Tyrone, but didn't know his last name. He keeps four horses here and pays for full service."

"Full service? Like getting the windshield washed?"

LaVon chuckled. "Some of us buy our own feed and come out daily to take care of our horses. Others want that all done for them. Costs more, but they don't care."

"How much more?"

"A lot. I'm just renting the stalls here for my two horses, and that runs me three hundred a month for each. To have the full care runs about four-fifty per horse. Multiply that by four, and that guy is paying big bucks."

"And he's making those big bucks on the backs of young children." Sarah hadn't realized how angry that thought made her until the mare moved away from a particularly hard swipe of the brush. She patted the horse. "Sorry, girl."

For a few minutes they concentrated on taking care of the horses, and the only sound to be heard was the swish of a tail chasing flies or a nicker of appreciation. Then LaVon paused and looked at her across the back of his horse. "You want to tell me more about this case?"

Sarah chuckled. "Nice try, counselor. We agreed to keep the job off limits. Remember?"

LaVon smiled and led his horse into the stall. Then he walked over and did the same for the mare. When he emerged from the stall, he took the brush out of Sarah's hand, then gave her a long look. "When can we have dinner?"

The question caught her off guard. The other agreement they'd made was to avoid anything that looked like a real date. Although there wasn't any reason for that now. Not like it was when they'd first met when he was defending that kid accused of murder. Still, she did worry about any possible conflict of interest that could come up in the future. Not to mention conflict with Angel. "What about—?"

He touched a fingertip to her lip. "We've made so many excuses for not acting on what we feel. No more excuses."

Before Sarah could respond, he lowered his head and brushed his lips where his finger had just been. The heat was immediate and so intense, Sarah stepped back, breathless. "I need to…"

"What?"

"Stop. Think."

"What you need to do is decide," LaVon brushed his knuckles down her cheek in a soft caress, his smile making her knees weak. "I have enjoyed our rides. The occasional coffee in the afternoon. But I do like nighttime the best."

Sarah took a deep breath and another step back. His intentions were all too clear. "Can I get back to you on that?"

He nodded with a wicked grin.

While she was driving home—alone—Sarah wished she could just tell the man yes. Tell herself yes. They'd been dancing around this attraction for over a year. Was it time to stop the dance? Whew. That thought scared the shit out of her.

117

Chapter Fifteen

• •

Monday, March 18

Marcella walked toward where Ricardo was leaning against the back of the portable school building, a faded wooden structure much in need of a new coat of paint. It was late afternoon, their usual time for meeting; a good time when school had been out for a couple of hours and the area was deserted. Normally she wasn't afraid to meet him and get some product. That was how he always referred to it. As if he couldn't say the word "dope."

But today was not a normal product buying day, was it?

She tried to hide the tremors of nerves, but she was afraid he could see her hands shaking so she stuffed them into her pockets. It had been easier to act tough in front of those cops the other day. Ricardo was another story. Even though he adopted a stance of nonchalance, and his pretty-boy features tried to render him as a nice guy, she knew better. She'd seen what he had done to her cousin Hector when Hector skimmed some money.

"Wassup?" Ricardo said as she drew near.

Marcella shrugged. "I need some stuff."

Ricardo rubbed his fingers against his thumb in that age-old gesture that said "money."

"Don't got no money."

"You never had that problem before."

"Yeah, well. Work's been slow. Not a lot of tips."

"Way I heard it. You were in the slammer. Not working at all."

"Well, yeah."

118

A couple of crows flew in and landed on the asphalt by a nearby dumpster. Ricardo seemed to find their scavenging extremely fascinating. The birds squawked and skittered across the pavement, and Marcella felt her nerves doing a similar dance.

Finally, he turned and looked at her. "You know this is a cash and carry business."

She nodded.

"So? What? You want me to just give you some of my product? Like a gift?"

"No." Marcella swallowed hard. "I know you don't do stuff like that. Just thought, like maybe I could sell a little for you. Make enough to pay for what I need. You get the rest."

"I like the profit margin I got."

Marcella had no idea what he meant. What the hell was a profit margin? Ricardo was always acting like he was so smart. Using big words and talking like he didn't come from no slum in Mexico. But Marcella knew. His sister Rosita had been in her class at school. That's how Marcella connected with Ricardo in the first place. She'd never even done drugs until Rosita offered her a hit one day in the girl's bathroom.

That had been five years ago when they were thirteen. She was shocked the first time Rosita made the lines of Cheese right there in the stalls, but it didn't take Marcella long to get hooked. She was soon buying her own and sharing with her friend during a break between classes. They did it quite frequently, and she was always afraid they'd get caught, but it never happened. The few times a teacher walked in, she ignored the girls. It was like the teacher didn't see, or didn't want to see. Didn't care.

Part of Marcella was always relieved when the teacher walked back out, but a small part of her wished the teacher would stay. Would maybe care enough to want to stop the girls. Kind of like that detective said the other day about finding a way out of the pull of the drugs. So far, nobody in Marcella's life had ever cared enough to say they didn't want her to throw her life away.

Maybe if they had …

"You want something or not?" Ricardo took a step toward her, so close she could smell the sting of tobacco on his breath. "I'm not hanging here all day."

"I told you. I don't have no money."

"You could maybe pay me another way." Ricardo smiled, revealing yellowed teeth and brushing a strand hair off her face with a lingering caress.

Marcella stepped back, shoving his hand away. She was desperate, but not that desperate. And she certainly didn't want him to know her sexual experiences were limited to the relationship she'd had with Jeremy for two years before the jerk dumped her. She hadn't been with anyone since. Some of her friends talked about trading a quick blow job for some dope like it was no big deal. But her stomach recoiled at the thought of having some guy's junk in her mouth. She hadn't been able to do it for Jeremy, so she sure as hell would not do it for some guy she barely knew.

"Tell you what," Ricardo said. "Since Rosita likes you, I'll front you a small amount. See what you can do to earn a buck with that. Then we'll talk again."

Ricardo reached into his jacket pocket and pulled out a small plastic bag that held little balls of yellow dust. He palmed the bags, then passed them to Marcella, who quickly put them deep into her purse.

"Bring cash next time or else." He punctuated the threat by grabbing his crotch, then laughed.

Marcella didn't laugh. She walked away, trying her best to appear nonchalant, despite the fact that her legs were shaking so much they threatened to give out before she could get away.

What on earth had she gotten herself into?

Chapter Sixteen

• •

Tuesday, March 19

Days of digging hadn't turned up anything to pin the murder of Felicity Santos on her father, and Sarah wasn't sure if she should be relieved or disappointed. While she hated the thought of a father killing his own kid, it would be nice to catch a break in the case.

What they had found out was that Santos ran his own small trucking company. In fact, the business was so small it was just him and one flatbed. Sarah wondered how they paid for the large home they lived in, guessing that he didn't make much money as an independent driver, but then Angel had reminded her that extended family lived in the house. They all probably contributed. Sarah also wondered where he had gone to "work" that day they'd questioned him. The business was run out of a back room in his house, so it's not like he had to go to an office. It was just something else that kept niggling at her. It wasn't like she really wanted to nail him, but she'd just like to either definitely take him off the suspect list or find something. Being halfway in between was never a good place.

Ryan had called first thing this morning to say he had some new information on the drug route from Mexico to Dallas, so he was now sitting on the edge of Sarah's desk sharing said information. "All the attention the DEA has focused on the major north/south routes has forced the cartels to change it up," Ryan said. "They're using some of the smaller highways coming up from the border and circling around to Dallas."

"Once they make it through the border check, what difference does it make?" Sarah asked.

"The bigger highways and freeways are more heavily patrolled," Ryan said. "And more officers there have K9s they use on routine stops."

"Rural departments have K9s too."

"True, but not as many as the larger departments." Ryan shifted his weight to his other hip and turned as Angel walked up. He gave her a smile and Sarah swore she saw a bit of red creep into her partner's coffee and cream complexion.

"Pull up a chair," Sarah said.

When Angel was settled, Sarah turned back to Ryan. "Tell us about this new route."

Ryan quickly recapped what he'd already told Sarah, then continued. "A state trooper pulled a truck over on Highway 79 just west of Tyler. It had ten bricks of black tar. When they ran the plates, they were registered to an Emillio Santos.

"Our Emillio Santos?" Angel asked.

"Yes, Ma'am," Ryan said in his most endearing southern drawl. Which was funny because Ryan was originally from New York and seldom drawled.

"How did you find out?" Sarah asked.

"The Smith County Sheriff. He's a friend of mine. Figured I might want to know about that Dallas connection." Ryan grinned again. "So. Who's up for a road trip?"

They got the okay from McGregor, and two hours later, Ryan was introducing Angel and Sarah to Sheriff JD Jones. On the way to Tyler, Ryan had explained that he and JD had grown up together in Brooklyn, so Sarah was surprised when she saw the man. The Sheriff was wearing boots, jeans, a white cowboy shirt with silver snaps, and the biggest hat Sarah had ever seen. Over all, he looked like he could have ridden out of a classic old western movie. She shook off the mental image of him galloping up to the station on a big black horse and tying the mount to a hitching post and offered her hand. "Pleased to meet you."

The sheriff shook her hand soundly and gave Angel a brief nod. Was it an intentional snub or just that the man was in a hurry to get them set up to interview Santos? By the look on her partner's face, Sarah guessed that Angel considered it a snub.

"We put the guy in the interrogation room and kicked up the heat on the thermostat," Jones said. "Let him sweat a little bit. He's back here."

Jones led them to a small room toward the back of the building and opened the door. He let the three detectives in first, then closed the door before taking a stance in the corner of the small, windowless room. The sheriff had not been kidding about the sweat. It glistened on Santos' forehead and the room reeked of a strong sour odor. Santos' arrest seemed to have diminished him. He no longer had the bluster and bravado he'd displayed days earlier. He slouched in his chair and didn't look up when the detectives took seats opposite him.

On the drive from Dallas the trio had decided that Ryan would take the lead in the interview, since Santos had not responded well to Sarah or Angel. Sarah didn't think it was just because they were women, but figured it wouldn't hurt to let Ryan go man-to-man. When Ryan opened with a soft approach, she was a bit surprised.

"Mr. Santos. Let me offer my condolences on the loss of your daughter."

The only response was a brief flicker of what could have been alarm, as Santos glanced quickly at Ryan, then lowered his gaze to the pitted and scarred wooden table that had seen better days and probably hundreds of interrogations.

Ryan waited a moment, probably to see if Santos would fill the silence. But he didn't. He also did not respond to any of the questions Ryan asked about the dope.

Well crap, Sarah thought. We're getting nowhere fast.

Then Ryan stopped the questions and just sat there for a moment before leaning forward. "You need anything?" Ryan kept his tone soft and easy. "Coffee? A soft drink?"

Santos shook his head.

Well, Sarah sure as hell wanted a cup of coffee. And she also wanted this cat and mouse game to stop. "You're a sorry excuse of a father," she said, her voice hard and cold.

He didn't respond, just lowered his head even further.

"What man would leave his family. His grieving wife. And do this."

"You no understand."

"Oh, I understand." Sarah leaned into his face. "I understand you are a disgrace. You dishonor your daughter."

The man covered his face with his hands. The detectives waited, but he said nothing.

"You're in deep shit here, Santos."

Sarah's abrupt comment had the desired effect. He looked up with genuine alarm in his expression.

"We find out this dope you're carrying is connected to your daughter's death, that's a serious capital crime." Sarah leaned even closer to him, and there was nothing soft in her tone.

Santos shook his head. Back and forth, back and forth. "No. No. There is nothing."

"Murder one with a drug connection. That means the death penalty, doesn't it, Ryan?" Sarah glanced at Ryan, who nodded.

"We'd hate for your wife to have to grieve another loss," Angel said. "If you can't help us out here, we can't help you out."

For a few minutes there was no sound except the rattle of chains holding Santos' feet to the table legs and his heavy breathing as he shifted in the chair. The detectives waited him out.

"What can help?" he finally asked.

"How long have you been transporting drugs?" Ryan asked.

"One year."

"How often?"

"I no understand."

Sarah leaned forward again. "How many times have you driven drugs from Mexico to Dallas?"

"Maybe he needs an interpreter," Sheriff Jones offered.

"Do you need someone to help you understand?" Angel asked.

Santos shook his head. "Me English okay."

"Then answer the question," Sarah said. "How often have you driven with the drugs?"

"*Una Vez al mes.*"

Sarah looked at Angel, who had better Spanish. "Once a month," Angel said.

"Ok." Sarah turned back to Santos, who was nodding. "Where do you deliver them?"

"Dallas."

"Where in Dallas?" Ryan asked.

"I no tell. They hurt my family."

"Haven't they already hurt your family?" Angel asked.

More vehement head shaking. "No. They no do that."

"How do you know?" Angel asked.

"I know."

Everyone waited a beat, then Ryan asked, "Do you belong to the Zetas or La Familia?"

"No! No!" The emphatic denial was accompanied by wide, terrified eyes.

"But you deliver their drugs."

"They make me."

"How?"

Santos shifted, making the chains rattle again. "I owe money."

"You do drugs?" Angel seemed surprised.

"No. Is for ... something else."

"What something else?" Sarah asked.

"For my *hermano*. To come to America. But then it not enough."

Sarah knew what he meant that time. "You mean you paid a coyote to bring your brother over?"

"*Si.* Two thousan dollar. Then he wan two thousan more. I could no pay."

"So. He came up with a way you could settle the debt."

"*Si.* I mean, yes. His cousin work with Zetas. Say I can do things for them."

"Where is your brother now?" Ryan asked.

"Chicken farm."

"Huh?"

"Rogelio. He go work on chicken farm."

"Does your family know what you're doing?" Angel asked.

"Brother, yes. Wife, no."

"Would your brother make any trouble? Cause the cartel to strike back and kill your daughter?"

The second reminder of the death seemed to shake Santos to his core. There was a palpable hush in the room, and the detectives waited while the man wiped the sweat from his face with a rumpled handkerchief. Sarah wondered if some of the moisture on his cheeks was from tears, and she was tempted to feel sorry for him. She had to resist that temptation though. She could remember her uncle, who had been in law enforcement, telling her that sympathy was a detective's worse enemy. Then John, her former partner, had reinforced that. "A perp is basically a con man," John had said. "He'll do anything to make you believe he didn't do it, including trying to twang your heartstrings."

Sarah had laughed at the image of a person twanging her heart like a guitar string, but the lesson had stuck. Don't be soft for a perp.

"If the cartel had nothing to do with your daughter's death," Sarah said. "What're we supposed to think?"

Santos looked up, startled. "No understand."

"Is there a reason you might want her gone?"

"What you say?" Santos tried his best to stand, dark eyes wide again. "No. No. I no hurt my daughter."

"The only thing I can't figure out is why." Sarah looked over at Angel. "You have any ideas?"

Angel shrugged, then Ryan said. "Maybe the daughter found out about Daddy's dirty runs?"

"Is that it?" Sarah turned a hard look on Santos. "You killed your daughter to protect your own ass?"

Santos shot out of his chair as far as the chains would allow and screamed. "No. Is wrong. No."

Sheriff Jones took two quick strides and pushed Santos down with a large hand on the man's shoulder.

As Santos sank to the chair, he seemed to deflate again. Sarah stood and pushed her chair back. "Time for a break. I need coffee."

Ryan and Angel stood, too, and Jones gestured to the prisoner. "What about him?"

"You want a drink?" Angel asked Santos.

The man shook his head, then lowered it to his hands as if his neck had lost all its strength.

"You going to prosecute him here on the drug charges?" Ryan asked a few minutes later as they sat around JD's office with steaming mugs of surprisingly good coffee. "Or can we have him in Dallas?"

"He's all yours." JD leaned back in his chair and put his very large, very fancy boots on his desk. "Much as I'd like to have another notch on my gun belt, so to speak, I can give this one up. Save my county some money in prosecution fees and save me a heap of paperwork."

Listening to the exchange, Sarah was amused by the way the sheriff seemed to slip in and out of good ol' country boy vernacular. As if picking up on her amusement, he said, "Folks in these parts like their sheriff to be a bit like the Duke himself."

"The Duke?" Sarah asked.

"You know, 'Howdy partner.'" JD did such a good imitation of John Wayne, Sarah had to laugh.

"I never was a fan," she said.

"Sacrilege girl. Sacrilege."

"We'll get transfer papers in the works," Ryan said.

"You want another go at him first?" JD asked.

"Naw. Let him stew for a while." Ryan finished his coffee and set the mug down. "Maybe he'll be ready to talk by the time we get him up there."

~*~

The detectives got back to Dallas late in the afternoon and there was just enough of the day left to make a quick report to McGregor, then head on home. Sarah thought about stopping at Kenny's for a juicy burger and a beer, then remembered Amber. Shit. The girl was stuck in the apartment with no food. Every day since Sarah had taken Amber in, she meant to do some grocery shopping and fill up the refrigerator, but she'd never done more than stop at a deli and pick up dinner. Which is what she was going to do tonight. She was too tired to do anything else.

Juggling the bags from Jason's Deli and her keys, Sarah tried to unlock the door, but it opened before she could get her key inserted in the lock. Amber stood there, arm in a sling, and a not-very-happy look on her face.

"Where have you been?"

"Pardon me?" Sarah meant it as questioning Amber's attitude, but the girl stepped aside as if Sarah had asked her to move.

"You left me alone all day with nothing but stale bread and peanut butter," Amber said, following Sarah into the kitchen. "I hate peanut butter."

Sarah resisted the impulse to snap back. Instead, she put the bags of food on the counter. She reached down to pat Cat, who wound his orange body around her legs. He was probably hungry, too. Then she turned to Amber. "Be happy I brought supper."

Amber sidled up to the counter and peeked in a bag. "What is it?"

"Salad and a roast beef sandwich."

"I don't eat meat."

"Then try one of the Fancy Feasts. It has tuna. Cat likes it."

"Very funny."

Sarah took a few minutes to calm herself by getting some chow for Cat, and topping it with a bit of the good stuff. It did smell like tuna.

Once he was settled in the corner, she washed her hands and then pulled the takeout containers from the bags. Then she got silverware from the drawer. Obviously, Amber wasn't going to help.

Sarah didn't mind eating out of a plastic dish, but hated those little white plastic forks that bent if you tried to pick up more than one leaf of lettuce at a time. She pushed a container over to Amber and slammed a fork down. "Eat or go hungry." Then she picked up her dish and started toward the living room.

"Boy, someone's in a pissy mood."

The comment stopped Sarah from exiting the kitchen. "You talk to your mother this way?" Without giving the girl time to answer she finished with, "It's no wonder she threw you out."

The stricken look on the girl's face made Sarah wish she could reach out and snatch those words back. "Listen, I'm sorry."

Amber gave a slight wave of her hand. "No. It's okay. You're right. My mouth is too smart for my brain."

"You and me both." Sarah set her food on the little table in the kitchen, and then took Amber's food over, motioning to the girl to sit. "What do you want to drink? Water or water?"

"Vodka."

Sarah shot her a look. "What did I say about—"

"It's a joke. Chill already."

After they were settled and had eaten part of the salad Amber asked, "So, how was your day?"

Sarah almost laughed. Talk about a crooked conversation path. But she didn't feel much like laughing. She looked at the girl across from her who'd been tossed from her home, abandoned by parents who couldn't hate the behavior but still love the child. And she couldn't shake the image of that young teen she'd seen lying on the cold autopsy table. Neither deserved the fate they had been given. She gave a quick shake of her head, and resumed eating, pausing again after a few bites.

"It's been a crap day, if you really want to know," she said.

"I do."

Sarah let that response sit for a moment, taking a couple more bites of her salad, then she put the fork down. "It's possible we're looking at a father who might have killed his kid. I don't understand how somebody could do that. How could a parent dislike a child so much? Especially a child who was such a good kid."

"As opposed to a bad kid like me?"

"I didn't say that."

"Yeah, right."

"Listen." Sarah did nothing to keep the sharp edge out of her voice. "You aren't a bad kid. Just a kid who's made a lot of bad choices. It's time to start rethinking those choices."

129

Amber concentrated on pulling the meat out of her sandwich, not responding and not meeting Sarah's eyes.

Sarah sighed. Whatever. She was too tired and emotionally drained to deal with any more drama.

Chapter Seventeen

•••

Tuesday, March 19

Tyrone pulled his Ford Escalade into the parking lot, which was empty except for Franklin's black Trans Am, parked next to the silver Tahoe he recognized as belonging to Chavez and Manuel. The lot was dark, except for the headlights of cars reflecting off the metal doors of an old building, but Tyrone could still see the figures gathered in front of the building. Franklin was leaning against the front fender of his Trans Am, sipping on a huge to-go cup from 7 Eleven. Two Mexicans stood between the vehicles; hands thrust deep in the pockets of their jeans. Chavez was tall and thin, but Manuel had the more traditional Mexican build, short and squat. People often misjudged his stature and found out later just how strong the small man was. He could take down a rival in the time it took to blink, and he unloaded a truck faster than anyone Tyrone had ever seen.

This deserted warehouse offered the seclusion and privacy they needed when a delivery came up from Mexico. Chavez and Manuel would meet the drivers here and unload the crates of auto supplies and get the bricks of heroin out of where they were secreted in false bottoms. Then they would repack the crates and send the drivers on to deliver the rest of their load. The legitimate part of their load. It was only after the drivers were gone that Chavez would call Franklin to come and take possession of the dope. It was better that way. A nice smooth operation that ensured there was no direct link from the drivers to Tyrone and Franklin. Tyrone was especially proud of having thought of it.

Easing the SUV next to the car, Tyrone killed the engine and got out. He had no idea why Franklin had called him here. His partner hadn't given a reason when he'd called. He'd just said, "You better come to the warehouse."

Tyrone nodded briefly to the two Mexicans, then looked at Franklin, whose head and face was nearly swallowed by the black hoodie. "What's the problem?"

"Santos never showed."

"He call?"

Franklin shook his head and took a loud pull on the straw.

"What time was he supposed to be here?" Tyrone asked.

"Eight."

Tyrone checked his watch. Almost ten. Then turned on Chavez and Manuel. "You waited two hours before calling Franklin?"

"We thought the hombre just be a little late. Didn't realize so late." Chavez glanced at his partner, as if looking for confirmation.

"Fuck!" Tyrone kicked an aluminum can, making it clatter along the blacktop.

"Hey man. The neighbors." Franklin accompanied the remark with a chuckle.

Tyrone looked at the broken windows on both buildings flanking the parking lot, and shook his head. Who was he going to wake up? The rats? Franklin always thought he was so funny. Tried too hard to be like those wise-assed sidekicks in those mystery books he was always reading.

"Maybe the truck broke down," Franklin said.

"He would've called."

"Uh-huh." Franklin took another loud sip of his tea.

"He never be late before, Mr. Tyrone," Chavez said.

"I don't like this," Tyrone said. "What else was Santos bringing in?" He directed that question to the Mexicans.

"Auto parts," Manuel said. "Go to plant in Arlington next."

"Okay," Tyrone said. "You guys go on. We're your first call if you hear from Santos."

"Huh?"

"If Santos calls you, you call us. *Comprende?*"

"Ah, *Si, senor*." Chavez wasted no time getting in the car. He started the engine even before Manuel was all the way in. Tyrone smiled. He liked the way he could keep the hired help hopping.

Franklin took one last noisy pull on his drink, then tossed the cup. It rolled in a dull rattle toward the aluminum can Tyrone had kicked. "Customers are waiting."

"I know." Tyrone paced for another minute, then stopped to lean against the car next to Franklin. "How much do we have?"

"Ten kilos."

Tyrone did the math. He was good at that. Numbers were his friends.

"That's roughly 9,875 bumps. What do we have already made up?"

Franklin held up a finger, opened his cell phone and made a quick call. Another layer of protection between them and the dope dictated that processing be done at another site by other people. Franklin and Tyrone never had to touch the product, unless they wanted to.

"What'd he say?" Tyrone asked when Franklin hung up.

"'Bout twenty-five thousand."

"With another ten, that'll only hold us for a week. We need to cut it deeper."

"Whoa, nigger. Hold on?"

Tyrone shot his partner a glacial look.

"You cut deep, the Cheese be unstable," Franklin said.

"You think I don't know that? If you have a better idea, let's have it."

Franklin shrugged. "Chill, bro. Just saying. Dudes start dying, we be fryin'."

"I'm aware," Tyrone said. "I'm the one who reads the newspapers."

The wind picked up a little and they both watched it play with the abandoned drink cup for a moment, then Tyrone started for his car. "I'll call Mexico. Let them know Santos didn't show. See if we can get something shipped up."

"What about Santos? He be a pussy. He get picked up. Fucker'll trip all over his tongue talking."

"Not a problem. He can only lead the cops to an abandoned warehouse. Not to us or our operation."

Tyrone slid into the driver's side of his car and pulled one of the throwaway cells from the glove box. He kept a supply there for calls he couldn't make on his regular cell. This was one of them. The Mexican contact called himself Carlos, but Tyrone was sure that was not his real name. Carlos had taken over when Hector abruptly disappeared. Tyrone knew better than to ask what happened to Hector. He just did business with Carlos as if it didn't matter. But on some levels, it did matter.

Hector had been small time. Didn't work with the big cartels, and that's the way Tyrone liked it. Less violence that way. He was an enforcer when he needed to be, but he drew the line on some of the tactics of the cartel that included killing whole families, raping women and children, and cutting off fingers and hands while victims were still alive. That was sick. Just plain sick.

When one of Tyrone's workers got out of hand, a single bullet to the head was enforcement enough, especially when the execution was done in front of other workers. They tended to toe the line after that.

Tyrone punched in the numbers he'd memorized and waited until Carlos answered. Then he told him that Santos had not shown. "That is not good, my friend," Carlos said.

"Too bad he didn't get the message when his daughter died."

"Yeah. Too bad." The words came across the line almost like a sigh.

"What now?"

"Maybe man too stupid to learn."

It sounded like the final word on the subject, but Tyrone knew better. Carlos would not let it go, and it was in their best interest to stay on the good side of Carlos. "You want us to take care of him?"

"No. We find him and handle it."

"Okay." Tyrone hung up, and Franklin pushed off from the side of the car and asked, "What was that about the kid?"

"Nothing."

"Didn't sound like nothin'. Carlos whack the daughter?"

Tyrone gave him a hard look, and Franklin shook his head. "Oh fuck. Say it ain't so, brother."

Tyrone didn't respond. Franklin looked stunned for a moment, and then he started pacing. "Man, nigger. I din't sign up for no shit like that. Not killing kids."

Tyrone grabbed Franklin by the arm to stop the pacing. "*We* didn't kill no kid. Got it? It's all on Carlos. And he got Santos back in line, didn't he?"

Franklin pulled free and stepped back. "*We* do bidness with Carlos. That puts us deep in the shit."

"What? You turning into a pussy?" Tyrone stepped close. "Huh? Lost that killing edge?"

"It ain't like offing some gang-banger."

"So? What're you saying?"

For a long moment Franklin said nothing, then the steel in Tyrone's eyes made him step down. "Nothin'." He shook his head. "Nothin'."

Franklin offered a hand slap and turned to go to his car. Tyrone watched his partner amble away, the two of them parting as they had so many times. But this time was different. This time, Tyrone wasn't sure that Franklin was in one hundred percent. And if he wasn't?

Chapter Eighteen

....

<u>Wednesday, March 20</u>

In the morning, Sarah decided not to stop for Hussain's great coffee, heading straight to the station instead. She was eager to see how things stood with getting Santos up from Tyler. Walking in the Capers area, she saw ADA Jessica Franklin hustling her way to the detectives' desks. "Ryan informed me about Santos," she said, leaning a hip against Angel's desk. "We're getting the transfer papers ready. I asked why he's coming here when the drug charges are in Smith County, and Ryan said you're looking at Santos for murder? For his daughter. Really? I didn't get anything on that."

Sarah walked around to the other side of her desk and pulled out the chair. "He's a possible at this point. That's all. But we thought if we could put some pressure on him, he might crack."

"You have anything that points to the father?"

"No evidence yet," Sarah said. "Just suspicions. His reactions to his daughter's death were all wrong. And now that we've discovered this drug connection, we've got to wonder about that. She was supposedly a straight arrow. If she found out what he was doing, that could've been a problem."

"Detective, I can't make a case on speculation."

"Give us time," Sarah said.

"Okay, then. We'll file on the drug charges when he gets here."

With that, Jessica left and Sarah went to the break room to get a cup of coffee. Angel was there adding sugar and cream to her mug. "Just saw Jessica," Sarah said. "Papers are in the works for getting Santos."

Angel stepped back to give Sarah access to the coffee. "She know when?"

"Nope." Sarah poured coffee into one of the mugs on the counter. "Maybe later today."

"We could hope," Angel said over her shoulder as she walked out.

Before leaving the break room, Sarah took a swallow of her coffee so it wouldn't slosh over the edge of the cup as she walked back to her desk.

It wasn't five minutes later that Gladys, the woman who took her role as "keeper of the gate" very seriously, buzzed Sarah on her cell to say there was someone at the front who wanted to see her. Taking one last swallow of coffee, Sarah stood and walked to the main area of the department where she saw Juanita standing on the other side of the low gate separating the waiting area of CAPERS from the bullpen than held the desks of the detectives. The woman was wearing a skirt and a silky-looking blouse with a scarf around her neck. Nervous fingers worried the ends of the scarf. "You wanted to see me? Sarah asked.

Juanita nodded. "I ... we ... heard from Emilio. He called last night from the jail."

It wasn't a statement that invited a response, so Sarah just stood, waiting.

"He is scared. Worried."

"He should be."

"No. You don't understand." Juanita paused and took a deep breath. "I need to tell you about him."

"Okay." Sarah nodded to Gladys to unlock the gate and she ushered Juanita in. "You don't have school today?"

"I couldn't. I mean, my sister. She needs me."

Passing Angel's desk, Sarah nodded to her to follow, and the three of them went into one of the small interview rooms. "It's more private in here," Sarah said to Juanita as she pulled metal chairs to the table.

After they were seated Sarah asked, "What do you want to tell us?"

Juanita had lost some of that staunch assuredness she'd shown in previous encounters, and she slouched a bit in the chair, still fidgeting with the ends of her scarf. "When will Emilio be here?"

"We're waiting on official paperwork." Sarah said.

"Oh."

"How long have you known about him transporting drugs?" Angel asked.

Alarm widened Juanita's dark eyes. "We didn't."

"Never?" Angel pressed.

The woman shook her head.

"How long has he been making the drives to Mexico?"

"*No se.*" Juanita seemed to catch herself and repeated in English. "I don't know."

The woman was clearly getting more nervous, so Sarah decided to ease the pressure a bit. She smiled and asked casually, "Did he ever take Felicity when he drove?"

Juanita took a moment, then answered, "Yes. Sometimes in the summertime. Like a vacation."

"Is it possible she knew about the drugs?"

Alarm crossed the woman's face again. "Oh, no. You don't think …?" She let the rest of the question fade, then found her voice again, stirring in agitation. "You want to blame Emilio? Point your finger at the nearest Mexican?"

When Juanita paused for a breath, Angel started to speak, but the other woman raised a hand to halt her, speaking with more force. "He would not. He is good man. Would not hurt his daughter."

Sarah reached across the table and put a calming hand on Juanita's arm. "Settle down. We're not accusing him. Just gathering information."

Juanita held Sarah's gaze for one defiant moment, then let her hands settle in her lap, and Sarah asked again. "Do you think Felicity might have seen something on one of those trips. Something she shouldn't have?"

The silence was deafening as the woman thought for several long minutes, then she sighed. "Maybe. She was a smart girl, and very watchful. She might have seen something. And…"

She let that sentence trail, so Angel prompted, "And?"

"Sometimes ... there was a man ... Emilio met him in the garage ... but I should not say. Not get Emilio in more trouble."

"What is more important?" Sarah asked, her voice soft. "Protecting your brother-in-law or finding out who killed your niece?"

Another long silence hung in the air; the room virtually charged with the electricity from the tension in Juanita. Then she took a deep breath. "Emilio. He might do bad things. I don't know. But I do know he love his daughter very much. No harm her."

"Okay," Angel said. prompted again. "Tell us about the man in the garage. How often did they meet?"

"I don't know. I only saw once when I came home from school meeting early. Strange car in driveway and garage door up."

"Did you get a good look at him?"

Juanita nodded. "Headlights shine on him and Emilio. Then Emilio close garage door."

"Did your brother-in-law tell you who the man was?"

"No. He no speak of it. But the man ... he no good."

Sarah noted that the longer they talked, the more Juanita slid from the articulate teacher they had met the day the young girl had died to someone not well-versed in English. "How did you know?" Sarah asked.

"His eyes. Hard. No window."

Sarah understood exactly what the women meant, and she glanced at Angel, who nodded. No surprise there. They both had dealt with enough perps to know about eyes that didn't reveal anything.

"Describe this man?"

Juanita closed her eyes while she spoke, almost as if she was conjuring a picture in her mind. "Black. Late twenties. Dress nice. Not like punks on the street."

Angel stirred a bit at that last comment, but Sarah held up a hand for her to be silent while the woman continued.

"Would you recognize this man if you saw him again?" Sarah asked.

"*Si*. Yes."

"Can you stay? Look at some pictures?"

Juanita nodded.

Sarah motioned for Angel to follow her out of the room. "Check with Ryan," Sarah said. "See if he can pull together an array that includes Tyrone."

"You think Santos was mixed up with him?"

"I don't know. We don't even know who all Tyrone is tied to. Let's just see what happens with the photos."

After Angel left, Sarah went back into the room with Juanita. "Can I get you anything? Coffee? Water?"

"Water, please."

Sarah brought a bottle of water. "You need anything else?"

Juanita shook her head.

Sarah sat down and watched the woman take small sips of water, unscrewing the lid then screwing it back on in a rhythm that was almost a ritual. Nerves, Sarah thought, and she didn't blame the woman. It had taken a lot for her to come in today.

It wasn't much longer before Angel came back with the photos and walked over to the table. "I'm going to put these out in a row," she said. "Don't say anything until they are all out there. Then take your time looking over them."

Sarah watched Juanita's eye twitch as each photograph was laid out. Then the woman did as Angel had instructed. She scanned them slowly, carefully, finally putting a finger on one. "This man. I think he *es* the one."

Despite the fact that she had chosen the picture of Tyrone, it wasn't a good ID if she only thought he was the man. "Look at them all again," Sarah said. "We need you to be sure."

"Hokay." The word was soft, hesitant, and Sarah hoped they weren't losing her.

"Take a minute," Angel said, in a friendly, conciliatory tone. "There's no hurry."

"*Gracias.*"

Juanita took another sip of her water, then looked at each picture for a few seconds each. Then she once again touched Tyrone's photo. "It was him. I am sure."

Keeping the elation out of her voice Sarah said, "Thank you."

Angel gathered the photos. "I'll let McGregor know. See if he wants to let Chad and Ryan bring him in."

Sarah nodded and Angel stepped out of the room.

"Who is he? The man?" Juanita asked.

For a moment Sarah thought she was asking about McGregor, but then she realized the woman hadn't gotten past the man in the photo.

"Sorry. That's not information I can give you." Sarah stood and motioned to Juanita to follow her. "I'll take you out."

Juanita grabbed her purse and the bottle of water. "What should I say to my sister?"

Sarah knew she couldn't keep this woman from telling her sister about coming to the station, and maybe that was okay. Perhaps the other woman needed reassurance. "Tell her we're doing everything we can to keep her husband safe."

"What about the man?"

There was no doubt what Juanita meant, and Sarah wished she'd asked someone else to walk the woman out of the department. She liked her, and respected her family loyalty, but professional boundaries were crossed at one's peril. She sighed and paused for a moment to look Juanita in the eye. "You can tell your sister that you identified someone who might have put pressure on your brother-in-law. But that's all you can say. You understand?"

"Yes." The response was firm, and Sarah saw again the woman who had impressed her the first time they'd met. She nodded in acknowledgement.

After the woman walked out, Sarah went back to her desk and sat down with a sigh. Hopefully, Tyrone could be picked up quickly, and maybe the end of this case was in sight. She leaned back in her chair and pulled her thoughts from the case, turning to another worrisome situation. Amber. She couldn't stay at the apartment forever, and she was still reluctant to change her way of life once her arm was completely healed. It was going to be back to dancing as far as she was concerned. They'd argued about it at breakfast this morning; if you could call standing at the counter and sharing a bowl of cereal with Cat breakfast. Amber had been sitting at the table munching a Pop Tart.

Most days started that way; the day ending with Sarah coming home with pizza or Chinese takeout, or the occasional nod to nutrition from Jason's Deli. Not that it was much different from when Sarah was alone, but still, Amber could do with more substantial meals., as well as something better to look forward to than dancing in The Club.

Maybe Becky from CPS could help. They'd met a few years ago when Sarah worked a double homicide that had left an infant an orphan. Becky had worked quickly to get the baby placed with the mother's sister, not letting the child stay in the limbo of a foster home for long, and Sarah had been impressed with the woman's compassion, as well as her ability to get shit done.

Sarah used her cell phone to call and was pleased to catch Becky at the office. "Hey, girlfriend. What's up?" Becky said.

"Got a favor to ask."

"No 'how you doing' first?"

Sarah chuckled. "Sorry. How're you doing?"

"Too late, girlfriend. We're past that now."

Sarah chuckled again. "Are we past being friends?"

"Nope. So, whatever it is, lay it on me."

"Remember that girl Amber I was trying to help last year?"

"Sure do. She still walking on the wild side?"

"Not only that. Guess where she's currently living."

"Get out of here." Becky paused and Sarah heard a snort of laughter before Becky continued. "That is not the kind of roommate you be needing."

"Tell me about it."

"No. Tell *me* about it."

Quickly Sarah recounted the circumstances that had landed Amber at her apartment, finishing with, "It'd be great if you could help me figure out some options for her. I'm hoping with a little more persuasion, she might be closer to changing her lifestyle this time around."

"She's all grown up. I don't do adults."

"I don't want you to put her through the system. Just come talk to her as a favor to me. Just once."

Sarah realized she'd been pleading when Becky laughed, then said, "Okay. Stop whining. When do you want to co this?"

"As soon as possible. I really want to get her started on a better future."

"Not to mention out of your domicile."

Sarah chuckled. "That, too."

"I guess I could squeeze you in between my last home visit and visiting my own home tonight."

"Great. Smother me with guilt."

"You will owe me big time for this."

"I know. Send me the bill."

After settling on a time to meet, Sarah hung up, just as Ryan strode toward her desk. "Where's Angel?" he asked.

Sarah cocked an eyebrow. Was his question personal or professional? He seemed oblivious to her non-verbal attempt at humor, so it must be serious. "Briefing with McGregor. What's up?"

"We lost our CI."

"Christ." An image of the pretty young girl flashed through Sarah's mind. "Lost as in ..." She let the question fade, not wanting to voice her worst fear.

Ryan shook his head. "She's not dead. Just scared. She tried a few times to get something on Tyrone, but her contact wouldn't budge. Never said anything she could bring to us. Then he started to get suspicious."

"Did he hurt her?"

"Roughed her up. Told her there'd be more if she didn't stop asking questions."

"Ah, man."

Ryan pulled a chair over and straddled it. "It wasn't pretty."

"Did you pull her?"

He nodded. "But we didn't want to trigger an alarm. Told her to hang around. Make another buy or two, but stop trying to get information."

"What about after that?"

"Trying to convince her to go home. Far away from here."

Sarah smiled. Seems like they were both on the same page with trying to keep the girl safe. "The good news is that we might not need that girl anyway."

Ryan's face lit up with interest, and his smile broadened when Sarah told him about Juanita coming in and giving the ID on Tyrone. Then the smile got even bigger when Angel walked into the area.

"What are you both grinning about?" she asked.

"I just told him that we can nail Tyrone."

Angel held up a hand. "Let's not get carried away. Him having some kind of meeting with Santos is far from a slam-dunk."

"What did McGregor say?" Sarah asked.

"It's worth a conversation. He gave the go-ahead to pick up Tyrone."

Ryan stood abruptly as if energized by the news. "Okay. Let's go."

"Do you know where to find him?"

"I know his usual hangout. Worth checking. I'll grab Chad. Either of you want to come along?"

Sarah bit her lip to keep from smiling at the thought of Chad and Ryan and Angel together. Angel might be oblivious to the fact that Chad had not gotten past his interest in her that had been ongoing since they'd first met two years ago, but anybody with a brain could sense the electricity between her and Ryan. And Chad had a very fine brain indeed. Much as she'd like to see this play out, Sarah couldn't spend the rest of the afternoon chasing Tyrone down. She had to get Amber squared away. "I'm out," she said with a wave of her hand. "Taking some personal time."

Angel gave her a quizzical look to which she responded, "The problem in my apartment."

"Another break-in?" Ryan asked.

Sarah chuckled. "No. But that might be easier to handle than what I've got. Angel can fill you in while you track down The Man."

Chapter Nineteen

Wednesday, March 20

Tyrone picked Franklin up on the corner of Jackson and South Griffin where he'd told him to be at four o'clock.

"Whassup?" Franklin asked as he slid into the car.

"Need to take care of some things."

Franklin seemed to accept that for the moment, and Tyrone went to Central Expressway and then drove south, hooking up with I45, then continuing south. Franklin played with the radio, finally settling on a country rock station. He bounced one leg in time to the music for a while, then looked outside when Tyrone slowed for the exit to the Trinity River.

"Hey. Where we going? We got no bidness down here by the river."

"Going to show you where my daddy used to take me fishing."

"We gonna catch us some?"

Tyrone didn't answer. He just drove slowly along the service road until coming to a gravel drive leading off into the wooded area. This was where gravel had been dug for roads in the 90s, so the river area had deep holes that filled with water during rainy seasons. The sun was slipping beyond the trees as dusk settled in, and Tyrone welcomed the darkness. It would make what he had to do easier. Franklin had been his partner for a long time, and Tyrone wished there was another way. But Carlos had made it abundantly clear. There could be no weak links in the chain. Tyrone wished now that he hadn't told Carlos about Franklin losing it the other day. Santos was being taken care of, so nothing could come back on Tyrone or the Mexican connection as far as the driver was concerned. But still, Tyrone had to make sure that everything was okay on his end. He knew that if he didn't, someone from south of the border would come up and make sure. Maybe the someone who had done the girl and maybe it wouldn't just be Franklin that was taken care of.

After nosing the car in under the branches of a tall oak near the end of the graveled road, Tyrone nodded to Franklin. "Let's go for a little walk."

There was a brief hesitation, then Franklin got out of the car. Tyrone led the way to the bank of the river, then turned as Franklin sidled up beside him. "We can't fish if we ain't got poles."

"I'll get them in a bit. Listen to the soft sound of the water moving. Enough to calm a man, isn't it?"

Franklin hefted a rock and tossed it into the river. "That's what I like to do. Make a big splash."

"Give me your gun."

"What?" Franklin turned to face Tyrone and the Glock 45 that was pointed at him. "What the hell, man?"

"Give me your gun."

Franklin took a half step away from Tyrone. "Wait a minute. Is it cause what I said about offing the girl? I don't care about that any more. What's done is done. I won't talk or nothin."

"We're way past promises, Franklin." Tyrone hesitated for just a beat, then finished. "I'm real sorry about this. But I don't have a choice."

Then he pulled the trigger.

Franklin crumpled to the ground. Tyrone stepped closer, pointed the gun at Franklin's head, and shot him again, just to be sure. Then he took a moment to rein in his feelings. No reason to be sorry for what had to be done. Quickly, he undressed the body and rolled it into the river. Another pang of something soft hit him. He never thought he'd end up killing someone here. Here where he had good memories of his father. The only good memories of the man who'd run off a couple of months after the last fishing trip they'd taken to the river. Tyrone had been nine. Didn't understand the way of fathers. Didn't know anything about how to survive without one.

Tyrone shook that thought, and the softness, off. It wasn't the time to be thinking with his heart. He'd learned how to survive, and survival meant no weak links. That's the hard lesson Carlos had taught him. "Do what has to be done."

He took Franklin's gun and knife, as well as the cash from the wallet, then rolled everything else into a tight clothing sausage. It could cook in a burn barrel under the freeway where the homeless gathered. They'd appreciate the added fuel for roasting their hotdogs.

~*~

Angel and Ryan waited for Chad down in the lobby. She was way too comfortable with this white guy who had the easy smile and vivid blue eyes that almost matched her turquoise ring. All her life she'd been warned away from "whitey." The same way she'd been warned away from friends with the flu and people who used drugs. It wasn't until she'd been on the force for a while that she'd come to the conclusion that some white people were just fine. It was that conclusion that had her butting heads with her father all the time. She smiled. Her daddy would blow up if he knew the thoughts she sometimes had about this very fine man who stopped his restless pacing and looked at her. "What?" he asked.

"What, what?"

"You're smiling."

"Oh."

"Hey, guys," Chad said as he exited the elevator and strode toward them. He paused a step, looking from one to the other. "What's up?"

Angel tried to pull the professional mask down. "Ready to roll?"

"Uh, sure."

Angel snuck a glance at Ryan as they pushed through the door. A big grin lit up his face. *He must really be enjoying this.*

"Where we headed?" Angel asked when they were settled in an unmarked squad car, Ryan driving.

"Ricky's Pool Hall." Chad answered from the front passenger seat.

The awkward little dance they'd done to determine who was sitting where had almost been amusing, but Angel hadn't laughed. She wasn't unaware of the tension between the two men. A dead person could have felt it, and she quite frankly didn't know what to do about it. Chad had not lost his interest in her, despite the fact that she'd made it clear a year ago that it wasn't reciprocated. And she was damn sure that personal shit didn't belong on this ride. She'd decided that perhaps if she stayed in the back the two roosters would relax their crops and spurs.

"It's his usual hangout spot," Ryan added. "If we're lucky we'll find him there."

The din of conversations, a TV playing, and pool balls clacking stopped abruptly when the three cops walked into the pool hall. People stopped what they were doing as if they were actors on a movie set and the director had called, "Cut."

Ryan waved to the guys at the tables on the far right of the room. "Carry on, fellas. We didn't come to arrest anyone for a little friendly bit of betting."

Feet shuffled and pool cues slapped the white ball on various tables, as Angel led the way to the bar. She hitched one hip on a barstool and the bartender, a short rotund man about fifty with a huge moustache, ambled over. He eyed her and the two other cops warily. "Help you?"

"Hope so," Chad said, laying his ID on the scarred wooden surface of the bar. "We're looking for Tyrone. Been told he hangs here."

"I can maybe get you a drink," the man said, a tremor in his voice that was incongruous with his outward demeanor. "Kinda short on information."

The action at the tables slowed again as the men, and a few women, strained to listen to the conversation at the bar.

Ryan lowered his voice and leaned closer to the bartender. "We don't need you to affirm that Tyrone uses this place for meeting his crew. We know that. What we don't know is if he's here now. In the back somewhere."

The bartender shook his bald head, a very slight movement that was almost imperceptible.

"Any idea of when he'll be in?" Chad asked.

The bartender looked from her to Ryan, then back again. "Nope." He waited a beat, glancing at the patrons who were still trying to catch the drift of the conversation, then added in a low voice, "Listen. I just serve drinks and stay clear of anything else goes on here. It's healthier that way. These aren't nice people."

"The healthy meter will go up about ten degrees without Tyrone around here," Angel said.

"Jesus, lady. Lower your voice."

"Just trying to help you out," Angel said with a smile. She slid a card across the bar. "Call us next time he comes in."

The bartender snatched up the card and palmed it.

Chad leaned in and spoke softly, "Better do what the lady said. We can bring a load of shit down on you. The folks who hang here won't like that."

Ryan thumped a forefinger on the bar. "Think about it."

The detectives turned and walked out of the place, pausing for a moment on the parking lot, just a few feet from the door. "What now?" Angel asked.

Before either of the men could answer the door burst open behind them and a woman bustled out. It was one of the women who'd been at the pool table, a tall brunette with a little too much around the middle and makeup that looked like it had been applied by a palette knife. Without looking at them she said, "Let's walk. I'll talk."

Angel stepped up beside the woman, with the men trailing a step behind. "I'll make this quick," the woman said. "I don't like Tyrone and his pals dirtying up the place where I like to play with my friends. Understand?"

She glanced quickly at Angel who nodded, then resumed. "He was in here earlier today. Alone. His second-in-command Franklin wasn't with him. Tyrone was on his phone off and on for an hour. Then he high-tailed it out of here. I never seen him ditch this place so fast before."

"Any idea where he went?"

The woman stopped for a beat and gave Angel another quick look. "That man is bad news. I don't get all up in his business. If you get my drift."

Angel got it. She was well acquainted with people who didn't get up in each other's business, legitimate business or not. But especially *not.*

"That's all I got to say." The woman broke off and walked briskly toward a Ford pickup that had enough dents to be a survivor of crash competition. Angel didn't try to stop her. It had taken balls to come out to talk to them.

The detectives got into the unmarked car, Angel in the back again. After Ryan pulled out of the lot, she asked, "You think whatever was going on with Tyrone had something to do with the shakeup south of the border?"

"Could be."

~*~

"Who's this?" Amber asked as Sarah brought Becky into the living room where Amber was sprawled on the couch with pillows and a bag of chips.

Becky strode forward and extended her hand. "Hi. I'm Becky Pickett from Child Protective Services."

Amber shot a quick glance at Sarah. "CPS? You called CPS on me? I'm not a fucking child."

Sarah held up one hand—the one that wasn't holding the pizza. "Relax. She'll treat you like an adult if you act like one."

"I didn't want to be here any more than you want me," Becky said to Amber. "I could be home eating real food."

Sarah chuckled and took the pizza to the counter that separated the living room from the kitchen, calling out, "You want wine or beer?"

"Wine."

"Beer."

Sarah turned to see Becky giving Amber one of her signature hard-ass looks. "How old are you, child?"

"I'm not a child."

Becky cocked her head and tapped her foot until Amber dropped her defiant glare. "Okay," the girl said. "I'm twenty."

"Close enough," Becky said, then turned to Sarah. "But don't tell my boss I okayed a beer for this underage girl."

"Did you stop the pain meds?" Sarah asked.

Amber nodded, so Sarah pulled two beers out of the refrigerator and set them on the counter next to a glass and a bottle of wine. Then she put paper plates and napkins out for the pizza. Cat wound his way around her legs, so she gave him a few chows before the humans settled down to eat.

"Okay," Becky said, lifting a piece of pepperoni from the pizza. "What do you want from me?"

"Huh?" Amber paused with her beer halfway to her mouth. "I thought you were here to tell me what to do."

"Nope. If you're old enough to have a beer, you're old enough to decide for yourself."

"You mean I can go back to the club and dance?"

"Is that what you want to do for the rest of your life?"

Amber shrugged and took a bite of pizza, cheese stretching in a long line from her mouth to the slice. Sarah sat back and let Becky handle things. She was very good at handling things.

"I mean it," Becky said after taking a sip of her wine. "You gotta think about pole-dancing at fifty. You want me to show you what fifty-year-old boobs look like? They ain't pretty."

Becky put her glass down and made a move like she was going to unbutton her blouse. Amber snorted beer through her nose. "No! Please."

Sarah choked on her own beer and wiped at the moisture with a napkin, glad that Amber had stopped Becky. There was no way she wanted to see her friend's boobs either.

"Well, girl. You got a plan B?" Becky spoke calmly, as if no beer had been spilled.

Amber shrugged again. "I never thought of making one."

"Okay. Here's the deal, girlfriend."

"I'm not your girlfriend."

Becky ignored the slight edge of hostility in Amber's voice. "We can be friends or we can be enemies. Your call."

When Amber didn't respond, Becky went on. "Sarah here told me about what happened last year. Then the fire and all a few days ago." She gestured at Amber with the point of a slice of the pizza. "You are one strong young woman. And those of us who are strong can come out on top, no matter what."

"You sound like a preacher," Amber said.

"Well, my daddy was a preacher. Over in Mississippi. But I learned about being strong from my mama. We learn best from our mamas. Don't you think?"

"Maybe."

The word was spoken softly, with no edge of sarcasm or hostility, and Sarah relaxed against the back of the sofa. Becky had the girl now.

As they finished the pizza, with more wine for Becky and another beer for Sarah, she listened as her friend outlined some options for Amber, including housing and financial help to return to college.

"When you were in school, what were you going to major in?" Becky asked.

"I'm not kissing up or anything," Amber said. "But I thought about sociology. Because of that boy. The one that my friend Tracey liked. You know, Sarah. The boy her father tried to buy off."

"What?!" The word exploded from Becky's mouth, then she just shook her head. "Why do I always act so surprised at something like that? The girl was white and the boy was black, right?"

Sarah shook her head. "Hispanic."

"Same difference," Becky muttered. "Just a little lighter skin tone."

"That didn't matter to me," Amber said. "That he was Hispanic. Doesn't matter that you're black either."

Becky sighed and glanced at Sarah. "Ah, the idealism of youth."

The women were quiet for a few moments. Sarah watched Amber fold a piece of pizza into a narrow triangle, then take a bite.

Becky finished her wine, then set the glass down. "So, you think you want to go back to college?"

"I guess."

"There be no guessing about it, girl. Either you do or you don't. Don't be wasting my time."

"Okay."

Again, the response was soft and polite. Sarah liked the direction this was going and watched with great interest as her friend did her magic.

‐*‐

Santos stood when the tall burly sheriff, JD Jones, came to the front of the cell. "Get up here, Santos. You're going for a ride."

Santos rose from the steel bunk, slowly looking from the sheriff to the deputy, eyes wide with apprehension. "Go where?"

"Some folks in Dallas want to talk to you."

"No! No go to Dallas."

"Well now, *senor*, you don't really have a choice, do you?"

Santos froze for a moment, his heart beating a wild rhythm in his chest. He didn't want to go to Dallas. Tyrone would surely kill him. "Please. No. *Por favor.*"

"Judge's orders. Turn around and stick your hands out this slot."

Two deputies joined the sheriff, and after taking a hesitant step forward, Santos paused.

"Come on," Jones said. "No point in stalling."

Turning, Santos put his hands out and felt the cold steel of the handcuffs as they clicked shut.

"Okay," Jones said. "Step back."

Santos did and the sheriff unlocked the cell door. The two deputies came in, one on each side of Santos. They grabbed him by the upper arms, holding him in grips so tight the bones in his arms ached with the pressure. Silently, they walked him out of the station, where a large white van, with the Cameron County logo painted on the side, sat in the front drive. Another deputy opened the back doors and moved out of the way as the men flanking Santos pulled him roughly inside then pushed him down on an empty bench seat. The man by the door said, "Take it easy. No need to kill the guy."

The remark surprised Santos, and he turned quickly to meet the man's gaze. A little smile played around the man's mouth. Did he think he made a joke?

"Never you mind," one of the deputies said. "You're just here to drive."

"Yes, sir." The man saluted, but there was a hint of arrogance to the gesture.

Santos noted the discord between the men for just a moment and might have wondered more about it had he not been so absorbed in his fears. Nothing good waited for him in Dallas, and that was much more serious than a lack of respect.

Chains rattled as the deputies wrapped them around Santos' ankles before securing them to the large metal rings riveted to the floor. Once his feet were secured, one of the deputies unlocked the handcuffs and motioned Santos to bring his arms around to the front. The cool steel of the cuffs encircled his wrists again.

Then one of the deputies sat down on the bench opposite Santos, and the other one exited the van, slamming the rear doors closed. A heavy screen separated the back of the van from the front seats, and a few moments later, Santos saw the two deputies get inside. The engine rumbled to life and the van rolled out of the driveway. There was a slight bump as it turned onto the street in front of the station.

The deputy across from Santos said nothing as the van settled into a fast, yet steady pace, tires humming along the pavement. The man leaned against the backrest and closed his eyes, but Santos was sure the man wasn't sleeping. Not that it mattered. There was no way for him to escape, so he would go on to face his fate, whether it was prison or Tyrone. And maybe, before either of those things happened, he'd get a chance to tell the cops who really killed his daughter. That the detectives believed he had killed Felicity weighed heavy on his heart. How could they even think that he would have done such a thing?

Thinking about his beautiful *la hila*, now cold in the ground, never to laugh or smile again brought a tight constriction to his throat and the warmth of tears to his eyes. The tears surprised him. They were the first he'd allowed since that awful day. He swallowed hard, then took a deep breath. He would not let this weakness show.

Santos leaned back and tried to copy the deputy in the pretend sleep. Or maybe even real sleep. That worked for about ten minutes, then a voice from the front sliced the silence, "Why're you taking the state highway? Interstate's faster."

"Not necessarily," came the reply and Santos opened his eyes. He leaned forward so he could look in the front and he saw the driver turn to the passenger for just a beat. "It's a straight shot to Dallas on 19."

The other deputy waited a moment, then said, "Sherriff Jones always uses the Interstate."

"Don't worry. I cleared it with him."

"Yeah?" There was a pause as if the man was waiting for an answer that didn't come. "Well, then. Guess it's okay."

Nothing more was said, so Santos settled back, not sleeping, but rolling slightly with the rhythm of the of the van. It was a different rhythm than in his big truck, but just as comfortable if one didn't fight the movement. He figured they'd gone about halfway if his mental mileage counter from his many trips to Dallas from the border was correct, when the van suddenly lurched and skidded with a scream of tires. Santos was pitched violently from side to side, the chains digging painfully into his ankles and his head slamming into the wall of the van with a hard crack.

The deputy in the back with him wasn't wearing a seatbelt and he was tossed from his seat like a piece of baggage when the van came to a shuddering halt. He landed with a loud thud on the floor but was able to pull himself up. "Don't you move," he said to Santos, brandishing his gun. Then he called out to the men in front, "What the hell's going on?"

A gunshot was the only answer.

The deputy in the passenger side of the van slumped over.

The deputy across from Santos called out again, a frantic edge of panic in his voice, "Merle. You okay?"

Merle didn't answer.

155

The next sound was of the van door being jerked open. Santos could see the driver's head disappear as he was pulled out. Desperation in his voice, the man shouted, "Wait. The deal was—"

The man never got a chance to say what the deal was. Another gunshot rang out. The deputy with Santos said, "It's some kind of ambush. I'll—"

Whatever the officer's intent was, it was cut off when the body of the van was peppered with a barrage of bullets. Santos couldn't tell how many slammed into him, but he knew he'd been hit. Many times. So had the deputy with him. The man had a small hole in his forehead and a crimson stain was spreading across the khaki of his uniform shirt. Santos knew the deputy was dead. He'd seen lifeless eyes enough to know, and he wondered why he wasn't dead, too. But if this was the cartel, and there was little doubt about that, it wouldn't be long.

The spray of bullets stopped as abruptly as it had started, and the back door of the van opened. The last thing Santos saw was the muzzle of the semi-automatic swinging around the edge of the open door.

~*~

After thanking Becky profusely for her help with Amber, Sarah drove back to the station to wait for the arrival of Santos. Around five o'clock she started to get worried and called the DA's office. "Hey Jessica, you got our guy over there?"

"Who? Santos?"

"Yeah. Thought he was leaving Tyler at three this afternoon. We haven't seen him."

"He was to go straight to you guys. No stopping here."

Sarah tapped a finger on her desk and thought a moment. "Okay. If we don't hear anything in the next thirty minutes, I'm calling down to Tyler. That cool with you?"

"Want me to handle it?"

"No. I got it. Took some personal time earlier, so I'm good. You go home to your family."

"Okay. But call me on my cell if there's a problem."

"Will do."

Sarah hung up and watched the time slide around on her watch for five minutes. Then she got up and walked to the break room, grabbed a cup of what pretended to be coffee this late in the day, and paced. Back and forth, back and forth between the coffee machine and the door. Where the hell was their perp?

Finally, she couldn't stand the wait any longer. She tossed the sludge left in the Styrofoam cup and went back to her desk. She found the Tyler sheriff's number in her contacts and called. When he answered she said, "Sorry to bother you, but I'm just checking on Santos. Was there a holdup on the transfer?"

"Nope. The van got off before three. Give or take a minute or two."

"He never arrived."

"What?"

"He's not here."

"That's not good."

"Yeah. Tell me about it. You heard anything from the deputies doing the transport?"

"No. Didn't expect to unless they ran into trouble."

Sarah glanced at the clock that showed the time at 5:45. "Okay. Something must be wrong. They're well past the usual drive time."

"Hold on. I'll ring one of the men."

Sarah waited for a few seconds, then JD came back. "No answer."

"Any idea what might have delayed them?"

"Nope. They weren't to make any stops."

"Was Santos the only transport?"

"Yup."

Sarah didn't know what to say. She snuck another glance at her watch. Coming on to 6:00 now.

JD broke the silence. "Hold on. I just got an urgent call."

Sarah could hear muffled conversation in the background, then the sheriff was back. "Holy shit. A guy called in an accident. Said he ran up on a police van all shot to hell. Just about halfway to Dallas."

Sarah groaned. "Santos?"

"Looks like it. Man said there was a prisoner shackled in the back and three deputies. All dead."

Sarah took a moment to absorb the news then shouted into the phone, "And it was just now spotted? It's a fucking freeway. Pardon my French."

"They weren't on the freeway. They took highway 19."

"Was that the assigned route?"

"Hell, no."

It took a moment, but then the most important question popped up. "We have to assume it was the cartel that did it. But how in the hell did they know where the van was going to be?"

There was no answer.

"Sheriff," Sarah said, her voice soft. "How did the cartel know?"

"Someone had to tell them." The sheriff's voice was tight with emotion.

Sarah gave him a moment to recover, then said. "Okay. We're going to have to look at everyone who knew about the transport. And the timing. My end and your end."

"Yeah." The word came out on a sigh. "Two of my guys had been with me for years. I can vouch for them."

A long moment of silence followed, then Sarah dared, "The third?"

"A new transfer from Bryan County. Just got here a few days ago."

"Cartel country?"

"Yeah." Coming on another long sigh.

Sarah waited a beat then asked the tough question. "You think he might have …"

She could picture the sheriff wiping his large hand down his face. It was a gesture she'd seen when meeting him in person. "It's possible. Let me do some checking. And I gotta get some backup for the deputy who took the call. He's in the middle of a fucking mess."

"Gotcha. I'll wait to hear back."

Sarah hung up, then immediately dialed McGregor's number. He answered with a gruff, "Yeah?"

She didn't waste time of pleasantries. "Bad news, Lieu."

"Tell me."

"Our witness got iced."

"What!?!?"

She held the phone away from her ear until the reverberation died down. "He never showed. I called Jones down in Tyler to see if there'd been a delay on his end. While we were talking, a deputy rang in to say there'd been an attack on the truck."

"Oh, my God."

"Most likely it was a hit."

"Fuck." The word was accompanied by rhythmic slaps on his desk. The sound only slightly muffled by the phone.

"My sentiments exactly. We need to find out who might have alerted the cartel about the transport."

"Jones think it was one of us?"

"Never implied. Just said we both need to check our people. Makes sense. He's going to get back to me."

"Oh, Christ." McGregor paused for a long sigh, then finished. "I'll let the ADA know. Without Santos we can't arrest Tyrone."

Sarah didn't respond. McGregor knew she didn't have to be told. And she knew he just needed to vent. The case had just been blown to hell.

Sarah hung up with McGregor and called Angel. They'd talked briefly while Sarah had been waiting for Santos to arrive. That was before Sarah's current bad news would trump Angel's bad news that they hadn't found Tyrone. Angel had let her know that Chad and Ryan were going to hang around places where Tyrone might show up. Angel was going home, after a much-needed stop at the dojo.

That had all seemed like a good plan until …

"This could only be a problem, you calling me again," Angel said.

Quickly, Sarah told her about the latest developments.

Sarah thought about asking Angel if she'd talked to anyone. Anyone at all about the transfer plans, but stopped the words before they could escape. Trust was not built on questions like that. Instead, she asked if Angel would come with her to talk to the family again. "They can't hear it on a television newscast."

"Not looking forward to that visit," Angel said.

Chapter Twenty

•••

<u>Wednesday, March 20</u>

"Noooo!" The word exploded in the room, then became a high keening. That from Mrs. Santos after Angel broke the news as gently as she could. She had been relieved to see the sister there, too, but any support she expected from the woman was obviously not going to materialize.

Juanita wrapped her arms around her sister but didn't remove her icy glare from the detectives. She let lose a torrent of Spanish then switched to English. "You did this. You and—"

Angel held up a hand. "No. You don't understand—"

"We understand. *Policia* the same. Here. Mexico. Make no difference."

Unable to find words, Angel tried not to flinch from the hostile glare.

"Juanita, we—"

Sarah was cut off by a slashing gesture from the woman. "Go. Now. Do not come back."

"The investigation into your niece's death is still ongoing."

Juanita rose in one swift motion and spread her arms as if herding reluctant children. "Go. Do *not* come back!"

Angel glanced at Sarah who gave a small nod.

"We're so sorry for your loss," Angel said as she walked toward the door, but she doubted the women heard her. Juanita had collapsed back on the couch with her sister, and both women were rocking back and forth. Words of Spanish were exchanged through their tears, and Angel was glad that they had each other.

The detectives walked out the front door to a yard that held only a couple of discarded soda cans and a flyer for the local Taqueria. It wouldn't take long for the yard to once again be overflowing with family and friends in an instant replay of the community support following Felicity's death.

"God! Hate to just walk out like that," Sarah said as they made their way to their cars. "Just drop a bomb on them and leave."

Sarah gestured expansively with the words, and Angel paused. "Don't start getting all crazy about it. We didn't have a choice."

"I know. It's just—"

"Just nothing." Angel leaned on the roof of her car. "We are the last people that grieving family needs."

It took Sarah so long to respond, Angel wondered if her partner was going to blow again, but then the woman sighed. "You're right."

Angel chuckled. "Did I actually hear those words from your mouth? I'm right about something?"

"Oh, come on ..." But Sarah didn't finish. She gave Angel a smile, then opened her car door. "See you in the morning. I'm guessing McGregor called you even though I was supposed to tell you about the meeting first thing."

"Of course, he did."

Sarah gave a wave of her hand, then got in her car and drove off.

Emotions still reeling from the encounter with the bereaved women, Angel decided to stop by to see her folks. She desperately needed the calming influence of her mother. She wasn't sure how things would be with her father. A frosty wind had blown through their relationship when Angel told him she wasn't going to listen to his hateful, bigoted talk any more. The few times she'd been back to visit and share a meal after that, it had seemed like Spring was not coming to warm things up between them. Phone calls had replaced visits, and in a recent conversation her mother had said that Angel's father was mellowing just a bit, but Angel wasn't betting on it. Her father did tend to hang on to a perceived wrong until it turned rotten in his hands.

The tangy aroma of cumin wafting from her mother's white chili met Angel when she walked into the kitchen. Her mother always called it chicken chili, a fact that had made Angel smile when she realized the possible reason. Ah, that deep vein of bigotry. Her mother was at the stove, stirring the pot and humming a tune Angel couldn't place. "Hi, Mama."

Martha turned, and a broad smile brightened her face, deepening the hollows around her mouth. "Angel." The single word spoke volumes, and Martha put the spoon down to open her arms for her daughter.

Angel always felt safe and comfortable in her mother's embrace, so she held it for several heart-soothing beats before pulling away.

"What a nice surprise," Martha said. "Put another bowl on the table."

It was always taken for granted that when one of the kids dropped by at dinner time, they would stay to eat. No invitation needed and no decline accepted.

Angel opened the cupboard to the left of the sink, the door made from beautiful distressed wood that her father had used when they'd done a kitchen upgrade a number of years ago. The wood was stained dark with layers of matte varnish, and Angel took a moment to run her fingers along the silky finish before taking out a soup bowl.

Her mother started with the usual litany of questions. How are you? Are you eating? Are you seeing anyone? Not pausing long enough for Angel to answer any of them before the next rattled along.

"Martha? You talking to yourself again, or to the beans?" Gilbert stopped in the doorway and Angel turned, locking eyes with him.

After a beat she said, "Hello, Daddy."

"Angel." He gave a brief nod and turned, walking away with legs stiff.

"I thought you said he was over it, Mama."

"Okay. I was wrong. I thought he was. You know how he gets all riled up about something, then simmers down after a while." She went back to stirring the pot on the stove. "I thought it was long enough."

"Should I go?"

"No. Stay."

"Dinner won't be pleasant."

Martha chuckled. "Maybe him not speakin'll be better than him yelling."

Angel nodded, then took her bowl into the dining room. She saw that there were only two other places set. "Is LaVon not coming?" she asked her mother when she went back into the kitchen. "He's usually scrounging dinner every day."

"He called me earlier. Said he'd miss tonight."

"Did he say why?"

"No. And I didn't ask. Not right for a grown man to be asked that by his mother."

Angel was right. Dinner was not pleasant. An icy silence hung over the table, and each clink of a spoon against a bowl hammered against Angel's nerves. Her father ate quickly, head down as if the beans and onions and chicken in his bowl were the most interesting things he'd seen in a decade. Angel found she had a hard time swallowing around the lump of emotion in her throat, so she finally put her spoon down.

"You need to eat up, honey," her mother said. "Can't have you getting all skinny on me."

"What I need," Angel said, looking at her father and fighting to keep her voice level. "Is to be treated like an adult. Allowed to have my own opinions."

Into the hush that followed, Gilbert finally said, "Thank you for supper, Martha. It was good."

Then he pushed back from the table and walked out of the dining room without even a glance toward Angel.

"Oh, Mama." Angel fought the tears that wanted to run down her face.

"I know." Martha reached over and touched Angel on the arm. "Just give him time."

"Time!?" Angel realized her tone had been too sharp when her mother pulled back. "I'm sorry, Mama. But all I do is give him time. What does he give me?"

"Child. He gave you life. He gave you a home. He gave you the means to an education."

"But, Mama. I'm not a child. And I know the good things about Daddy. That's why this rift between us hurts so much."

"So maybe you should take the first step. Go to him and—"

"What? Apologize? I have nothing to apologize for." Angel got up and carried her bowl into the kitchen where she scraped the contents into the trash.

Martha followed with the two empty bowls and put them in the sink. "So, you're happy to just let things be."

It wasn't a question, just a statement, but Angel knew an answer should follow. "No, Mama. I'm not happy. Not happy at all. But you know what I said last time we had this talk. I will not bow to his ways. Not anymore."

Her mother gave her a long look, then turned to add soap and water to the sink. Angel felt it then. A slight tremor that altered the space between them. Her mother wouldn't choose sides. Couldn't choose sides.

Angel turned to leave, saying softly, "I'm sorry, Mama."

-*-

Before going home, Sarah stopped at the grocery store and picked up fixings for salad and a couple of steaks. Her current roommate might enjoy something other than pizza and Cheez-Its, and Sarah couldn't remember the last time she had something that could pass for healthy eating.

Walking into the apartment, Sarah didn't see Amber in her usual place on the sofa. She took the bags of groceries into the kitchen, calling out, "Amber? Where are you?"

"In here."

Sarah followed the sound to her bedroom, where Amber was slowly packing underwear in the small black duffle Sarah had bought for her. "What are you doing?"

Amber turned and gave her a look. The smart-ass one that Sarah found both infuriating and endearing. Her grandmother had probably had the same reaction when Sarah was a teen, throwing that look of disdain that conveyed the same message. "Are you dense? Can you not see what I'm doing?"

"Okay. Clearly, you're packing. Although it's going to take a long time one-handed. I guess I should have asked you why."

"Moving out. Ms. Becky found me a group home where I can stay."

Sarah sat down on the bed next to the duffle. "Oh. Well. I figured you'd move out sooner or later. Just didn't figure it would be today."

Amber grinned, mischief sparkling in her gold eyes. "Ms. Becky told me about your dilemma."

"What dilemma?"

"Needing me gone so you can have your life back."

"What?"

The chirp of Sarah's phone interrupted the conversation, and she glanced at the text. It was from LaVon.

Can I see you tonight?

I'm not sure. I'm...

Another text from LaVon overrode her response.

You might want to check your front door.

Sarah glanced from her phone screen to Amber. "Um ... I need to ..."

"Go ahead," Amber said.

Sarah strode to the front door and opened it as wide as the security chain allowed and saw LaVon—flowers in one hand and a bottle of wine in the other. "I hope you have food,' he said, with just a hint of mischief.

Before Sarah could come up with a response, Becky stepped up behind LaVon. "You going to keep this fine man standing outside your door all night?"

Sarah released the security chain and opened the door wider, just as Amber came out of the bedroom. "Ah, Ms. Becky," she said. "I'm about ready. First I need to meet 'this fine man.'"

LaVon, appearing unruffled by the appearance of two other people, handed the flowers to Sarah and reached out to Amber. "I'm LaVon. LaVon Johnson."

Amber shot a grin toward Becky. "So, this is the dilemma you told me about. Mighty nice dilemma."

"What the hell?" Sarah sputtered.

"Never you mind," Becky said, picking up Amber's duffle. "I'll tell you all about it tomorrow. Including where I'm taking Amber."

Amber gave Sarah a one-armed hug and whispered in her ear. "Thanks so much. For everything."

Passing LaVon, Becky said, "Don't you go hurting my friend. You hear?"

"Yes, Ma'am."

Sarah stood motionless for a few moments, at a loss for words for perhaps the first time in her life.

"Do you have glasses for the wine?" LaVon asked, moving further into the apartment.

"Well, um, nothing fancy. Just Mason jars."

"Mason jars it is." He set the bottle down on the counter beside the grocery bags and looked in them. "Ah. Dinner. Were you expecting me?"

Sarah was starting to get her wits and her words back. "It was for me and Amber."

"Great. Dinner for two. Shall I cook?"

"You cook?"

"Of course. My mama taught me how to be self-sufficient."

Sarah took two small jars out of a cabinet and set them out for the wine. Then she took a larger jar, filled it partway with water and put the flowers in it. "I've never had flowers before."

"Really?" LaVon looked up from his task of opening the wine and the banter was gone from his voice. "I'm glad I could remedy that."

His gaze held so much meaning, Sarah had a hard time looking away. "Should we cook the steaks?"

"Whatever you want."

Chapter Twenty-One

∙∙

Thursday, March 21

S arah slipped out of bed and looked at the body next to her. *Oh my God. What have I done?* She scrambled to find her sleep shirt in the tangle of sheets and blankets. The nightshirt she hadn't even put on last night. She hadn't put anything on after LaVon had so carefully undressed her, but she needed something between her and the chill in the room. Truth be told, she needed something between her and the man who was sleeping in her bed. She studied the steady rise and fall of his chest. The early morning sunlight filtered through the slats on the window blinds and cast stripes across his bare torso. While his face and arms were a dark brown, the rest of his body was the color of bronze and more muscular than one would expect from a man who spent most of his time at a job that used mental muscles more than physical.

Walking quietly into the bathroom, Sarah wondered how on earth she was going to tell Angel she'd slept with her brother. She closed the door and leaned against the sink. The woman was going to go ballistic. But then, maybe Angel wouldn't have to know. It's not like they were best friends in high school who shared stuff like this. But would LaVon tell?

Oh, hell!

After a few months of sexual attraction and push-pull between them, LaVon had issued the challenge with that kiss at the stable. He'd reminded Sarah that they no longer had the professional conflict of interests to stand in their way, although Sarah reminded him that they had plenty of personal issues that should warn them off, namely

Angel Johnson. But last night ... Oh, last night. The way he'd just come over, all smiles and barely disguised innuendos. They were just supposed to have dinner. That was all that had to happen, and she still wasn't sure how they got from dinner to her bed. Maybe it was a fire in his dark brown eyes that ignited a fire in her belly.

Sarah turned away from the sink and walked over to start the shower. There was a discreet tap on the door. "Can I come in, Sarah? I, uh, really need to use the facilities."

She crossed to the door and opened it, relieved when she saw he had pulled on his jeans. She wasn't ready for nakedness this morning.

"Good morning," she said, stepping around him to go out.

He stopped her with a touch on her arm, then leaned down to brush her cheek with a kiss. "Good morning."

All so nice and polite and almost ... genteel. Sarah chuckled at the sharp contrast to the riotous sex of last night. Neither one of them had been genteel as they'd stripped off clothes and tumbled into the bed.

A few moments later, Lavon opened the bathroom door. "You left the shower running."

"So I did."

They stood there for a moment, just looking at each other. "This is awkward," he finally said.

"A bit."

"Should I help you pay your water bill?" He cocked his head toward the shower, and Sarah burst out laughing.

"Only if you want to."

"I'd feel more inclined if I got to use some of that water."

"Go ahead. I'll wait."

He took her hand and pulled her into the bathroom. "We've wasted too much water already."

He dropped his pants and stepped into the shower, holding the curtain back just far enough to get in. "You coming?"

Sarah hesitated just for a moment, then shucked off her shirt and joined him.

~*~

Sarah walked into the squad room and stopped by her desk to get a notebook. Just in case something important came down at the meeting this morning. Angel was already at her desk, and Sarah avoided direct eye contact, afraid something of the thrill of that morning shower would show in her eyes.

"You okay?" Angel asked.

"Fine."

Actually, more than fine. The morning lovemaking had been just that. Lovemaking. Thinking about it brought the heat of a blush to Sarah's face. The night before had been raw, reckless lust, but this morning had been tender and ...? Sweet. LaVon was a romantic to the core, and he made her feel like a cherished woman in ways no other man had. Not even Paul, whom she had thought was a forever man.

Was LaVon a forever man?

That question stopped her short. It was way too soon to even start down that path. Especially with his sister looking at her with all kinds of questions in her eyes.

When her cell phone rang, Sarah picked it up and checked the caller ID. LeVon? What on earth? She turned her back on Angel and answered the call, speaking as quietly as possible. "What are you doing calling me at work?"

"I miss you."

Trying her best to keep her voice soft and calm Sarah said, "Really? We've been apart ... what? An hour?"

LaVon responded with a soft chuckle. "I forgot to tell you to have a good day."

'OMG' as Amber would say. Just the sound of his voice made a wave of desire creep over her entire body. She was turning into a teenager with a crush.

"You there?"

"Yeah. Sorry."

"I should get to work."

"Yeah. Me, too. See you, uh, later." Sarah hit the end-call icon and slipped the phone back into her purse. Needing a moment to regain her composure, she used the ruse of looking for something in the stack of papers on her desk, avoiding eye contact with her partner.

"You ready?" Angel asked.

"Yeah." Sarah grabbed the notebook and a folder and followed her partner to the conference room. Jessica Franklin was already there with McGregor and Chad. Ryan came in a few moments later.

After everyone was seated and pleasantries exchanged, McGregor cleared his throat. "Everyone up to speed on Santos?"

Nods all around. "Okay," he cleared his throat again. "You know this is just procedure, but I have to ask. Did any of you talk to anyone about Santos coming up here? Mention the time?"

The unanimous response was no.

"Good. I didn't think so, but I had to ask."

"We get it," Chad said.

McGregor nodded an acknowledgement to Chad, then turned to Jessica. "What about your team?"

"I did the transfer papers myself. Anyone could've seen the copies in the files, I guess, but there's pretty tight security in that area. Nobody from outside could have easy access."

"But your team?" McGregor pushed.

Jessica bristled a bit at the question before answering, her face hardening and her tone becoming clipped. "We have no problems."

Silence hung in the air for a beat, electric in the room, and Sarah felt a tinge of sympathy for her friend. Then McGregor dipped his head in what could have been a nod of apology and tensions eased.

"Sarah? Any ideas?" McGregor asked.

She shrugged.

"Did Santos know he was being moved? Maybe he told his family and they—"

Jessica cut Angel off with a raised hand. "That's not the way it works, Detective. Prisoners are not privy to any information about a move."

More silence followed that, although now it was not laced with so much tension.

Into the silence came the buzz of Sarah's phone. She retrieved it from her jacket pocket and checked the screen. When she saw the caller ID she said, "It's the sheriff in Tyler."

She swiped to accept the call. "Kingsly here. Can I put you on speaker?"

"You secure?"

"Yes. In conference with a few colleagues trying to figure out what went wrong with the transfer."

"Okay."

Sarah put her phone on the table and hit 'speaker.' "Okay, JD. Go ahead."

"The problem was down here," JD said without preamble.

"You figured that out pretty quick." Sarah said.

"It was easy once the real deputy was found."

"What's his story?"

"No story. He's dead. His body was found close to the Rio Grande."

"You mean one of the men on the transfer wasn't legit?" McGregor asked, heat in his voice.

JD took a moment before answering. "Yup."

McGregor slapped the table so hard the phone bounced. "How the hell did that kind of screwup happen?"

Again, there was a moment before the sheriff answered, this time his voice stiff. "The transfer van came from Cameron County. Our van was making a run to Houston with another prisoner. Since I was short-handed, the Cameron sheriff said he'd send one of his deputies to drive. That man never made it to Tyler, but the one who did had all the right ID."

"Ah, shit!"

"Yup." JD paused for a beat then added. "If there's nothing else, I gotta sign off. I'm being sucked into a mudhole here."

"Sure. Sorry about the shouting," McGregor said. "Thanks for letting us know."

"You bet."

Sarah hit the disconnect icon and they all sat in another strained silence for a beat. "Now what?" Angel finally asked.

171

"We're back at square one," Chad said. "Nothing to hold Tyrone on even if we find him."

"Okay, we start over," Sarah said.

"Not exactly," McGregor said. "We now know a lot more about this whole drug operation of Tyrone's than we did before. And maybe we can put the squeeze on him."

"Right," Ryan put in. "We don't have to tell him that Santos is dead. Put him in the box and dangle the threat of a witness who's willing to testify."

"Hold on there." Jessica stood and put her hands over her ears. "This is going in a direction that I don't need to hear. I know nothing about any threats and lies. I'm out of here."

She gave Sarah a brief smile as she passed. It was a smile of understanding. Jessica wouldn't want to be privy to any details but, short of police brutality, she also wouldn't care how they got what she needed to prosecute Tyrone.

~*~

Sarah was contemplating lunch when McGregor buzzed her. "Meet Bert out at the river. He's got a floater. Here're the coordinates."

"No address?"

McGregor hesitated just a moment then said. "It's The River."

Even though he couldn't see her, Sarah nodded. Everyone knew The River meant the Trinity. And there weren't a whole lot of businesses along the shores with street addresses.

"Take Angel."

"Sure thing, Boss." But McGregor had ended the call after her first word. She sighed and stood up, giving Angel a nod. "Lieu wants us to take a look at a floater."

With the help of GPS, they had little trouble finding the spot where police cars and forensics' vans were pulled off the dirt road about fifty yards from the shoreline. A tech crew in protective clothing was huddled near a bloated lump on the ground. Drawing near, it became clear what that lump was. "Oh my God," Angel said, pressing a hand to her mouth. Most of the face was gone.

"This your first floater?" Sarah asked.

Angel nodded.

"Good thing we didn't have lunch first."

Angel swerved and headed to the bushes.

Bert ambled over to where Sarah had stopped about fifteen feet from the crew and the body. "Your partner going to pass on the up close and personal?"

Sarah chuckled. "Looks like it."

But Sarah didn't move any closer. "Got an ID?"

Bert shook his head. "He went in in his altogether."

Roberts, who'd been hunched over the body, stood and snapped off his latex gloves, then looked at Sarah. "Anything else before we take him away?"

"Any idea of TOD?"

"From the condition of the body I'd guess he hasn't been in the water more than a day or two. But that's just a guess. You know the rest of my crime-scene sermon."

"Yeah. Wait for Walt to do his job."

Roberts nodded, then motioned to his crew to finish up. Just in case this might be the place the man was killed, the techs spread out and started walking a thirty-foot perimeter around the body, bagging anything that looked out of place. Since people considered the great outdoors their personal garbage dump, there were a lot of things that looked out of place. Sarah did not envy the techs their job.

Sarah moved back to the squad car, Bert and Angel following. Sarah leaned against the front fender on the driver's side. "So, what's hinky about this one?" she asked Bert. "Lots of people drown in The River."

"Besides the fact that the body was naked?"

"Yeah. Besides that."

"The missing face and the bullet hole in the back of his head."

"That'll do it." She looked to Angel who was still a little pale around the lips. "You okay?"

Angel nodded and joined her partner in the car-lean. "You think the man was shot and put in the water here?" she asked Bert.

"No tellin' where it happened. Bodies can float for miles."

Sarah let out a deep sigh. "So, we don't necessarily have a crime scene."

It wasn't a question, but Bert answered anyway. "Nope. And we may never find one. He coulda' been killed anywhere and dumped from a boat."

Bert pulled out a handkerchief, and wiped the beads of sweat on his forehead. "Heating up. Even for spring."

"You want to take the lead on this one?" Sarah asked.

"Nope." Bert stuffed the handkerchief into a pocket in his wrinkled brown slacks, then adjusted his tie, which bore hints of more than a few lunches, but Sarah knew under the sloppy façade was a damn fine detective.

"Lieu figures your case is stalled so you can take this one." Bert said. "Simms and I are on a string of burglaries along Mockingbird. Be on stakeout for the next couple of days. Got a tip on where the perp might hit next, so Simms is already there."

Sarah let out another deep sigh. "Okay, we'll wait for Walt to get here."

Bert gave a brief salute and shuffled over the sandy gravel to his car. Not that he had to salute. They were at the same rank. It was just his way. He did it to everyone, sometimes even the officers in blue.

Sarah turned to Angel. "You're going to get teased for that." She made a vague gesture toward the bushes where Angel had puked.

"I'm used to it. The white girls at school toughened me up."

There was an edge in Angel's voice that scraped across Sarah's patience with the chip on Angel's shoulder, but she decided to hold back the sharp response that had wanted to escape restraint. Maybe not responding was the best way to handle it at the moment.

Besides that, Walt had just pulled up with the wagon right behind him. Sarah gave him the few minutes it took to don his protective gear and check the corpse, before moving. "I'll talk to Walt," she said to Angel. "No need to come."

Despite that offer, Angel followed Sarah over to the body. Walt was carefully examining the bullet hole in the head when the detectives drew near. "Cause of death is easy," he said without looking up. "Even if I find water in his lungs when I have him on the table. It's the bullet that started it all."

"Any guestimate as to TOD?"

Walt sat back on his heels and regarded Sarah with a hint of amusement. "Really detective? How many times do we need to have this dance?"

Sarah smiled. "I'll dance with you any time, Walt."

He hrumphed and turned back to the body.

"Bert said something about the skin on his fingers peeling," Angel said. "Will prints be possible?"

Sarah glanced at her partner. Huh? Apparently, Angel must have gotten over the sick and come close enough to hear what Bert had said. And she hadn't puked again. Good for her.

"We'll try," Walt said without looking up. "That's all we can promise."

"Okay. Let us know when you're ready to do the post," Sarah said.

"Sure thing."

Back at the station, Sarah sat at her desk, trying, with various degrees of success, to read over the material they'd gotten from Vice on the Dallas drug scene. The more she read about what was known about Tyrone and his partner, Franklin, and what couldn't be proven, the more frustrated she got. She remembered seeing Tyrone that day she'd been riding with LaVon. The cold look in his eyes and the smirk. Almost as if he knew she was PD and he was challenging her. And the young kids riding with him? His dealers? So young all of them. Probably only middle-school age. They should have been playing games with their friends. Going out to dinner with their family. All those things normal young kids do. But they had not looked like normal young kids. Somewhere they'd lost the innocence of childhood.

Sarah slapped the folder shut. "This waiting around doing nothing is killing me," she said to Angel who was intently studying something on her computer monitor. "Going downstairs to get candy. Want anything?"

Angel shook her head and Sarah checked the pocket of her jeans to make sure she had a few bills. Halfway to the door, she met Ryan who was walking in with three cups from Starbucks. The brilliance of his smile could have powered an entire city block. "Coffee and a happy face?" Sarah said. "Please tell me it's because you've solved the case. Caught all the bad guys and championed justice in Dallas."

Ryan chuckled, taking the coffee to Angel's desk, where he offered her one. "Your favorite," he said.

Sarah bit her bottom lip to keep from reacting. She didn't even know Angel's favorite, and the woman could say what she wanted, but there was definitely something happening between these two. "And mine?" Sarah asked, still fighting to hold back the smile.

"Didn't know how you like it. But I brought plenty of creamers and sugar. Just in case."

"Thank you." Sarah avoided a direct look at either of them as she pulled her chair over to sit by Angel's desk. Ryan pulled a chair from a nearby empty desk.

Angel and Ryan were strangely quiet for the next few moments, so Sarah jumped in with the obvious question. "What brings you here bearing gifts?"

"You know Tyrone's partner, Franklin? Nobody's seen him for a couple of days."

"Is that unusual?" Angel asked.

Ryan shrugged. "Hard to tell. They aren't always together. But usually connect up every day or so at their favorite hangout."

"And they haven't?" Sarah asked.

Ryan shook his head. "There's a buzz about his absence on the street. But nobody knows anything for sure."

"What's the buzz?"

"That Tyrone has been unhappy with his partner for a while."

"What's Tyrone saying?"

"Nada."

"Why don't we bring him in?"

Sarah glanced at Angel. "We have nothing on him."

"Nothing except we know he's a goddam drug king pin."

"But we can't prove it," Ryan said.

"Right," Sarah said. "But maybe Angel's on to something. Tyrone doesn't know we don't have anything on him."

Ryan shook his head. "He'll see through that old cop cliché in the first five seconds. Don't forget how intelligent he is. If we were dealing with Franklin, that'd be another story. He's pretty street smart, but doesn't have it up here." Ryan tapped his forehead.

Sarah picked up her coffee cup to take a sip, then slammed in down on the desk so hard coffee surged over the top. Angel grabbed a couple of napkins to save some of her case notes she'd been entering into the computer. "What the hell?"

"Could Franklin be our floater?" Sarah said.

"What floater?" Ryan asked almost on top of Angel saying, "That's a stretch, isn't it?"

Sarah held up a finger to Ryan and addressed Angel. "Think about it. Some of the details mesh."

"What floater?" Ryan asked again. "What details?"

Angel dropped the wet napkins into her trash can, letting Sarah finish telling Ryan about the dead guy at the river and his estimated TOD.

Ryan pulled on his upper lip while he listened, apparently not discounting the idea. When Sarah was finished, he said, "But we don't know who he is, right? The dead guy."

"No. His face was blown away. Or eaten away by the fish. Walt's still trying to figure that one out." Sarah went to her desk and retrieved the pictures of the deceased. Angel glanced away as Sarah showed them to Ryan.

"Oh, geez." Ryan said.

"Yeah. Pretty bad," Sarah said. "But it could be Franklin. Right?"

"I don't know. I never saw him without his face."

"Ryan," Angel said sharply. "Some compassion here."

"Yeah. Sorry."

"So, what about it?" Sarah said. "Can we work Tyrone over for this? Tell him we know this is Franklin. And we know he offed him?"

Ryan started to shake his head, and Angel leaned forward. "Wait. This is different from some vague, 'we got proof' thing. Run a positive ID of the floater by him. See how he reacts."

"And if he doesn't? If he just lawyers up?"

Angel shrugged. "Then he does. We can still hold him for twenty-four hours. Maybe longer."

"And maybe by then we get an ID. And this is Tyrone's partner." Sarah tapped the picture. "And unless some gang war cropped up while we weren't looking, there's a good chance Tyrone had something to do with blowing this guy's face off."

"I'm convinced Tyrone has something to do with everything," Angel said. "From the murder of that little girl in the park. And killing God know how many other kids with that street drug. It's all connected. I'm sure of it."

"She has a point there, Ryan," Sarah said. "So, what say you? We pick the little weasel up?"

"He's anything but a little weasel," Ryan said. "But let's do it."

~*~

An hour later two uniformed officers were outside the back door of Ricky's Pool Hall where Chad had reported Tyrone was occupying his favorite table. Chad had been keeping an eye on the place ever since the news about Franklin had started circulating on the street. There was always the chance that Franklin could show back up but the more hours that passed without a sighting made that seem less and less likely.

They'd gone in quiet. No lights. No sirens. And Sarah pulled the unmarked car to the curb a half a block down from the entrance to the club. Ryan had just hung up from the latest update from Chad, who was now inside. "Tyrone's still in there. Just drinking his tea. Not talking to anyone."

"Who's he got with him?" Angel asked from the backseat.

"Chad's pretty sure he spotted at least four who could be muscle. Didn't see weapons, though."

"Doesn't mean they don't have any."

"Right." Ryan glanced at Sarah. "How do you want to play this?"

Sarah already had her car door open. "Just go in and grab the bastard. I'll take the lead. You guys cover me. Tell Chad we're coming in."

Ryan nodded and pulled out his cell, talking quietly and briefly while the trio walked toward the club. Then he hung up and nodded to Sarah.

"Okay," she said and pushed through the door.

At first it was like walking into a cave, all blackness after the brightness from outside, but when her eyes adjusted, Sarah could see Tyrone sitting about four tables in. He was alone. Barely missing a beat for the adjustment to the lighting, Sarah strode over to the table, holding her badge out in front of her. "Dallas PD, Tyrone. Stand up."

"What for?"

"I'm arresting you on suspicion of murder."

For a moment, nobody moved. Not Tyrone. Not the cops. Not the other people in the club. Then Tyrone let out a small laugh. "Who is it that I'm supposed to have murdered?"

"Let me see. I have a list here somewhere." Sarah patted her jacket pockets, never taking her eyes from Tyrone. While his lips had shone amusement, his eyes had not.

"Very funny, officer."

"It's not a joke, asshole."

"Besides that rather dubious list, what exactly do you have that legitimizes an arrest?"

Sarah leaned close to his face. "We found your partner."

A barely perceptible flicker of worry flashed through Tyrone's eyes, then they went blank and cold again. "I don't believe you."

"Believe this," Sarah grabbed his arm and started to pull him out of the chair. "Tyrone Vane. You are under arrest for the murder of Franklin Gibbs."

There was a rustle of chairs as two men at a nearby table stood. Sarah glanced over quickly, in time to see Ryan and Angel step forward. "Stand down," Ryan said in a voice that rang with authority. But the men didn't move and the unease in the room ratcheted up to a point of explosion.

Everything froze for just a beat. Even the air didn't move. Then the explosion came. The two men pushed the table into Ryan and Angel as Tyrone jerked his arm away from Sarah and bolted toward the back. Chad was off his barstool in a flash, but he was too close to the front. Too far away to stop Tyrone who made it to the back door with Sarah ten feet behind him.

Tyrone blasted out of the back door and saw the two cops in a patrol car blocking his way to the mouth of the alley. Quickly, he turned and raced down the other way, the officers piling out to run hard after him. At the end of the alley, he scrabbled up on a dumpster and hurled himself over the fence, ripping his pants in the process and leaving tufts of blue denim like little souvenirs.

One of the officers followed, barely breaking stride as he clambered up the pile of debris to the dumpster and then going over the fence. Sarah pulled up short, taking a moment to catch her breath. No way was she going over the fence. "Follow your partner," she called to the other officer as she whirled and sprinted toward the patrol car. She jumped in and backed out of the alley with a roar of engine, scream of siren, and screech of tires.

On the street, Sarah dodged through traffic and made a hard left at the corner. Half a block down, she saw Tyrone shoot out like a bullet and tear down the street in the other direction. A few seconds later, a uniformed officer came barreling out, paused to take a quick look, then raced after Tyrone. Sarah gunned the engine and drew abreast of Tyrone, who then swerved into the next alley.

Sarah made another hard left and bounced the patrol car over bags of garbage, a discarded tire, and drawers from a broken-down dresser that were strewn on the alley floor. Surprisingly, Tyrone was staying ahead of her. He was like a goddam Olympic runner. He pushed a galvanized can over in her path, and for a moment, Sarah hesitated. Then she mentally said to hell with it and pressed hard on the accelerator, blasting into the metal can with such force the steering wheel shook in her hands. She white-knuckled it, closing the distance until she was close enough to stop and jump out of the car. Tyrone was ten feet from the fence at the end of this alley, but Sarah was only five feet behind him.

She reached down to her last reserve of strength and leaped forward, grabbing the back of his jacket. For a second, she was afraid he would slip out of the jacket and race away, but she managed to pull him down. She fell heavily on top of him, thankful that he took the brunt of the slide across the concrete. Then she put a knee in his back and pulled out her handcuffs just as the uniformed officers came to a panting stop beside them.

After getting the handcuffs secured, Sarah stood and pulled Tyrone up. Through gasps to catch her breath, she read him his rights, ending with, "Run again and I'll shoot your ass."

Then she turned to the uniformed officers. "You didn't hear that last part, right?"

"No, Ma'am."

"Take him in and book him."

Chapter Twenty-Two

....

Thursday, March 21

S arah jogged back toward the pool hall, meeting up with the other detectives about halfway down the block. Apparently, the fight had gone out of Tyrone's backup muscle the minute he'd split and after Ryan told them that nobody there would be arrested. Yet. The not-so-subtle threat of that single word had quieted everyone down.

All that, Sarah learned after she got into the car that Chad was driving, Angel and Ryan in the back. "Thanks for the ride," Sarah said, settling in beside Chad.

"Any time, detective."

The banter and easy chuckles provided good relief from the stress, and Sarah's heartrate was almost back to normal by the time they pulled up in the station parking lot. They went straight to booking, where Tyrone was still being put through the paces. Sarah motioned to one of the uniformed officers. "Take him to interrogation room one when you're done here."

The officer nodded.

"Why don't you take a few?" Angel said to Sarah. "We'll bring McGregor up to speed, then meet you at the box."

"Okay. Thanks." Sarah found a nearby ladies' room and was shocked when she saw her reflection in the mirror. No wonder Angel had sent her on this side trip. She ran water and wet a couple of paper towels, wiping at the dirt on her face. Under the dirt was an abrasion high on her cheek that she hadn't been aware of until she touched it. Now it hurt like hell, reminding her of the spill she'd taken on her bicycle when she was a kid. She'd never known abrasions could hurt worse than a deep cut until she'd gone sliding across the gravel road for about ten feet. She'd ended up with scraps along her leg from ankle to thigh and limped around for at least a week.

Thankfully, the current abrasion was much smaller and didn't have bits of stone imbedded in it.

Her jacket was smudged where she'd slid across the alley with Tyrone, but wet paper would only make that mess worse. She pulled out a few dry towels from the dispenser and brushed at the smudges, not really making a dent in them. She sighed and carefully dabbed at her face again with a wet towel. Then tried a smile. Her face wasn't used to it.

Giving up on the smile, she made her way to the interrogation room. Angel and Ryan were standing outside, watching Tyrone through the glass. "Where's Chad?" Sarah asked.

"He volunteered to see McGregor. Give him the details of what went down at the pool hall," Angel said. "How's your face?"

"Okay." Sarah thrust her hands in the back pockets of her jeans and studied Tyrone. He was sitting back in the metal chair, feet crossed at the ankles, as if he was just hanging with some of his pals. "How should we to play this?"

"He has little use for women," Ryan said. "I should start."

"Be my guest," Sarah said. "If I went in there right now, I might kill him."

Tyrone didn't change his posture when Ryan walked in. He didn't speak, either.

Ryan leaned against the wall opposite the man cuffed to the chair. "We've got you on suspicion of murder and resisting arrest. Could even add assaulting an officer to the list. What do you think?"

"More like she assaulted me." Tyrone lifted his torn shirt, revealing the abrasions on his stomach and chest. "Maybe I file police brutality charges."

"Yeah. You do that. See if a judge gives a good goddam."

Ryan dragged one of the other chairs in the room toward the table and straddled it, crossing his arms over the back. "Since you'll be facing charges of murder and drug distribution, we'll probably get some latitude on what we had to do to bring you in."

"So soon after George Floyd maybe the judge give this poor black man some consideration. Sides, I don't know why you thinking I killed Franklin. Far as I know, he still alive. Just off on some trip or something."

"Yeah." Ryan slapped the folder on the table and slid the picture of the dead guy from the river out. Pushing it across so Tyrone couldn't miss it. "Maybe he took a trip down the Trinity all by himself. What do you think?"

"You think that's Franklin? That could be any nigger without a face."

"But he's your nigger without a face."

"You watch your mouth, white boy."

"Or what?" Ryan maintained a visual stand off for a moment. "You gonna send one of your goons after me?"

"Could happen," Tyrone said with a hint of a humorless smile. "Could happen."

Outside the interrogation room, Sarah turned to Angel. "What the hell?"

Sarah moved toward the door. She was going in there and kick some black ass. Angel put a hand on her arm. "Wait. Let Ryan handle it."

The door to the viewing room opened and McGregor stepped in, followed by Chad. "How's it going?" McGregor inclined his head to Ryan and Tyrone.

"It's not," Sarah said. "Tyrone's stonewalling. Ryan can't seem to make a dent."

"Maybe a night in jail will change that." McGregor turned to Chad. "Take him downstairs."

Chad nodded and exited the anteroom. He walked swiftly into the interrogation room and pulled Tyrone up. "On your feet, asshole. You're coming with me."

"Where?"

"To a nice little nine-by-nine room where you can think about things."

Tyrone tried to pull out of Chad's grasp. "You can't do that. I want a lawyer."

"Here's the deal," Ryan said, stepping up to help Chad control Tyrone. "That doesn't mean shit right now. No arraignment. No lawyer. That's the way it works."

~*~

After filling out her report, Sarah gratefully left headquarters and got into her car to head home. She was still sore from her tussle with Tyrone, just now noticing a stiffness in her right shoulder from slamming into the concrete. Keeping her left hand on the steering wheel, she rolled the shoulder, testing for any serious damage, finally concluding that stiff and sore was the extent of it.

She walked into the silent apartment, for a minute forgetting that Amber was gone. Hmmm. She'd kinda gotten used to the girl. So had Cat, obviously. He ran out of the bedroom mewling on high volume and almost tripped her as he wound around her legs. She gently nudged him away, and he immediately went to his food dish, pushing it with one paw as if wanting to make sure she saw that it was empty.

"Okay. Okay. Just hang on a minute."

Sarah went into the bedroom, shrugging out of her jacket along the way. That she tossed on the bed to deal with later, but her weapon immediately went into the nightstand drawer. She changed into shorts and an over-sized t-shirt, kicked off her shoes, and padded barefoot back to the kitchen to fill Cat's bowl and maybe her own stomach.

~*~

Angel was almost out the front door of the station when Ryan hustled up. "Let me get that for you." He pushed the door open.

"How kind of you," Angel said, putting on a sweet Southern accent.

"Hey, that's pretty good," Ryan said.

For a moment they just stood there, eyes locked, then Ryan grinned.

Heat rose on Angel's cheeks and she was glad that the blush could probably not be seen. "We can't keep doing this," she said.

"Doing what?"

She grasped for a response. "Looking at each other."

"Okay." Ryan turned to look at the DPD parking lot where cars stood in neat little rows.

"Do you always just joke around?"

"No." He turned back, his face now dead serious. "I just don't know how …" he gestured vaguely. "I'm not good at this."

Angel moved away from the door and leaned against the side of the building. "I don't know if there should be a 'this.'"

"You don't feel it?"

Part of her wanted to say no. It would be so much easier. Loving this man would complicate her life in innumerable ways. And she had no doubt that loving was part of what was happening between them. His attentiveness that she found so charming. The ease with which they could tease and banter. The attraction that was growing with each encounter. Even at the coffee shop where she'd met him a few times, trying to kid herself that having coffee together wasn't like dating.

"Well?"

The one-word question stopped the train of thoughts and she met his gaze. "I do feel it. But…"

"But?"

"This." She held her arm close to his. Creamy brown next to ruddy white.

"Doesn't matter." He took her hand and raised it to his lips.

The touch was fire, and when Angel gasped, Ryan kissed her hand again.

"I can't have sex with no white boy," Angel blurted.

Ryan chucked. A deep seductive sound. "That would do for starters. But I want so much more."

Chapter Twenty-Three

● ●

Friday, March 22

Sarah was on her way to the interrogation room when her phone pinged with a message from Gladys that someone was there to see her. It was urgent, according to the visitor. She was surprised to see Juanita standing on the other side of the gate, twisting a handkerchief as if wanting to kill it.

"Let her in," Sarah said to Gladys, then motioned Juanita to follow her to her desk where she pulled an empty chair over for the woman to sit. "What is it?"

It took several moments before the woman spoke. "I want no trouble."

"Are you in trouble?"

Juanita shook her head. "Emilio. He was in trouble."

"We know."

"More than that. The driving."

Sarah sat forward. "You knew he was transporting drugs."

Juanita lowered her gaze for a moment, attacking the handkerchief in her hands again.

"Did you?"

The question was harsh and the woman looked up quickly. "*Si*. Yes. But only me. Not my sister. I heard Emilio talk on phone one day."

"When was that?"

"Few days ..." her voice faltered. "Few days before Felicity."

Sarah drew in a breath, then asked. "What did you hear?"

"Emilio say he not drive for drugs anymore."

187

"Do you know who he was talking to?

Juanita shook her head.

"Was that all?"

Another head shake. "Emilio say, 'Threats no work.' His voice hard and strong. Then he listen before saying, 'One more time. That is all.'"

Juanita paused and seemed to gather some inner strength to sit a little taller and lift her chin. "Then you arrest Emilio."

"But in between—"

"Yes. In between, my niece is killed."

Sarah thought about the implications for a moment. It was very possible that the killing of the girl had been a horrible message to Santos that he couldn't just quit. But who delivered the message? Someone local or an out of town enforcer? And who was Santos talking to that day Juanita heard him?

'We'll check phone records to trace the call."

Juanita shifted in her seat and used the handkerchief to wipe a tear that had dared to slip across her cheek. "He didn't use house phone. Always had another. Private. Secret. Even Camille could not touch."

Damn! Probably a burner. Sarah started to stand. "Well, thanks for coming in. Your information is most—"

"That is not all."

Sarah sat down abruptly, inviting Juanita to continue with a small hand gesture.

"Emilio. He call when he was arrested in Tyler."

"Did you talk to him?"

"No. He only talked to my sister. But after, she told me. She was very upset."

"About?"

"He told her he did bad things. With bad people. Afraid what bad people will do. What they did."

Sarah held up a hand. "Wait! Did he say what they did?"

Juanita didn't answer right away. A small sob choked her for a moment, then she took a breath and said, "Not exactly. Emilio. He say he sorry. He didn't mean for anything bad to happen, especially not Felicity."

Sarah had to hold back anger and sadness as her mind called up the image of that poor girl lying in the park that horrible Sunday morning. What bastards could kill a child to threaten a father?

"So, he thought whoever he was working for killed your niece?"

Juanita nodded, then a few more tears escaped her large dark eyes. Sarah sat still, letting the moment of shared sadness linger a bit longer.

Then Juanita pulled herself together once again and stood. "That is all I came to say. Please do not tell my sister I did this. She no want to tell. Is scared."

"I understand." Sarah rose and escorted Juanita toward the gate. "I'll see if we can offer any protection until we get whoever did this."

"*Gracias.* Thank you."

Before going to the interrogation room for another run at Tyrone, Sarah swung by McGregor's office to let him know about what Juanita had reported.

"Too bad she didn't catch a name," McGregor said when Sarah finished. "Especially if that name was Tyrone."

"Yeah, but it does give us the most direct line away from the father as a suspect. And we know it was not a blooding ritual. Narrows the field."

"Okay. Go see what our guest has to say for himself. Angel's already there."

~*~

"Did you sleep well last night, Tyrone?" Sarah asked.

"I've had better accommodations." His voice was rich and velvety and completely without rancor.

"I'm sure you have." Sarah took a seat across from him, placing her notebook on the scarred top of the table. Angel leaned one shoulder against the wall near the door.

"Am I free to go now?"

"Not yet. We'd like to continue the conversation from last night."

"Oh, about last night." Tyrone smiled, an expression that looked anything but friendly. "As soon as I'm out, you'll be hearing from my attorney. Unlawful detention. I might even charge police brutality."

"Brutality?" Angel stepped forward. "Nobody laid a hand on you."

"But I got an awful stiff neck from sleeping on that hard metal cot in the cell."

"I thought you were such a big strong man," Sarah said. "And here you are, whining like a baby."

Tyrone stood abruptly, pushing against the table and making it move a few inches toward Sarah. "Watch your mouth, bitch!"

Sarah didn't flinch, neither did Angel. Both women stood firm, holding his gaze without a hint of fear in their eyes. They had the upper hand. This was their house, and he knew it. He could try for intimidation all he wanted, but intimidation only worked on his turf. Not here.

The eye-fuck held for several long, tense seconds, then Tyron slowly sat back down.

A strained silence followed, interrupted a few moments later. Not by words but by loud popping sounds from outside the room. Firecrackers? In the building? Sarah glanced over at Angel. "What the hell was that?"

"I don't know. Gunfire?"

Sarah gave a slight shake of her head as more rat-a-tat noise sounded.

Angel beat her out to the hall where they could hear what still sounded like firecrackers going off. Officers in the CAPERS department sprang from their desks in a frenzy of movement that upended coffee cups and knocked papers off desks.

The noise was definitely not firecrackers going off. It was clear now that gunfire was coming from one of the lower floors. Sarah stood at the door to the interrogation room and motioned to Burtweiller, who was the closest officer. "Help me out here. Take this scumbag down with you. Then have some Uniforms hold him.

Then see where McGregor needs you and Simms. We might need to evacuate the building."

Burt shot her a quick salute, and grabbed Tyrone by the arm, pulling him toward the stairs, joining the stream of officers who were headed that way. All following the protocol that no elevators were to be used in the case of a bomb threat or other possible attack on the building. Angel and Sarah followed quickly, joining the throng of other police personnel in the halls and staircases, all racing down to the lower level of headquarters. As they neared the lobby, the sound of gunfire intensified, and Sarah was the first one to the stairway door. She eased it open a crack and looked out. "Oh, my God!"

"Can you see the shooter?" Angel asked.

"No. Shots are coming from outside."

"People down?"

"Yeah. But I can't tell if they're hit. Maybe just down for safety."

The gunfire stopped, making way for an abrupt, deadly silence. Nobody moved. Sarah held her breath.

"Is it over?" Angel asked, voice barely a whisper.

"Don't know." Sarah pushed the door open a little further, crouched and slipped into the lobby, gun drawn, nerves taut. She saw Hank, the duty officer, peeking over the top of the information desk, his gun drawn, too. He motioned with the barrel toward the front window where bullets had smashed through, scattering pellets of glass across the marble flooring. Two civilians were still down, a man and a woman. She crawled over to them, relieved to see they were not hit. "No. Stay down," she said when the woman started to rise, panic in her eyes. "Wait until the all-clear."

"Oh, my God. We had no idea." The woman looked wildly around.

"About what?"

"He ... a man ... gave us a note to give to the officer here."

Sarah turned quickly to Hank. "What note?"

"This one." He raised a piece of paper. "Says he came here to kill a bunch of cops."

"It appears he's failed."

191

"Maybe not," Hank said. "He's in a van outside. Says it's rigged with explosives."

"Shit." Sarah turned back to the couple. "We have to get out of here. Can you crawl with me to the stairwell?"

They nodded.

"You, too, Hank," Sarah called out. "Nobody's staying here."

By the time Sarah and the other three made it back to the staircase, McGregor was there with a couple of other lieutenants. Most of the other officers who had come down a few minutes earlier were gone, including Angel. Sarah hoped they were either out the back, or safe in the shelter in the basement. "The gunman's parked out front with explosives," Sarah said.

"Yeah. We know." McGregor nodded to Hank. "He called upstairs. We're evacuating. Everyone outside through the back doors."

As he spoke, McGregor ushered the civilian couple toward one of the other officers, telling them, "Go with him." Then he turned back to Sarah and Hank. "Anyone else in the lobby?"

"No sir," Hank said. "We were lucky. Two minutes before, we had a group of boy scouts come in for a field trip. Chief Dorsett had just taken them into the elevator."

"Okay. Let's go."

They made their way to the first floor, then took another staircase to the basement. Streams of people were exiting through the doors normally used for deliveries. Sarah was relieved to see the Chief and the kids moving safely toward a far corner of the block. Looking around quickly, she strained to catch a glimpse of Tyrone and his watchdogs, but couldn't spot him. McGregor's cell phone chirped, and he answered. Sarah watched a myriad of expressions cross his face as he listened, then he said, "Got it."

"What?"

"SWAT's been mobilized. Officers are at the first-floor windows, ready to take a shot."

They exchanged a look, both keeping the question to themselves. What if the building blows? Death was always hovering in the background of any officer's day. They all knew the risks. But right now, Sarah had a greater appreciation for the SWAT team that was sometimes too quick on the trigger. The officers needed to be damn quick today.

Then she heard a loud screech of tires and a van rounded the corner of the building and roared past.

"Son of a bitch," Hank said. "That's him."

"The shooter? You sure?" The questions came from Sarah and McGregor at the same time.

"Yeah. It's his van."

The whap, whap, whap of the police helicopter drowned out any other attempt to speak. It cut a path between headquarters and Cockrill Avenue in pursuit of the van.

Again, Sarah looked around at the milling throng of people, checking on Tyrone, but she didn't see him or Burt. A little niggle of unrest shortened her breathing a little more. Should she trust that Tyrone was safely in custody? Or should she give in to the worry?

Angel appeared out of the crowd. "Where's Tyrone?"

"I sent him down with Burtweiler right after you ran out. Haven't seen either of them since."

"Let's start looking." Angel waved an arm at the right-hand edge of the crowd. "I'll start on that end."

"Okay." Sarah moved off in the other direction. It was hard to conceive of how many people still worked in the old headquarters until a moment in time like this, with hundreds of people lining the back of the building and spilling out onto the streets. There was no traffic, so obviously roadblocks had been set up as soon as the shooting started. While Sarah didn't always agree with the brass, or support their policies, she had to admit they didn't waste time when there was none to waste. She'd made it about halfway through the throng, when she spotted Burtweiler, who was in a heated discussion with a young officer in uniform, who held a bloody handkerchief to his nose. As she drew close, she heard, "How'd he get the drop on you?"

"We were being jostled pretty good coming out. He just threw an elbow into me and melted into the crowd."

The niggle of unrest blossomed into full-fledged panic. Oh shit!

"You let my perp get away?" Sarah poked the young officer in the chest with her finger. "Jesus Christ! He's wanted for multiple murders."

The officer took a step back. Whether it was from the force of her words or the force of being prodded so hard in the chest, Sarah didn't know. Nor did she care at the moment. "We had him," she continued her rant. "We had the fucking murderer in custody. And now he's gone."

Burt put a hand on her arm. "Take it easy. Shit happens."

"Shit happens!? You're goddamed right shit happens. And you know what?" Now she turned back to the other officer, whose nametag read 'Jenko.' "When shit happens even worse shit happens."

"I'm sorry, I—"

"Sorry don't cut it." Sarah was red-faced with rage and screaming.

"Sarah!" Burt took her arm again, but this time the gesture was not one of gentle persuasion. She felt his fingers dig deep into the flesh on her upper arm. "Stop. This isn't productive."

She shook out of Burt's grasp, then sighed. "You're right." Turning to Jenko, she said, "I guess it would be pretty contradictory of me to say sorry at this point."

A slight shrug was the only response.

"But I shouldn't have railed against you."

"You're entitled," he said. "I let you down."

"No, this whole fucking mess let me down. Let us all down."

"We good?" Burt asked.

Sarah nodded.

"Okay. I need to get this officer's broken nose checked out."

Watching Burt guide Jenko toward an ambulance a bit further down the street, Sarah took a deep breath to steady her roiling emotions. She wondered how much longer they'd be stuck out here and whether there really was a bomb. Then that wondering turned into a really scary thought. Had Tyrone had any part in this? Did his power extend to that level?

"Sarah."

She turned at the sound of her name and saw Angel weaving her way through the throng of people.

"Where's Tyrone?" Angel asked when she stepped next to Sarah.

"In the wind."

Angel looked around as if wanting to verify for herself, then she turned back to Sarah. "Crap!"

"My thoughts exactly."

Sarah spotted McGregor who was talking on his cell phone and motioned to Angel to follow her. As the women drew near, he finished the call and put the phone in his pocket. "That was the bomb squad. There was a pipe bomb near the front of the building. They have it and are taking it to the disposal site."

"Can we go in now?" Angel asked.

"Not yet. They want to check the whole perimeter of the building." He turned to Sarah. "Did you fire your weapon when all the shooting started in the lobby?"

She shook her head. "Just Hank fired."

"Good. We don't need you on the seventy-two-hour mandatory leave right now. You have to push Tyrone hard. Find a crack and get him to break."

"We need to find him first."

"What?!" The word came out like an explosion and McGregor's face reddened with the effort.

Briefly, Sarah brought him up to speed on what had happened with the officer escorting Tyrone out during the evacuation.

"Son of a bitch!" The words were still explosive, but the red was slowly leaving his face. Sarah was glad. She always feared one of McGregor's pressure-cooker type reactions would burst a major blood vessel. Even though he'd quit drinking, he was still a heart attack or stroke waiting to happen; eating junk food, smoking, and eschewing any form of exercise.

"We need to get an APB out as soon as possible," Sarah said.

"We need to get back into the building," Angel said. "Can't do shit out here."

It took another hour to sort everything out. McGregor got a call on his cell from the SWAT team. When he closed the call, he told the nearby officers, "A sniper took out the shooting suspect."

That news was greeted with a cheer, then he told them that forensics was just waiting for the go-ahead to get their equipment to scour the van. And the bomb had been safely detonated.

"How soon will the building be clear?" Sarah asked.

"Any time now. No other bombs were found."

It actually took almost another hour before people were back inside. Sarah stopped by the restroom before heading to McGregor's office. Angel, Chad, and Ryan were already there when she walked in. Due to the perpetual state of messiness of the lieutenant's office, seating was at a premium. Angel had the chair directly across from the desk. Chad was in a metal folding chair situated between two stacks of folders that may have been propping the chair up. Or vice versa. Sarah wondered if the chair had been moved in the last decade. Chad started to rise and she waved him off. "Appreciate the offer," she said. "But I'll hold up the other side of the door." She nodded at Ryan who had one shoulder against the wall.

"Okay. Here's what we gotta do," McGregor said. "I'll get the APB out, but my guess is Tyrone's gone to ground. Anyone disagree?"

Nobody did.

"How about we reach out to the press?" Angel asked. "Let them report that we're looking for Tyrone as a person of interest in a murder investigation? Set up a hotline for people to call."

McGregor groaned in chorus with the other three detectives. "Hotlines are a pain in the ass. Every weirdo between here and Houston will call."

"Sure. But there's a chance that in the midst of all those, someone will call with good information." Angel said.

"Let's try a couple of other things first," Sarah said. "We need somebody on the inside at Ricky's. Surely one of his lieutenants there will know where he is."

"No doubt," Ryan said. "But we can't go in. They know us."

"And we can't send in any other officers," Chad said. "Those guys have cop radar that never fails."

"What about your CI, Ryan?" Angel turned to look at him. "You think she'd do it?"

Ryan shook his head. "She is out completely. Got so scared of that dealer she was trying to get close to, she left town."

"I know someone who could work out." Sarah stepped closer to the desk and told them about Amber.

"Wait a minute." McGregor held up one hand. "We can't send a civilian in there."

"She's not just any civilian. She's street smart and tough as old boot leather. She played a key role in bringing down that woman who killed the Clemment girl two years ago."

Angel swiveled to look up at Sarah. "But she's got a busted arm."

"It's almost healed."

McGregor gave a little shake of his head and pulled a bottle of Pepto-Bismol out of his desk drawer. He took a hefty swig while glaring at Sarah.

"Does she play pool?" Chad asked, half in jest.

Sarah smiled, then shrugged. "But if anybody can figure a way to blend in and pry some info loose, it's her."

Ryan shifted his weight to his other foot, drawing their attention. "It just might work, Lieu."

McGregor didn't respond for a long, strained few moments. Then he took another pull on the pink bottle. After putting it back, he said, "That's a last resort. We'll see what the APB does over the next twenty-four hours. I'd rather try the media and a hotline first."

"Thought you didn't want—"

McGregor waved a hand to interrupt Sarah. "I'd rather do that then put a civilian in jeopardy. Consider her our plan C."

"Okay," Sarah paused then added, "What's our plan B?"

"I'll let you know when I think of one. For now, you talk to that reporter at Channel Eight. Get her a picture of Tyrone." He pointed at Ryan. "Get someone on his house."

Ryan nodded.

"What about some protection for the Santos family?" Sarah asked.

McGregor wiped sweat from his forehead with a nasty-looking handkerchief and nodded. "I'll see if Walsh can put an Undercover over there. Better than a Uniform."

Sarah tried not to think of when that handkerchief might have been washed last. What a stark contrast to the white one Juanita had used for some tactile reassurance.

"That's it. Get out of here," McGregor said, waving a hand. "Get the hell out of here and catch that bastard."

Chapter Twenty-Four

• •

Friday, March 22

Walking into the bar, Sarah scanned the room and saw Bianca already seated at a booth halfway to the back. The daytime presence of the reporter was a stark contrast to the on-air person who sported fresh makeup and impeccably styled hair. Bianca's long black hair was pulled back in a tight pony tail, and only a touch of lipstick added color to her face. Not that she needed it. She was every inch a Spanish beauty and Sarah would have killed for the flawless skin and perfect white teeth that sat in a neat row.

Sarah slid into the booth across from the reporter. "Thanks for agreeing to see me."

Bianca nodded. "I'm like a stray puppy. Hard to get rid of."

The waitress stepped up. "What can I get you ladies?"

"Glenfiddich, with a touch of water and one ice-cube." Bianca glanced at Sarah. "You're buying, right?"

"Right." To the waitress she said, "I'll have coffee. Neat."

Bianca chuckled. "So? Cops really don't drink while on duty."

It wasn't a question, so Sarah didn't bother to respond. Instead she got to the point. "We need your help with something."

Now Bianca laughed. "Really. You push me away whenever I'm at a crime scene and now you want my help?"

It was obvious that was a question. "You had to figure it was something like that when I called," Sarah said. "You had a choice to come or not."

The waitress came with their drinks, and while she set them down on little white cocktail napkins the two women held a visual standoff.

Finally, Bianca lifted her glass. "And it's my choice whether to stay or not."

"Of course."

Sarah gave the reporter time to take a couple of sips of her whiskey, then slid a brown envelope across the table. Bianca opened it and took out a picture. "Tyrone?"

"You know him?"

"Of course. We know who runs the drug business in Dallas."

"We need to find him."

"Wait a minute." Bianca held up a hand. "That's police business. Not mine. It becomes mine when there's a story to tell. No story as far as I can see."

Sarah took a swallow of her drink, then leaned forward to talk quietly. "Here's the deal. We had him. Then in the confusion of evacuating headquarters during the bomb scare, we lost him."

"Your chief said nothing about that when we interviewed her after the all-clear."

"Yeah. Well, can you blame her? It wasn't one of our stellar moments."

Bianca chucked at that, and Sarah felt her feelings toward the reporter shift slightly off of the extreme negative pile. Maybe she could actually like the woman. She watched Bianca swirl the golden liquid in her glass, then said, "Can you show his picture tonight? There are phone numbers you can post for people to call."

"What's in it for me?"

Ah, a bit of the old Bianca was back. "We'll give you an exclusive when we catch Tyrone."

"Can I have that in writing?"

"Are you kidding? We're not working out a plea deal here."

Bianca didn't respond. She took a slow swallow of her drink, then set the glass down with a dull thud.

Tamping down the surge of frustration that was building, Sarah leaned forward and said, "What you have is my word. And where I come from a person's word means something."

Finally, Bianca put the photograph back in the envelope and stood up. "I'll take it to the news producer. He has the final say, but I don't think there'll be a problem."

The switch from obstinate to agreeable was so fast, it took Sarah a couple of seconds to catch up. "Thanks. I'll be in touch."

"Sure thing." Bianca started to walk away, then paused. "We don't have to be enemies you know. We both just have jobs to do."

Sarah nodded. For the sake of the reporter and for herself. It had been two years now since the press was definitely against her. Newspaper headlines and stories on television all painted her as that evil white cop who shot a young black boy. The fact that the black community had all risen up in protest, screaming in outrage made for good soundbites and kept the interest going for weeks. Through it all, Sarah was grieving the loss of her partner, John, and hating herself for having to kill that kid. But she had no choice after the kid shot John and turned the gun on her. But those facts were buried deep in the stories, and most people just heard about the white woman and the black kid. And nobody seemed to care about her pain.

Sighing, Sarah looked up, to say something else to Bianca, but the woman was gone.

~*~

Angel was at her desk when Sarah got back to the station. "Ryan got Grotelli to put a couple of Uniforms on Tyrone's house, and the pool hall. How'd it go with our favorite reporter?"

"Good." Sarah slipped off her jacket and put it across the back of her desk chair before sitting down. "It should be on the news at five."

"Does McGregor know?"

"Yeah, I called him on my way back. Hope he can fill the phone banks. Not my idea of a great way to spend an evening."

Angel chuckled. "Mine either. I'd rather play pool."

Sarah swiveled her chair to face her partner full on. "You play pool?"

"No. Just thought maybe someone should be inside the pool hall tonight. Catch a little chatter. Maybe pick up a lead on our man."

That pronouncement stunned Sara for a moment, then she said, "Why not wait to see if we can get the OK for Amber to do some recon?"

"Better me than a civilian."

"What does McGregor say?"

"Didn't ask him."

"What!?"

Angel waved a hand in a dismissive gesture. "Like you always ask?"

"That's different."

"Oh. Really?"

Sarah stumbled for a response to that, a verbal trip that Angel didn't miss. She smiled.

Sarah finally found some words. "What if they recognize you?"

"I was just a black dot in that little drama the other day. Nobody will remember me. They were all too busy looking at you and Ryan. The white folks stand out. Especially white cops. And I bet they wouldn't even recognize Chad."

"He's going with you?"

"Maybe."

"Let me amend that. He's going with you. Statement, not question."

Angel gave her partner a hard look. "Since when do we need a man to protect us?"

"That's not what I mean. I don't care who you get. You just need backup, and it can't be me or Ryan. As you so carefully pointed out."

Angel's ice melted, and she offered a slight smile. "Okay. I'll get backup. Happy?"

"Yes."

~*~

When Angel called Ryan and told him her plan, asking for someone to back her. Maybe someone who could act as her date, he had much the same reaction that Sarah did, only stronger. She wasn't surprised at his flare of concern. He was a little bit of the old-school man who saw that line between male and female very distinctly, and while she did like it that he brought her coffee, always remembering her favorite. And he didn't pressure her to take their relationship to the next step, she didn't like the fact that he saw her as needing him in a way she didn't.

Ryan finally wound down, and Angel said, "If you've got that all out of your system, can I tell you my plan?"

She interpreted his silence for assent. "I'm just going to hang out. Have a couple of drinks and listen. I'll leave my gun and badge at home."

"Whoa, wait a min—"

'No. You wait. I'll take my other weapon. It'll be fine."

Ryan didn't say anything for a long moment, then he sighed. "I'm sorry. I should trust you."

That was something else Angel appreciated about this man. He wasn't afraid to admit he was wrong. Her heart melted just a little bit more.

"So, who can be my date tonight? And don't say Chad. I thought about asking him, but I think if we walk in together, some of those guys will make us. He's been there too often."

"Yeah. Let me see if my guy Darren is willing to go undercover. He's about your age, and he'll definitely blend in, if you get my drift."

Angel chuckled. "You afraid to say he's Black?"

"Nah. Just thought I'd rattle your chain just a bit."

Oh, he'd done more than rattle her chain in the past few weeks. He'd rattled her heart, and Angel knew when this case was over, and they all had time to breathe, and maybe talk about more than strategy, she and Ryan had a mountain of things to discuss.

Chapter Twenty-Five

∙∙

<u>Friday, March 22</u>

At eight that evening, Darren pulled up in front of Angel's little house in a shiny metallic gray Trans Am with the requisite loud muffler that could have roused people sleeping in the next county. Angel, wearing tight red leather leggings and a gray scoop-necked jersey top, opened the passenger door and slid in. "Didn't really want my neighbors to see me in this get up," she said, "but I'm sure they're all looking to see what all the noise is about."

Darren gave a little chuckle and pulled away from the curb with another rousing rendition of muffler music.

"You're enjoying this aren't you?" Angel smiled at him.

"Yes Ma'am, I am. And I must say you're looking mighty fine."

If not for the brief meeting earlier, she might have been concerned about another man making a move on her. But not to worry. He was married with two young children, and so devoted he'd shown her pictures at their brief meeting earlier. He'd also been a little reluctant to take off his wedding ring, but then Ryan had reinforced the importance of Darren being Angel's boyfriend, not her husband. Luckily, there was no tell-tale mark of the ring on his finger.

Darren chuckled and then asked, "What do you plan to do when we get there?"

"Do you play pool?"

"I know my way around a table." He paused a moment to check traffic before a turn, then asked, "You?"

"My father taught me. Pool was kind of a family affair." Thinking about those Saturday afternoons that she'd spent learning the game, and then getting good enough to almost beat her father brought a pang of sadness. There'd been many smiles and good-natured teasing along with the lessons in geometry that taught her and her brother how to sink the balls, and she missed that. The pool hall visits had slowed when LaVon went off to college, then her father's business had picked up, yet he still insisted on doing most of the jobs himself, only now and then hiring a neighbor boy to help with some of the heavy lifting. That had left little time for games.

Her heart broke a little at the thought that they might not ever play together again. Not if they couldn't get past this barrier that stood between them. Angel didn't want it to be that way, but she also knew that she could not be the first one to reach out and take a brick out of the wall. Not this time. She'd always done it, but now it was time for her father to step up.

And now there was the added complication of Ryan. He was slowly becoming an integral part of her life.

"Hey, girl. We're here." Darren gave Angel a glance as he turned off the engine. "You went away somewhere."

"Sorry," Angel said. "Just getting ready to forget I'm a cop for a little while."

"Don't forget completely."

Angel chuckled. "Don't worry. I won't."

They stepped into the dim interior of the pool hall and Angel paused just a moment to let her eyes adjust. Darren, playing his role completely, draped an arm around her shoulders and pulled her toward the bar. "Come on babe. Let's you and me have a drink."

Finding two empty stools toward the end of the bar they sat, and Darren motioned to the bartender. "We'll have two Coors. And keep them coming."

"Bottles or on tap?" The bartender asked.

"Tap."

The bartender expertly filled two frosty mugs with beer, making a nice head on each that let just a trickle of foam slide down the sides of the glass. He brought the mugs over, setting them on small white cocktail napkins. Angel lifted hers, took a sip, then swiveled her stool so she could watch the game in progress over at the tables. She drank slowly, not wanting to get loopy this early in the evening.

After watching the game for a little while, Angel got off the stool and walked over to the table to have a closer look. When a player attempted to bank a shot, the ball just missing the corner pocket, she put her finger on the side of the table. "This is where you should have aimed."

Suddenly all talk around the table ceased while several pairs of not-very-friendly eyes turned to her. She could feel the heat of their glares, but she didn't flinch, watching the player she'd dared to advise.

"What you tryin' to prove, bitch?" the man said.

Angel took a half-step back, feigning innocence. "Hey. Didn't mean nothin'. Just wanted to help."

"Don't need your help."

"Okay." Angel started to walk away.

"Wait." The man motioned to her with his cue stick, then tapped it on the side of the table in a rhythmic pattern, as if accompanying his thought process with a drum beat. Then he looked at Angel again. "Girl? You want to show me that shot?"

"Don't want to get all up in your business."

One of the other players called out, "Let it go, man. We don't need no bitch showin' us our game."

"Sure," Angel said. "I'll just go back to my man and my beer."

"First I wanna see that shot."

Angel nodded and motioned to the man in a silent request to use his cue stick. Then she lined up the balls as they'd been before the missed shot, chalked the end of the stick, and took careful aim.

Just like her Daddy had taught her.

The white cue ball smacked into the red three-ball and sent it spinning on a diagonal toward the bank. It careened off the side and rolled slowly toward the corner pocket. Rolling. Rolling. Rolling, until it dropped in with a swish of the net.

"Damn, that was good," the man said.

Angel returned the stick. "It's the angles. Simple geometry."

"You do that all the time?"

Angel shrugged. "Maybe."

The man tapped the stick against the table again. Maybe he really did need the action to stimulate his thoughts. "How about a little one-on-one?"

Even though that's what she'd been hoping for, the invitation caused sweat to pool in the middle of her back. She couldn't blow this.

"What about our game?" one of the other men called out.

"We're done." The icy glare he gave the others could have been used to chill every mug in the bar.

Up to this point, Angel had wondered who might be one of the top dogs in this pack but not any longer. This light-skinned black man with the Nirvana t-shirt and baggy jeans was it. While she still hadn't formulated a plan as to how she or Darren might get any information out of this evening's little escapade, she at least knew on whom to focus. And she could enjoy a game of pool while she was at it.

Maybe.

If her nerves didn't scuttle her.

"I'm Kiara," Angel said, using the pseudonym they'd agreed on earlier. She took one of the pool cues from the rack and turned to the man. "What's your name?"

The man laid a fifty on the side of the table. "Grant."

Angel looked at the bill and then at the man. Okay. then. Nobody was going to use a real name. She gave a little laugh and said, "Okay, Grant. Rack 'em up."

He gathered the balls and arranged them in the black plastic triangle, sliding it back and forth to settle them all, then he carefully lifted the rack and said, "Go ahead. You break."

Angel nodded and positioned the white ball to get ready for her shot. She chalked her stick, then leaned over the table, hitting the ball with enough force to send it careening toward the other balls. The formation broke with a loud clatter. Three balls went into pockets, two solids and one stripe.

"I'll take solids," Angel said, lining up her first shot. She sank one, then purposely missed her second shot.

Grant grinned, then sank three of the stipes before missing a bank shot similar to the one he'd missed before.

"That's a tough one to get," Angel said, chalking her cue.

Grant didn't reply, so Angel leaned over the table and sank two more solids, before missing a shot that was intended to push one of her balls out from between two of his.

He grabbed his cue stick and walked around the table, sizing up his next shot. Just as he was starting to lean over to line up on the cue ball, the front door of the pool hall opened and a young teen wearing a Nike jersey with the hood and the baggy jeans that every young black kid seemed to be wearing, breezed in.

Grant looked up, and the new guy hurried over and whispered something to Grant, who looked around quickly, then motioned the other guy to move into a corner, away from the table and away from the bar. They carried on a whispered exchange for a moment, none of which Angel was able to catch, then Grant came back to the table and scooped up the money. "We're done here."

He grabbed a hoodie off a nearby chair and hurried out with the kid.

Angel was frozen for a moment. No way could she simply head out after Grant. That would be too obvious. She walked quickly over to Darren, still carrying the pool stick, and said, "Why don't you go on home? I'm going to play a little more."

She'd spoken loud enough for her words to carry, and Darren seemed to get the unspoken message. He slammed his beer down on the bar top, sloshing half the contents in the process. "Bitch, you done playing with someone else."

"What I be done with." Angel poked him with the pool stick. "Is you telling me what I can do. Just get your sorry ass out of here."

"You got it!" Darren pushed away from the bar and stormed out.

The bartender sidled over as Angel finished her beer. "Your boyfriend stuck you with the tab."

"No worries," Angel said. "He has a tendency to do that. Quick temper. He'll get over it."

"Want another?" The bartender motioned to her empty glass.

Angel shook her head. She took her purse off the stool, pulled out some bills, and put a twenty on the bar. "Keep the change."

After slinging the purse over her shoulder, she walked over to replace the cue stick, and one of the guys stepped close. Too close. The whiskey on his breath made her stomach roil. "Thought you wanted to play another game."

"Changed my mind."

He reached out and touched her hair. "Pretty girl like you shouldn't be alone."

"Don't worry about me." Angel gave him a wicked smile. "I've got another friend I can call."

That seemed to take him by surprise, and he didn't try to stop her as she walked out the door.

She hurried to the next corner and went around it before stopping to pull her cell phone out of her purse and call Sarah. "I need back up to my backup."

"What happened to Darren?"

"He's following the guy who's going to lead us to Tyrone."

"Really? It worked?"

Angel could almost feel her partner's excitement. "Yeah. It worked."

"Okay. Leaving now. Going to call Chad. I think he's closer."

While Angel waited for either Sarah or Chad to show up, her phone pinged with an alert that there was a text. She opened it to see a message from Darren: Can you talk?

She texted back: Yes.

Seconds later her phone buzzed. Darren talked softly and quickly. "I'm outside a warehouse. It looks abandoned. The guys I was following went in. No lights. No activity."

"Where?"

Darren gave her the location, then Angel said, "I'll meet you there. Sarah's picking me up. Or maybe Chad."

"On the north side of the building. Facing away from Mockingbird."

"Okay."

Angel ended the call just as Chad pulled up in one of the unmarked cars. Okay. No Sarah for now. She slid into the passenger seat, and Chad punched the accelerator, sending them flying down the street. "Where we headed?" he asked.

Angel told him, then asked about Sarah.

"She's en route," Chad said. "Let her know where to meet us."

Angel pulled out her phone and called Sarah. After a hurried conversation, she ended the call and glanced at Chad. "She's five minutes behind us."

"What do we have there?"

Angel knew what he meant. "Two guys went into the building. Haven't come out. Unknown number inside."

"Good thing we got the cavalry coming." Chad smiled. "I called Ryan. He hooked up with Sarah."

Angel nodded and grabbed the aw-shit handle as the car careened around a corner and headed west on Mockingbird Lane. "It's two blocks up on the left. Get us there in one piece."

"Yes Ma'am." Chad grinned and eased up on the gas just a tad.

The grin reminded Angel of why she'd been attracted to Chad when she'd first met him. She'd pretended otherwise. For a lot of reasons, mainly her reluctance to let anyone get into her heart. It had been wounded long ago by that loser of a boyfriend who'd chosen drugs over her, and she'd been protecting that fragile part of herself ever since. Then Chad had come along with his easy smile and charming ways. But the flicker of romance had never gone past that. Just a flicker. At least for her.

And now there was Ryan, with his own charm and delicious smile.

She shot a quick glance at Chad again. He was a good guy. A really good guy, and she could care for him if she gave herself half a chance. That would be the smart thing to do. Her father could never object to her being with a black man, but he sure as hell would object to Ryan. If only she didn't have the feelings she did for Ryan.

The car swerved into the wide driveway leading to the warehouse. *Good. Focus on the job.* "Go around back," she said. "That's where Darren is."

At first Angel didn't see Darren's silver Trans Am. Then she spotted it at the far end of the building wedged in behind a broken-down van. Chad slowed his approach. Finally stopping with a tall pile of wooden crates and bins providing a bit of cover.

Angel slipped quietly out of the passenger side of the car, closing the door with a soft click, and she looked ahead to see Darren crouched tight to the brick just to the right of one of the doors leading into the abandoned warehouse. There was a loading dock further to the left, jutting up to metal doors that were as tall as they were wide. They were pitted with rust. Shards of glass from broken windows littered the expansive cement apron around this backside of the building, glinting like silver sequins thrown from some Gypsy hand.

Before Angel or Chad could move toward Darren, Sarah pulled up in another department-issue car with Ryan riding shotgun. Darren zigzagged his way over to the other detectives, using empty barrels that sat on tall stacks of wooden pallets for cover. Quickly, he told them that the two guys were still inside. "There could be others. I don't know."

Sarah nodded then pointed to him and Ryan. "Cover the big delivery door. We'll go in the other way."

Darren and Ryan dashed off to the left, while the other detectives cautiously made their way toward the smaller door, dodging from cover to cover. When they got to the door, Chad reached out and tried the knob. It turned. He motioned with his drawn weapon that he was going in. The other two nodded and followed his lead.

Inside, the air was still, heavily laden with a moldy smell that burned Angel's nose. The cavernous ceiling was supported by concrete pillars, and dusty broken cardboard boxes had spilled from some of the dilapidated shelving that ran in long rows, making it difficult to navigate the space. In the dimness, Sarah and Chad looked like shadows moving slowly from row to row before choosing one to go down.

Angel decided to go down the first row and was halfway to the far wall when she heard the muffled sound of voices coming from somewhere ahead. Moving as quietly as she could, she made it to the end of her row, then ducked back when she saw three men in a cleared space about fifty feet ahead. One of them, Tyrone, sat on an upturned barrel, the other two with their backs to her, but she recognized the stance of the man she'd played pool with.

Angel crept forward again, turning to keep most of her body hidden by the boxes on the shelving, then risked a quick glance to her left where she saw Chad poke his head around the end of the row next to her. She gave him a quick nod, then pulled back into her cover, straining to hear what the three men were saying. Their voices were hushed and what few words she could hear were in Spanish. Damn. She should have paid more attention to the Spanish class in high school.

She risked moving forward again and could make out, "Mexico." That one word could mean anything. They could be talking about a shipment coming from Mexico. Or they could just be talking about their families in Mexico, although that was a stretch her manic mind was making. What was clamoring in her gut was a conviction that they were discussing getting the hell out of Dallas and finding refuge in Mexico. All of them? Or just Tyrone? No way to know. But what she did know was this. They couldn't lose him again.

So far Angel had not seen any weapons, but she didn't doubt they were carrying. She just had to get the drop on them. She was about to put that thought into action when she caught a flicker of movement to her left. She glanced over and saw Chad move out of his cover with his weapon raised. "Police!" The word echoed off the concrete walls, seeming to bounce around the great expanse. "Hands up. Now!"

The tableau froze, then the situation spun out of control, and the next few moments played out in a series of flash cuts.

Grant and the kid whirl, pulling guns out of the front of their jackets.

They open fire.

Chad staggers.

Falls.

More gunshots echo in the cavernous room.

Tyrone dives behind the barrel for cover.

Angel fires.

Grant goes down.

The kid ducks behind one of the wide pillars.

Gunshots ping back and forth like some out of control Shooting Gallery videogame.

The sound of Sarah's voice stopped the whirling images. "Angel? You okay?"

She took a breath, then answered. "Yes."

Actually, not okay. Chad wasn't moving. She pounded a fist on her leg, fighting an impulse to run to him. That would be a mistake. A deadly mistake.

Sarah called out again. This time to the perps, "Give it up. You've got a choice. Walk out of here or be carried out in a body bag."

The response was a barrage of gunfire from Tyrone and the kid who had made it safely to cover.

Then there was silence. Eerie, frightening silence.

Looking to her right, Angel determined that she could go around the two rows beside her and come up behind the kid hiding behind the wide pillar. She risked a glance out and to her left. Sarah was peeking out three rows down. Using quick abbreviated hand gestures Angel let Sarah know what she was planning.

Sarah shook her head, clearly indicating that she was not happy with the idea.

Ignoring her partner, Angel stepped back and quickly moved to the end of her row and then along the perimeter wall until she could see the kid. Holding her weapon at the ready, she made a swift scan of the immediate area. From this vantage point, she couldn't see Tyrone, which was good. He couldn't see her either.

Taking a deep breath to steady her wildly beating heart, Angel quietly walked toward the kid with her weapon raised. When she was within ten feet of him, she called out in a quiet yet firm voice, "Drop the weapon."

He seemed to take forever to make his decision.

Then he turned, gun raised.

Mistake.

Angel fired.

Her shot invited more gunfire, and Angel stayed where she was, protected from Tyrone and any stray shot from Sarah.

When the gunfire ceased, she risked a glance toward where she knew Tyrone was hiding. Maybe she could get the drop on him, too, but then she saw Sarah coming up from the other side, moving silently toward Tyrone.

As if in an instant replay of Angel's moments earlier, Sarah got within ten feet of Tyrone then told him to put down his weapon and put his hands on top of his head.

This asshole did.

He turned to face Sarah with a mocking grin, nodding to her gun. "Go ahead and shoot me, bitch."

"No. I'll leave that to your roommates in the Pen. After you're sent away, we'll make sure they know you kill kids. They'll take care of you."

The grin slowly faded and Sarah cuffed him.

Now that the situation had been contained, Angel raced over to where Chad sprawled in a puddle of blood. His blood. *Oh God. Don't let him die.*

"Call an ambulance," she screamed.

Ryan stepped up beside her. "It's on the way."

When had he come in? And Darren? Was he inside, too?

Ryan hunkered down and started to put an arm around her. She shrugged him off. "No. Leave me alone."

She didn't even glance up to see if Ryan went away. Her focus was on Chad. Only Chad. The brightness in his eyes was fading, and she knew the life was slowly slipping away. She recognized the sign. She'd seen it before when sitting by her grandmother's bedside when she passed. "Oh, Chad. I'm so sorry. You deserved ... you deserved better than .... Better than this."

Angel was surprised to see a small smile tug at the corners of his mouth. A smile? What did that smile mean? "Dammit, Chad, don't you dare die. I'll ..."

What? What kind of promise can you make to a dying man that maybe you won't be able to keep?

Chad managed a word so soft and breathless it was almost carried away by Angel's own breath. But she clearly heard it.

"Okay."

Angel had no idea what he meant by that either, and she wanted to ask, but logic told her it was too late.

As she watched that final light in his deep brown eyes blink out, a flood of tears spilled out of her own dark eyes and fell like glistening raindrops on his face. She touched one of the droplets, letting it spread on her fingertip, then she brought it to her lips, tasting the saltiness that was tinged with a hint of the essence of Chad.

She sat for what seemed like forever, just looking at him, and then she felt another touch on her shoulder. She looked up to see Sarah. "The ambulance is almost here."

Ambulance? Someone must have called. *But it's too late.* To the question in Sarah's eyes, Angel gave a slight shake of her head.

Sarah whirled and paced in tight angry circles, muttering curses that Angel rarely heard even from a partner who could often put a member of a street gang to shame. If Angel was of a mind to, she might have joined the other woman in the tirade. But she didn't have the emotional or physical strength to do anything but sit here holding him and letting the cold from the cement creep into her bones. She didn't care about the cold.

For a few moments all Angel heard was the voice of her partner, then the scream of a siren grew louder, finally coming to an abrupt halt somewhere outside. She glanced over her shoulder and saw Sarah waving two EMTs over.

Angel was reluctant to move, but her training kicked in and she slowly stood, backing away to give the medics the space they needed. She felt an arm around her shoulder, and she turned, expecting to see Sarah again. Instead it was Ryan, emotion darkening his blue eyes to a depth she had never seen before. And she was sure she saw water pooling just behind his pale lashes.

Not saying anything, she let him lead her outside. Squad cars flanked the ambulance, and Darren was pushing the handcuffed Tyrone into the back of one of the cars. He wasn't being gentle.

Ryan started to steer Angel toward the car that she'd arrived in with Chad, but she quickly pulled back, shaking her head. "I can't."

Ryan seemed to understand the 'can't.' He took her to the other car, easing her into the back seat. Then he slid in after her and pulled her into his arms.

Angel wasn't sure what to feel. She wasn't even sure she could feel. She was numb. She was so cold, it was as if a winter wind had blown through the car, and she was relieved to be able to press her shivering body into the warmth of Ryan. It wasn't sexual. Far from it. It was comfort, and yet something much deeper than comfort. But she didn't have to put a name to it. Not right now. There was time for that later.

Chapter Twenty-Six

. . . .

Thursday, March 29

The slow creak of the wheels grinding to lower the casket into the freshly-dug grave sent a shiver down Sarah's spine.

Chad was in that casket.

She hadn't thought she would be burying another officer so soon after John. That had just been a little over two years ago. For some people, two years would probably seem long enough, but it wasn't. No time was long enough. It shouldn't be this way. She blinked back tears that burned her eyes. She didn't want to let them run loose. She snuck a quick glance at Angel who stood beside her, quiet and somewhat stoic.

She knew what her partner was feeling. The aftermath of the shootout at the warehouse with Angel hunched over Chad's body brought back too many memories of that alley where she'd done much the same when John was killed. Having an officer go down in the line of duty is one of the worst things that can happen to a department, and it's very hard on the officers closest to the victim. Sarah could only hope that Angel's grief would not cut us deeply and create nightmares as long as Sarah's had.

Chad's mother was on the other side of the yawning hole in the ground. She was a regal woman standing tall and looking anywhere but at the grave. Sarah had met her once when Chad was celebrating getting his shield. The celebration had included his extended family and his family at the department, making it a loud and joyous party.

Listening to the department chaplain spout platitudes about how Chad was now at peace, resting in the arms of Jesus, Sarah noted how the words seemed to slap Chad's mother, making her flinch. It was a slight movement, hardly more than a tic in the smooth cheek, but still unmistakable for anyone watching. Sarah couldn't imagine what the woman was feeling. She'd heard so often that the hardest loss in the world was the death of a child. She believed that but she had thankfully never felt it. And this poor woman had no other children.

Sarah took a deep breath and let it out slowly, then felt something brush her hand. She looked down to see Angel reaching for her. Opening her fingers, she let them intertwine with those of her partner who squeezed hard as the casket made its slow descent. They stood, neither moving, for as long as it took for the casket to finish lowering into the hole, then watched the family members drop handfuls of dirt and sprigs of flowers into the opening. The attending police officers did likewise, until only Angel and Sarah were left.

"Come on." Sarah urged Angel forward with a slight tug. "You can do this."

Angel didn't speak, but after a few moments of hesitation she followed Sarah and dipped into the loose dirt, letting it flow slowly out of her hand. Then she nodded and walked quickly away.

Sarah let her go.

*

Police officers, some in uniform and others in plain clothes, jostled for room at the bar that was overflowing with those who came to raise a glass for Chad. This was the way it was when one of their own went down. It didn't even matter if you knew the fallen officer. You just came to pay your respects. Sarah figured she'd attended far too many of these gatherings. Even one was far too many, but she knew the hope that she would never have to attend another one was futile.

Above the bar, a TV was on, sound muted, and Sarah looked up for just a moment to watch Bianca deliver the evening news. As promised, the reporter had her exclusive.

Sarah sat at a table in a back corner of the room not really wanting to mingle. She was nursing a second Rob Roy and trying to decide when she might be able to slip out without anyone noticing. She no longer had to worry about how Angel was doing. Her partner was being well taken care of by Ryan, and Sarah managed a little smile thinking about how good they looked together. She just hoped that when it was time for Angel to tell her parents about this white man in her life, they would have the same reaction.

Was that another futile hope?

She took a sip of her drink and then looked up when she sensed somebody by her table. "Jeanette. What a surprise."

"Hope I'm not intruding."

"No. It's just ..."

"A surprise. Yes. You said." Jeanette gestured to the chair opposite Sarah. "Can I?"

"Sure."

After Jeanette sat down, Sarah wasn't sure what else to say. The last time she'd seen John's widow was a few months after the funeral, and she hadn't known what to say then, either.

Sarah twirled her glass on the table, breaking the rings of condensation that had formed. "Want a drink?"

Jeanette shook her head, then spoke after another few moments of silence. "Chad was one of the good ones."

"Yes. Yes, he was." Sarah looked up to make eye contact. "Then John ...? He spoke of Chad?"

"He had a lot of respect for him."

"We all did."

There was another awkward silence, and then Jeanette nodded toward Angel. "How's it going? You know. With her? Your new partner?"

"She'll do." Sarah shrugged. "But she'll never replace John."

Jeanette gave Sarah a knowing look. "I know what you mean."

It took a moment for the full significance to register, then Sarah smiled. "Of course, you do."

After a few moments of an awkward silence, Jeanette stood. "Come by sometime. The kids do miss you."

Sarah nodded. "I'll try to do that."

As Jeanette made her way through the crowd, Sarah downed the last of her drink, ready to get up to make her exit, when McGregor settled his bulk in the chair the other woman had just vacated. He had a glass of amber liquid in his glass.

Sarah sat back down. "Lieu? You fall off the wagon? Not that I blame you." She glanced around the room as if that was explanation enough.

He shook his head. "Though I might need to find a group for ginger-ale addiction."

"That's a pretty safe addiction to have."

McGregor took a hefty swallow of the soda. "How you holding up?"

Sarah knew he meant more than just the immediate loss, but she didn't want to talk about it. She'd unload on Cat later tonight. "I fell off the no-cussing wagon when Chad went down."

"You were really trying?" He looked incredulous.

"Figured I'd give it a shot. Couldn't let you beat me out in the self-improvement department."

She followed that with a smile, and he chuckled, then motioned to her empty glass. "Want another?"

"Nah. I should go."

"How's your partner doing?"

"She's going to be okay." Sarah nodded toward where Angel was leaning into Ryan. "He's got her back."

"Good thing the department changed the policy about officers in relationships."

"Yup."

McGregor drummed his fingers on the table for just a moment, then asked. "Anyone new in your life?"

"You hitting on me, Lieu?"

He just gave her a look.

"Sorry. Knee-jerk reaction."

His gaze didn't waver. "Sounds like deflection to me."

For the briefest of moments, Sarah considered telling him about LaVon. In the years they'd worked together, he'd been more than her boss and a deep friendship had formed that allowed them both to share confidences. But she decided this was a confidence best shared with her feline friend.

"Just caught me off guard. That's all. Nothing to talk about."

"Uh-huh." His tone said he wasn't buying it, but their years of mutual respect kept him from pushing.

He took a long look around the room, then said. "Good turnout for Chad."

"He will be sorely missed."

"That he will."

McGregor finished his drink, then stood. "You take care of yourself, Kingsly. And your partner. Don't want to do this again."

Sarah gave him a quick salute. Words couldn't get past the sudden lump in her throat.

Chapter Twenty-Seven

••

Two Weeks Later

Angel was trying to concentrate on a file concerning a burglary in Highland Park, but the buzz of her partner's phone on the desk opposite kept pulling her attention away. She'd ignored the first few pings, but it kept going until Angel finally got up and walked around to Sarah's desk. Angel didn't know why her partner had left the phone. She usually took it with her, even to the bathroom. But whatever the reason, Angel had to stop that annoying pinging of notification.

Her intent was to just swipe the phone to decline the call and shut the thing up, but then she saw who the call was from. What? Angel picked up the phone and swiped to answer. "LaVon? Why are you calling Sarah?"

"Why are you answering her phone?"

"Because it was ringing and she's not here?"

"Where'd she go?"

"No fair, counselor. Don't keep deflecting with more questions. What the hell is going on?"

"You should ask her."

Spotting Sarah striding toward her, Angel said, "Okay. Maybe I will." Then she hit "end call."

Sarah frowned as she drew close to her desk and saw what her partner was holding. "What're you doing with my phone?"

"The thing is." Angel dropped the cell on the desk. "You must have forgotten to take it with you. Then it started buzzing with calls coming in. Kept breaking my concentration. So, I answered."

"What?" Sarah snatched up her phone. "You took a call?"

"I wasn't going to. I was just going to hit the button to decline. Then I saw who it was. And he wouldn't tell me why he was calling you."

"Oh, my God!" Sarah slumped into her desk chair. "Don't tell me it was LaVon."

Not a question. Just a statement, so Angel didn't respond at first. Then a bit of anger kicked in. "Why is my brother calling you? Please tell me it was purely professional."

Sarah hesitated, then shook her head.

"Damn." Angel leaned a hip against the desk and thought for a moment. "How long?" She gestured vaguely at the phone, not able to complete the question.

"Off and on for a while," Sarah said. "It's been complicated."

"I bet." Angel shook her head. "He never said a word."

"We wanted to wait. See how it played out. Figure out the ramifications."

The reality of what was happening hit Angel hard. Sarah and her brother? Together? She stood abruptly. "I don't want no honky bitch dating my brother."

For a moment all the animosity between the two women rose to the surface like lava boiling in a volcano. Sarah looked as if Angel had just sucker-punched her, anger seething in her eyes. Then something else. Pain? Angel took a step back from the intensity of the emotion rising off her partner like steam from a hot wet fire. She waited until the blaze went back down to Defcon 1 before giving a little shake of her head. "I can't believe I just said that."

Surprise replaced the pain in Sarah's expression. "What?"

Angel took a breath before responding. "What my father would have said."

Sarah didn't respond and Angel sighed. "I guess I never realized how prejudiced I could be."

Now Sarah sighed. "Welcome to the club."

That elicited a small chuckle. "What are we going to do?" Angel asked.

"About what exactly? Race relations or me dating your brother?"

"Both I guess. My daddy is going to explode."

"Spontaneous human combustion."

Angel laughed. The sound felt good to Sarah's ears and she smiled, then asked, "What about you and Ryan?"

"What do you mean?"

"You know, and I know."

Angel tried for a deflection. "That's certainly more than I know."

Tension crackled for a moment, then Sarah gave a small chuckle. "Listen to us. We're having a conversation, almost like two old friends."

Angel gave her a long silent look, then smiled. "Yes. It certainly seems that way."

"So? You okay with me and your brother?"

"Give me more than a minute to adjust."

"Maybe we could get together for a drink and talk about it. Say, in a week?"

Angel laughed. "That'll do."

⁓*⁓

Instead of going home after her shift ended, Angel went by the dojo. She always had her *gi* in a small duffle in the back of her car. She went into the ladies' locker room and quickly changed, nodding to the young blonde girl she frequently sparred with.

"Want to have a go at it?" Danielle asked.

"Sure."

A few minutes later, Angel snapped the chin strap on her helmet and went out to the gym. Danielle was already on a mat stretching, and Angel joined her for the warmup. Then they stood, bowed deeply, and faced off.

Danielle made the first move with a spin-heel kick that almost caught Angel off guard, but she ducked under it, poking a jab to Danielle's stomach followed by a backhand to her jaw. A sudden flurry of punches drove Angel to the edge of the mat, and she side-stepped, managing to land one feeble blow to the side of Danielle's head.

It didn't take long for the sweat to run in rivers down her back, and Angel fought for concentration. She should have known better than to spar when her mind was spinning off in a million directions.

Suddenly, Angel staggered under the force of a front-snap kick to her chest.

"Break!" Randy called out, and Angel was vaguely aware of the girl stepping back.

Struggling to recover the breath that had been knocked out of her, Angel leaned over and put her hands on her knees. She could hear the soft pad of Danielle's feet on the mat, then a hand touched her shoulder lightly. "You okay?"

"Yeah. Fine."

As soon as Angel could stand upright, she bowed to Danielle. "Another time?"

Danielle nodded, then moved off to practice patterns.

Randy took Angel by the arm and led her into his office.

A tall, rail thin man, Randy was Asian, but he'd never told anyone at the dojo what country he was from. The style of martial arts he taught was a mix of practices from many Eastern countries, and he spoke perfect English, with just the hint of an accent. But when he wanted to make a point, he channeled his favorite actor, David Carradine from the TV show "Kung Fu," using the accent and familiar references.

"You are not so often distracted, Grasshopper. It is not good to spar under those circumstances."

"I know." Angel smiled at the endearment. "I should've just worked off my stress by myself."

"Do you care to tell your old master what is troubling your mind?"

"You really want to listen to my problems?"

"We are community. We are family. You speak. I listen."

So, Angel told this wise old man about her partner. About her brother. About Ryan. About losing Chad. About the ongoing problem of bigotry in her family. She hated that she was still so estranged from her father, and she didn't know what to do about Ryan. Should she tell her father? Would her father ever change his mind about others? Could he ever accept her position? Or was this a point in their relationship when their paths would veer off and never connect again?

"You ask many questions," Randy said.

Angel nodded, not even sure what she expected back from him.

"When you are sure it is all in order up here," he paused and touched his forehead, "then you go down to here."

Again, he paused, this time touching his chest. "Listen to what your heart says you must do."

"I'd rather not do anything."

Randy laughed. "When life is most difficult, that is when we often want to crawl under a shell and stay there. But life also pulls us out. Tells us that there are wonderful things ahead if we walk through this dark place and come out the other side."

Angel nodded. She knew he was right. She couldn't avoid what had to be done. She bowed and said, "*Arigatou gozaimashita.*" Because of Randy's mixed bag of martial arts experience, she knew the words used in Karate were acceptable, but she still repeated them in English, "Thank you."

He bowed in response, and she left.

~*~

Sunday evening, Angel walked into her parent's house, pleased to see LaVon carrying a steaming plate of roasted chicken to the dining table. Her mother was right behind with a basket of dinner rolls. "Angel," Martha said, "sit down. We're about ready to eat."

Gilbert, already seated at the head of the table, gave Angel a tight smile as she took the chair close to him. Into the stilted silence, Martha offered a quick blessing for the food, then plates were filled and a three-way conversation ensued, with Gilbert pointedly remaining silent. When he was about to finish the last of his chicken and mashed potatoes, Angel knew he would then get up and leave the table. She put a hand on his arm. "Daddy, we have to talk."

His face wore a tight expression, as if he were sitting in a doctor's office expecting bad news. He didn't say anything, but he also didn't move, so Angel continued, "We're never going to agree on racial issues. I know that. And you know that. So, we have to agree to disagree."

"Now, wait a minute, young lady. You will not be lecturing me."

The force of those words exploded in the room and Angel bit her cheek to keep from an angry response. She took a breath, marshaling a calming mantra. *Breathing in, I calm my body; breathing out, I smile.* Then she said, "This isn't a lecture, Daddy. It's a conversation that we need to have. And we need to let it come to a conclusion."

Gilbert stood, ready to push away from the table, but stopped when LaVon said, "Daddy!"

That word was explosive, too, and Gilbert glanced over at his son. "What? You defecting, too?"

Angel looked to her mother, to gauge her reaction. But Martha just sat there with her hands in her lap, apparently okay with letting her children handle the situation.

Leaning closer to her father, Angel said, "I don't think all white people are bad people. That's where we disagree. You put them all together as the bad guys. I've seen plenty of bad guys. White and black. But those are individuals. Not the whole race, either color."

Angel paused for a moment, hoping for some response from her father, but none came. She sighed. "Okay. I know. I'll never convince you to change your mind about all white people. But I hope I can convince you to change your mind about one white man."

For the first time since the dinner started, Gilbert looked at her, alarm clear in his expression. "What are you saying?"

Angel took a deep breath and told him about Ryan. About how much she cared. About how much she didn't want to care. Watching the myriad of expressions—anger, fear, revulsion, hate—flash across her father's face, Angel wasn't sure which one would end up being the final one. Under the circumstances, immediate acceptance wasn't possible. She knew that, but maybe she could look toward something gradual. He had changed his mind before, glacial as the change came, so maybe there was hope.

She turned slightly to look at her brother wondering, and hoping, that maybe he'd speak up, too. She wouldn't expose him and Sarah. That wasn't her place. She waited a long moment to see whether LaVon would speak up, then he gave a slight shake of his head, and she knew. It was too soon for them to spring that information on her father.

She felt her mother's hand touch hers and she grasped it as if it was a lifeline.

For a few moments, Gilbert said nothing. He sat in a stony, frozen silence. Then he finally spoke. "This man. You love him?"

"Yes, Daddy. I do."

Another long silence filled the room, then Gilbert said, "That don't make me change my mind about all the history."

Angel sighed. "I don't want to change your mind about that. White people have wronged us in so many ways. For so long. And I understand how hard it is to let go of the anger. The blame. The frustration. All of those things that have fueled this great divide between us and them. I feel them, too, when I think of systemic racism and what it's done. But hanging on to those feelings. Letting them drive everything we do. That doesn't help us look to the other side and maybe close that divide just a little bit."

She paused to take a breath and to give her father time to respond. He didn't, so she went on. "I've learned to appreciate the strength and goodness that I've seen in my partner. I don't feel discriminated against. Or judged by her. We're equals. And we're partners."

After another long pause during which she mentally debated the wisdom of saying it, she added, "That's the same way I feel with Ryan. Equal. And loved."

Gilbert gave a snort of disgust, and Angel held up a hand, palm out to stop any more protest. "Listen to me. I didn't plan to fall in love with a white man just to spite you, Daddy. Hell, I didn't plan to fall in love at all. It just happened."

Her father didn't say anything in response, and Angel was surprised when her mother straightened her back and spoke. "Gilbert, these children of ours are no longer children. They be grown-up people who can make grown-up choices for themselves. And dammit, Gilbert, you have to let them make those choices!"

Angel was shocked to hear her mother swear. She couldn't ever remember hearing her mother utter any of the words she deemed "bad" words. And her father seemed just as surprised. His eyes widened and his mouth opened but nothing came out. Then he swallowed hard and said, "Okay, Martha. Whatever you say."

Stunned, Angel sat for a moment, unable to speak. Beside her, LaVon chuckled and said, "Could you say that again, Daddy? I'm not sure I heard it right."

Gilbert snorted.

Angel found her voice. "Thank you, Daddy."

His response was a muttered hrrumph.

But it was enough.

Chapter Twenty-Eight

....

Three Weeks Later

L eaving her apartment to head to the station, Sarah mentally reviewed where they stood with building a case against Tyrone. At first, the only good thing to come out of his arrest was closing down the flood of drugs into the Dallas area for a while. Not that drugs still weren't on the streets. It had just slowed to a trickle. And no more deaths from Cheese, thank God. But they still had no hard evidence to tie the scumbag to the murder of the girl in the park, or Franklin. The ADA was working an angle to try him on the deaths of the two girls in the restaurant, but the last thing she said to Sarah was that the case was a bit thin. It was going to be a hard sell.

Sarah stopped for a coffee, hoping to have a brief chat with Hussain, but she'd barely poured the coffee when her phone chirped with a text message. She put the lid on the container and pulled her phone out of her purse. The text was from Ryan: *Got something. Meet us in conference room B.*

That was it. Short and sweet.

Sarah paid for the coffee. "No time for talking this morning, Hussain. Gotta run."

He smiled and nodded. "Go catch bad guys, Miss police officer."

Sarah had to smile at his unwavering belief in her abilities, as well as his never-failing formality. It was always Miss Police Officer, no matter the fact that they'd known each other now well over a year.

When she got to the station, she put her phone in a pocket of her tan jacket, then locked her purse in her desk and headed toward the conference room. She walked in to see Ryan, Angel, and Ryan's

CI, the young Hispanic girl. Marcella. "Hope this means something good."

"Yup," Ryan said. "Grab a coffee and I'll let Marcella fill you in."

Having finished the takeout on the drive in, Sarah was ready for a second cup. She went the little sideboard and poured rich, dark liquid into a Styrofoam cup. When the aroma of good, fresh roast wafted up from the cup, she made a mental note to come to this room more often for coffee. This was definitely ten steps above the sludge normally found in the break room.

After she sat down, Ryan nodded toward the young girl. "Okay, tell these detectives what you said to me on the phone."

"It's like this. I was …" She gave a furtive glance toward Ryan. "Should really say what I was doing? No want to get jammed up."

Ryan shook his head. "No arrests will be happening here today."

The girl let out a breath. "Okay. Well, see, I went to see Ricardo. To score again. And that day he was like all nervous and jumpy …"

"Like how?" Sarah encouraged.

"Just, you know, nervous. Looking around. Couldn't stand still."

"He didn't act like this before?" Angel asked

Marcella shook her head. "He always tough. Cool. Has this swagger about him. You know, tough-hombre swagger. Never saw him like this before."

Sarah glanced at Ryan. "This is what you called us both in for?"

"It's just the setup. There's more." He gestured to Marcella to continue.

"Okay. So anyway, Ricardo asks do I want to get high with him. And I think why not? Then I won't have to pay. We go to his place. Take a few hits of the Cheese. Then Ricardo ……He starts talking …"

"And?" Sarah prompts.

Marcella took a sip of the water that was in front of her then she continued. "Ricardo, he say he scared. Never hear him say that before. Never. Then he say that a couple of small-time dealers vanish since Tyrone … you know."

"Since his arrest you mean?" Angel asks.

The girl nods, then words burst out. "Ricardo say Tyrone should fry for what he did."

"What?" Angel and Sarah say almost at the same time

"Murder get death penalty. Right?" Marcella asked.

"Yes." Ryan said

"So, Ricardo ... he knows about that girl that was killed."

"What girl?" Sarah asked even though she suspected she already knew.

"In the park ... back in the spring."

"What exactly does Ricardo know about this girl that was killed?" Sarah asked keeping the question and the tone of her voice non-threatening.

"Says he knows it was Tyrone what did it."

"How does he know that?" Angel asked.

"Ricardo and Franklin. They were pretty tight. Before Franklin disappeared, he told Ricardo that Tyrone kill that girl. And why."

"And why was that?" Ryan asked.

"To put pressure on man that was driving for them. Maybe it was the father."

"We need more than just his say so," Sarah said.

Marcella's leg started to pump up and down. "We want protection."

"We?" Sarah asked.

"Me and Ricardo. He have proof but—"

"What proof?" Angel asked.

"Voice recording Franklin made. Tells all."

Angel and Sarah exchanged a glance before Sarah said, "Where can we find Ricardo?"

Ryan slid a pen and pad of paper across to Marcella. "Write down an address. We'll bring him in. Keep you both safe."

"He might run," Marcella said. "He really scared."

"Okay," Sarah said. "Does he trust you?"

The girl nodded.

"Send him a text. Tell him we're coming. Tell him we will make sure nothing bad happens to him."

Marcella pulled out her phone and typed quickly, then looked up. "You sure? We be safe?"

Sarah nodded and watched as the girl finished the text, while Angel made arrangements for a uniformed officer to sit with Marcella and bring her more water and snacks from the vending machine. Then they all headed out to Ricardo's crib.

It was a dingy, rundown apartment building, just off Greenville near Gaston, and they went up three flights of dirty stairs that reeked of rodent piss. Ricardo's apartment was not even a step above the filth of the rest of the building, except it only reeked of weed, and Sarah was glad when the kid was willing to come with them, despite the obvious fear in his wide, dark eyes.

He was silent during the ride back to the station, where they stashed him in one of the small interrogation rooms.

"We're not going to jam you up," Ryan said after they were all settled around the table. "We just need to hear the recording. The one Marcella told us about."

"Marcella? She ok?" Ricardo asked.

"Yes." Sarah answered. "And you will be, too. We'll protect you."

Ricardo shook his head. "Not here. Not in Dallas. Not safe. Not safe."

"Okay. We'll see what we can do."

The kid waited a long moment, then pulled out his phone. "Hokay." He pressed a button and the detectives listened to a halting account of the murder that had started them down this rabbit hole of a case.

When it finished, they thanked Ricardo and left him. This time Ryan made arrangements for a bottle of water to be given to the kid.

"You okay, here?" Angel asked. "Want to pop over to Bek's for a burger. Missed breakfast and lunch."

"Sure." Sarah waved her off, then called McGregor to bring him up to speed, asking him to let the DA know they had evidence for the case against Tyrone. Then she went downstairs for a candy bar from the vending machine, eating it back at her desk as she started on the paperwork.

Close to an hour later, Ryan called to say that the ADA was ready to hear the tape. She saved the document she was working on, then hurried to the interrogation room, noting that Angel was back. Ryan must have called, her, too.

Jessica was in the viewing area and wasted no time once Sarah arrived. "What do you have?"

Sarah nodded to Ricardo who was inside, seated at the table, Angel across from him. "He's got a recording you need to hear."

"Okay. Let's do it."

Walking into the room, Jessica nodded to Angel, and then to Ryan who was leaning against the wall. Jessica sat down next to Angel. Sarah joined Ryan in holding up the wall.

"This is the assistant district attorney," Angel said to the kid. "She's the one who can ensure your future. One way or another."

Ricardo looked at her, alarm widening his eyes. "What you mean, one way or another?"

"What she means," Jessica said, "is that I can put you in witness protection, or prison. Depends on what you give me."

"The voice recording's pretty damning," Sarah offered. "Why don't we give it a listen, then talk about the boy's options?"

Jessica nodded, so Angel went to the door, where a uniformed officer handed her an evidence bag that held a cell phone. "For the record," she said to Ricardo. "Is this your phone?" She didn't let him touch it, but he could clearly see through the plastic. He nodded. So she slipped it out of the bag and queued up the recording. A moment later, Franklin's voice came through loud and clear. He'd even had the presence of mind to identify himself so there'd be no doubt who was talking.

When the recording ended, Jessica asked, "Why did Franklin send you that?"

"So I know. In case ... In case something happen to him."

Jessica turned to Angel. "You sure this is Franklin?"

Angel nodded. "We tracked the call back to a phone he had. A personal phone. Not one of the burners they used for business."

"While those details of Tyrone admitting to killing the girl are damning, it's still hearsay," Jessica said. "So, I can't nail him on that."

"Does that mean we're dead in the water?" Angel asked.

Jessica shook her head. "What's in the recording gives strong motive for wanting Franklin dead. We can put the little bastard away for a good long time for that. And if a jury believes that Tyrone had a hand in the young girl's death, not to mention all the kids who died from using Cheese, well … Get a few mothers and grandmothers on the jury. Show them pictures, and he'll be toast.

"I'll ask for the death penalty."

"So? I get protection?" Ricardo shifted in his chair, anxiety almost dripping off him.

"Are you willing to testify?" Jessica asked.

He gave a slow, hesitant nod.

"Okay. I'll start the ball rolling." Jessica stood. "Good job, detectives."

After Jessica walked out, Ryan stepped over to the table and looked at Ricardo. "You and Marcella will be safer in jail for now. We'll work on getting you a safe house as soon as we can."

Ricardo nodded again.

Ryan turned to Angel and Sarah. "I'll get him squared away. It's been a long day. Hell, it's been a long three months. Go home."

Sarah opened the door for Angel and they stepped out. "I'm not ready to go home," Sarah said. "You?"

"Not really."

"What do you think? Is it time we go have a drink together?"

Angel paused for just a beat, then nodded.

THE END

About the Author

M aryann Miller is an award-winning author of numerous books, screenplays, and stage plays. She started her professional career as a journalist, writing columns, feature stories, and short fiction for regional and national publications. Now she writes primarily mysteries, including the critically-acclaimed Seasons Mystery Series that features two women homicide detectives. Think "Lethal Weapon" set in Dallas with female leads. The first two books in the series, Open Season and *Stalking Season* have received starred reviews from Publisher's Weekly, Kirkus, and Library Journal. *Stalking Season* was chosen for the John E. Weaver Excellence in Reading award for Police Procedural Mysteries. Her mystery, *Doubletake*, was honored as the Best Mystery for 2015 by the Texas Association of Authors.

Among the other awards Miller has received for her writing are the Page Edwards Short Story Award, the New York Library Best Books for Teens Award, first place in the screenwriting competition at the Houston Writer's Conference, placing as a semi-finalist at Sundance, and placing as a semi-finalist in the Chesterfield Screenwriting Competition. She was named The Trails Country Treasure by the Winnsboro Center for the Arts, and Woman of the Year by the Winnsboro Area Chamber of Commerce.

Miller can be found at her Amazon Author Page her Website on Twitter and Facebook and Goodreads She is a contributor to The Blood-Red Pencil blog on writing and editing.

www.ingramcontent.com/pod-product-compliance
Lightning Source LLC
Chambersburg PA
CBHW020607180626
46810CB00007B/2677